If Wishes Were Horses

Karly Lane lives on the mid north coast of New South Wales. Proud mum to four beautiful children and wife of one very patient mechanic, she is lucky enough to spend her day doing the two things she loves most—being a mum and writing stories set in beautiful rural Australia.

ALSO BY KARLY LANE

North Star
Morgan's Law
Bridie's Choice
Poppy's Dilemma
Gemma's Bluff
Tallowood Bound
Second Chance Town
Third Time Lucky

Karly
LANE

If Wishes Were Horses

ARENA
ALLEN&UNWIN

First published in 2017

Copyright © Karly Lane 2017

Arena Books, an imprint of
Allen & Unwin
83 Alexander Street
Crows Nest NSW 2065
Australia
Phone: (61 2) 8425 0100
Email: info@allenandunwin.com
Web: www.allenandunwin.com

Cataloguing-in-Publication details are available
from the National Library of Australia
www.trove.nla.gov.au

ISBN 978 1 76029 183 9

Set in 12.4/17.6 pt Sabon LT Pro by Bookhouse, Sydney
Printed and bound in Australia by Griffin Press

10 9 8 7 6 5 4 3 2 1

MIX
Paper from
responsible sources
FSC® C009448

The paper in this book is FSC® certified.
FSC® promotes environmentally responsible,
socially beneficial and economically viable
management of the world's forests.

To the brave and loyal Anzac horses,
whose sacrifice has largely gone untold.

The ones they left behind.

Prologue

'Sophie, wait for backup.'

'There's no time, Mac. She's going to bleed out if I don't get in there and help her.'

'He's armed, Sophie. You can't go in there.'

Sophie slung the bag over her shoulder and closed the door of the ambulance. 'I'm not leaving that woman to die when we have a chance to save her.'

'I'll do it,' Mac said, trying to take the kit from her.

'You heard what he said—he'd only let me in. I'm going.'

Mac ran a hand through his short sandy hair and swore under his breath. 'He shot her, Sophie. You can't do this. Darrell's goin' to have a fit! The cops are on their way, just give it five minutes.'

'She doesn't *have* five minutes. I'll deal with Darrell when this is over. I'm going in, Mac,' Sophie said, pushing past her partner and heading towards the house.

As he stood in the doorway waiting for her, the man was clearly agitated and upset, though the rifle he held trained on her seemed steady enough. She tried not to look at it as she walked past him into the house. She was here to do a job. *Focus on the job.*

Her eyes jumped to the woman lying on the hallway floor. Seeing the amount of blood pooled beneath her, Sophie was immediately worried about how much she'd already lost. She approached her carefully, sending a quick glance around the room for any other victims and was relieved not to discover any. She crossed to the prone woman and knelt beside her.

'My name's Sophie. I'm here to help you,' she said out of habit, although the woman was not conscious. Sliding her fingers with practised ease across the woman's wrist, she searched for a pulse. It was there but faint, and now that she was up close, Sophie could also see the extent of her wounds.

Behind her the man paced. 'What's taking so long? Help her!' he yelled, coming to stand over her.

From the corner of her eye, Sophie saw the blood splattered across the front of his ripped t-shirt and forced herself to concentrate. She needed to calm him down. 'What's her name?'

'Mandy,' he finally muttered, reefing his eyes from the bloody gauze that Sophie was attempting to stem the bleeding with.

'We need to get Mandy to hospital,' Sophie said carefully, trying to keep the shaking she felt inside out of her voice.

'No. You're not taking her away from me,' he said, his voice turning cold and his watery eyes glaring down at her.

'No one's trying to take her away from you, but she needs a doctor or she's going to die. Do you understand?'

'I didn't mean to hurt her,' he said, his face crinkling into a mask of torment. 'She just wouldn't shut up. I told her to. I told her to shut up,' he yelled, wiping one forearm across his eyes but keeping the gun pointed on Sophie.

'Calm down, okay, mate? I know you didn't mean to hurt her, but I need you to put the gun down and let me help her.' This was not going as she'd hoped.

The wild look in the gunman's eyes did nothing to comfort her, and Sophie suspected he was on something. Any moment the police would arrive, and when he caught sight of them he was going to lose it completely. She had to get this woman out of there *now*.

'Sophie? Report in.' Her boss and old friend Darrell's voice crackled out of the radio on her shoulder.

As Sophie moved to answer him she felt the sudden cold, hard barrel of the gun press against her temple.

'Drop the radio!' the gunman yelled.

Sophie froze. Her heart thumped painfully against her chest. 'It's just my boss. Look, I need my partner in here to help me get Mandy into the ambulance.'

'No! No one else comes in. You help her.'

'I can't do any more. She needs surgery.'

'You do it!'

'I'm not a doctor!' she said, raising her voice in alarm. Quickly lowering it again, she squeezed her eyes shut to continue calmly: 'I promise she'll be safe. We'll take care of her.'

'No!' he yelled and pushed Sophie backwards, away from the woman on the floor. 'No one is ever taking her away from me, you hear?'

Sophie automatically lifted her hands in front of her, trying to placate him, ignoring the bright red blood on her gloves that belonged to the woman who was dying on the floor. 'Okay, okay. No one's taking her from you. What if you come too?' The last thing anyone wanted was a gunman in the back of an ambulance, but maybe if she could just gain his trust enough to get him outside she could get Mandy into the ambulance before the police arrived.

The sounds of cars pulling up with sirens blasting and lights flashing crushed this last glimmer of hope. Everything slowed down as she saw the rage in the gunman's eyes when he looked up and caught sight of the police. She saw the gun, heard the yelling, felt the pain of being pulled by her hair across the room. Staring at the end of a rifle, the hole gaping like a sinister tunnel between her eyes, Sophie knew there was no way he'd miss at this range. She wanted to drag her eyes away from the end of the barrel and plead for her life, talk him out of doing anything stupid, but she was frozen.

She could hear the gathering of armed police outside the house and knew Mac would be out there, beside himself with worry. She didn't want anyone to see her die like this.

Sophie knew all these people; she didn't want her grizzly death on their consciences. She was about to open her mouth to try to talk him down one last time, but before she could the world erupted around her in an explosion of noise and pain.

She was dead.

One

Hilsons Ridge, population 1100. The timber sign sat in the middle of a vividly colourful display of flowers. It was also a tidy town winner and an RV-friendly town, so the sign stated. This didn't tell Sophie much more about her new home, but at least everyone puts their rubbish in the bin and was welcoming to travellers.

On the map it hadn't looked too remote, being nearby a few larger regional towns scattered throughout the area. It wasn't until she'd turned off the major highway onto inland roads, which then became narrow ribbons of grey bitumen, occasionally shifting into sections of dirt and back again, that she realised the distance on the map didn't truly reflect the real difference in terrain.

The closer she got to her destination, the wilder the countryside became. Earlier she'd driven up a winding, somewhat nerve-racking mountain range, mainly rainforest, before passing lush green hilly paddocks populated by black and white dairy cattle with enormous udders. The bush here was more scrubby, the paddocks flatter than the ones she'd passed earlier, and the cattle were bigger and bulkier.

When Sophie had finally arrived, the main street looked a lot like those of the other small towns she'd driven through on her way out here: wide streets lined with heritage buildings, and a lot of dusty utes with dogs sitting patiently in the back.

Following the instructions of her Irish-accented GPS companion, Sophie located the ambulance station easily enough. She'd grown quite fond of him after pulling over somewhere outside Newcastle to change it from the condescending American woman's voice that had been previously set. There was no way she could tolerate her for another seven hundred-odd kilometres.

Parking in front, she got out and stretched her legs for the first time in hours as she surveyed the building before her. The Hilsons Ridge doctor's surgery was attached to the newer Multipurpose Services hospital, which serviced the area with one doctor and a full-time paramedic stationed in the same building. It had eleven beds, nursing staff and a small emergency department.

The hospital had been established as a way of diversifying rural and remote health care into small towns all across the state. Their patient load was mainly made up of the elderly, waiting for permanent placement in the nearest nursing home in bigger regional towns, and surgery recovery for patients who had been released from the bigger hospitals at Grafton or Inverell to convalesce closer to home. They also had the occasional low-risk pregnancy.

Sophie had heard how the small town had fought to keep its ambulance station only a few short years ago, when the health department had tried to centralise services to the larger townships over an hour's travel distance away. The community had reacted swiftly, and the support the local ambulance received had saved the station from closure. Sophie had been suitably impressed by the passion of the townspeople—it took a lot to change the minds of the powers that be once they'd decided to axe a station.

Sophie's boss, Darrell Mitcham, had been the one to suggest this transfer. At first she'd thought he'd lost his mind—Sydney to the middle of nowhere? But after the initial shock had worn off, she realised that maybe he was right. Maybe she needed something completely different for a while. Darrell had been stationed here twenty or so years earlier, back when every little town had its own ambulance station, before the health department became a corporate identity and began streamlining and grouping its stations. Never mind the fact that these bureaucrats rarely set foot outside the city and had no concept of the problems of distance in regional Australia. The difference between life and death in an emergency could be the fifty or so kilometres it took to travel to the nearest assistance.

Darrell had assured Sophie this would be a positive step. She wanted to believe him because she loved her job, but giving it up had been something she'd been seriously considering since coming back after her release from hospital a little over two months ago.

This was a new chapter in her life. She could do this. She *had* to do this: her old life was gone and there was nothing left for her back there now.

Taking a deep breath, she locked her car and headed towards the building.

∽

Slipping her sunglasses on top of her head, Sophie went through the front door and into a spacious waiting room. She crossed to the reception desk where a friendly woman in her late thirties smiled a welcome at her.

'Hi. My name's Sophie Bryant. I'm the new paramedic.'

The woman's eyes lit up and her smile widened as she jumped up from her seat and came around the front of the desk. Sophie didn't have time to blink before she found herself wrapped in a huge hug. 'Welcome to Hilsons Ridge. We've been waiting for you to get here.'

'Ah, thanks,' Sophie managed to stammer once released.

'I'm Janice and this is Trudy. Dr Tomovic is with a patient but he'll be out shortly. How was your trip?'

'Long,' Sophie said with a weary smile as she shifted her gaze to the second woman, who was approaching from where she'd been sitting in front of a computer screen. Sophie was a little relieved when Trudy seemed content with a smile and hello.

'Well, come on out the back and I'll get you a nice cuppa,' Janice was saying, taking Sophie's arm and leading her through the waiting room and down a long corridor to a well-appointed tearoom. Sophie would kill for a cup of coffee right about now, and the smell as it filtered through the impressive-looking machine beside the kitchen sink was enough to make her mouth start to water. Somehow servo coffee just hadn't quite hit the spot.

'So, this will be a bit of a change for you then,' Janice said as she sat down opposite Sophie, depositing a plate of home-cooked Anzac biscuits on the table.

Sophie reached for one and bit into it, barely managing to hold back a groan of delight. 'Yes, it will be, but that's kind of what I was looking for.'

'We're all very relieved that you're here. There wasn't much interest in the job and we were worried we'd lose the station again.'

'I guess it was good timing for both of us then,' she said with a smile.

'Any reason in particular for needing a change?' Janice asked, reaching for her own biscuit before eyeing her again.

None she was willing to talk about with a complete stranger, Sophie thought dryly. 'I'm in a position to move, and it was a good excuse to get out and see some of the country.'

'So no husband? No boyfriend?'

'No,' Sophie said in a tone intended to immediately shut down that line of questioning. It still hurt.

What *was* she? She was no longer married, but it wasn't by choice. Her husband, Garth, had died in a car accident, so technically she was a widow, but she hated that word. It sounded so . . . cold. She could be single, although she didn't *feel* single either. The last eighteen months had been rough.

'Oh good, here's Ado now,' Janice said, standing up as a slim young man walked into the room. Sophie noted the chiselled jawline, narrowing from high cheekbones and dark eyes. 'This is our new paramedic, Sophie Bryant.'

Sophie stood up too, and extended her hand to the man as he approached. Her head barely reached his shoulder, but she was used to everyone else towering over her. 'Nice to meet you, Dr Tomovic,' she said. She was also used to doctors who looked barely old enough to be out of university; although at closer range she realised he wasn't as young as she'd first suspected, possibly in his late thirties, but he had a youthful appearance that belied his age. There was a weariness in his dark brown eyes—the kind of look one carried from life experience rather than just the regular exhaustion of a harried doctor. She wouldn't mind betting he'd seen quite a bit of life's dark side.

'Please, call me Ado. It's a pleasure to meet you, Sophie.' Her name rolled off his tongue, sounding a little bit exotic with the underlying hint of an accent. 'I think we have a dinner planned for tonight, to welcome you. I'm afraid I'm fully booked until late this afternoon, but I look forward to catching up with you then. Janice will take you through to the station, get you settled and introduce you to the volunteers who'll be working alongside you. If there's anything you need, please just let us know. We want to make sure we keep you happy.'

'I'm fairly easy to please so I'm sure I'll be fine. Thank you.'

'Then I shall see you tonight,' he said, flashing a brief smile before he turned to leave.

'Ado's single too,' Janice supplied helpfully as both women watched the doctor disappear down the hallway. 'Anyway, let's get you sorted,' she said, turning businesslike in the blink of an eye. 'As we mentioned in your welcome email last week, there *is* an ambulance officer's quarters; however, it's currently undergoing some plumbing repairs. So, temporarily, we're putting you up at the pub. It should only be for a week . . . two at the most,' she amended, then caught the flicker of uncertainty that crossed Sophie's face. 'Oh, don't worry, the pub's lovely. It was refurbished a few years ago. You'll be more than comfortable.'

'So how long have you been without a full-time paramedic?'

'Going on three months now. Poor Percy stayed on as long as he could after his wife and kids moved overseas. He was all set to follow them, but they just couldn't get anyone to transfer out here. The volunteers have been covering a lot of the shifts, but they'll be pretty happy to see you too, I'd imagine.'

Sophie had heard about the program, but never actually been involved with it before now. To assist the only full-time ambulance officer in a small town, volunteers made up the extra staff and shared shifts. It was a system that was becoming more and more popular in remote parts of rural Australia where distance was an issue for any medical assistance.

They came to a set of electronic sliding doors, which separated the surgery from the rest of the building, and

Janice punched a code into a panel on the wall beside them before walking through.

∽

There were five volunteers currently staffing Hilsons Ridge station. The two younger women, Katie and Jackie, were farming wives in their thirties with children at home, while Margaret and Garry, a husband and wife duo, were in their early sixties. Sophie guessed John, the other male of the group, to be somewhere in his forties.

They'd all come in this afternoon specially to be on hand to meet her, and greeted her warmly. These five individuals were her new colleagues and the only people she could depend on for help out here. For the first time since arriving, the weight of that responsibility rested heavily on Sophie's shoulders.

Taking a tour around the small station, she noted with relief that they seemed to be well stocked and relatively up to date with equipment. Maybe that had been a bit of citified snobbery on her part, half-expecting to have to do without the usual state-of-the-art technology she'd worked with in Sydney. She felt a little ashamed of the assumption and vowed to try not to make the same mistake again. Talking with the staff as they showed her around, she was reassured that they were every bit the professionally trained operators she'd been told of before she accepted the posting. They *had* been handling the entire station alone without a full-time paramedic for three months, so it was safe to say they knew what they were doing.

The nearest town with a hospital and station staffed full-time was over eighty kilometres away. Any cases deemed beyond the volunteers' experience would automatically have the other station assisting, but because of distance the volunteers were more often than not first on the scene and required to treat the patients until assistance arrived to take over.

Katie, an outgoing blonde thirty-something, asked about her previous workplace.

'It was a lot bigger,' Sophie smiled slightly, 'but from what I hear you guys can have your busy moments too.'

Katie gave a shout of laughter and eyed her companions knowingly. 'I hope you didn't come out here looking for a relaxing holiday,' she grinned.

'Ah, no. Just a change of scenery, really.'

'Well, I expect you've got your wish there,' John, the dark-haired man in his forties, nodded. She'd learned earlier that he farmed a property a few kilometres out of town and had a background in the army. There was something about his quiet and reserved demeanour that Sophie found comforting.

'I can't say I've had to dodge kangaroos in the CBD very often,' she said dryly, only slightly exaggerating as she recalled the loping marsupial that had bounded across the road ahead of her as she neared town.

As they sat down in the ambulance staff room to brief her on the day-to-day running of the shifts, Sophie was pleasantly surprised at how everyone managed to fit in so easily. Katie and Jackie tended to do mainly weekends and were usually on opposite shifts in order to take each other's children during school holidays and evenings, whereas Margaret and Garry, who were recently retired, often took the less family-friendly shifts. John seemed to float in between and, except during sowing and harvesting times, could be counted on to fill any leftover spots.

Her old station could learn a few things from this crew: there was always someone bitching about something, and shifts were never this simple to organise. Maybe they were just breaking her in slowly.

'We're an easygoing bunch,' Katie smiled. 'We try to fit in around each other's family and work commitments, but we're all pretty much on call and ready to come in whenever we're needed.'

Sophie noticed that the vollies, as they referred to themselves, averaged between four and ten jobs a month, ranging from simple transfers to hospital to, occasionally, more serious accidents. It was certainly going to be a change of pace from her usual workload, but she reminded herself once again that this was what she needed until she got back on her feet again.

She hit save on her laptop and gave a relieved smile as they wrapped up the meeting, happy to have received a bit of an overview on how the station worked and what to expect on her first shift the next day. 'Thanks for coming in today, everyone. I'm really looking forward to working with you all and getting to know you a little bit better over the next few weeks.'

Sophie thanked Margaret and Garry for giving her directions to the pub where she'd be staying, and declined the offer of help with her luggage, leaving the station to let the last shift get back to work. The long drive had tired her out, and all she felt like doing right now was finding a bed and falling asleep for a couple of hours.

Two

Sophie dumped her bag on the end of the bed and looked around the room. Janice was right: this wasn't what she'd been imagining when she found out she'd be living in a pub. There was a comfy-looking queen-size bed, and a beautifully restored set of drawers and a small table sat by the French doors, which opened up onto a wide timber verandah. She had to share a bathroom but there were two, both clean and newly renovated and only a few doors down the hall. She'd lived in worse places, she thought, remembering back to her early university days doing her nursing degree.

She'd completed three years of the four-year course before realising it wasn't really her thing. She loved the patient contact, found the clinical training fascinating, but there was something about the hospital environment she wasn't fitting in with. While doing her placement in emergency she'd see the paramedics come in and hand over their patients to the hospital staff. Then one day Sophie witnessed something that would change her career and, in doing so, her whole life.

The doors had opened and a blast of activity had followed. Nurses and doctors had swarmed to the gurney that had just been rolled in, stats were called out as the two ambulance officers had given a handover on the move: a car accident involving two teenagers, both with serious injuries. As the paramedic closest to her had gone to leave, Sophie had seen that he was holding the hand of the young woman on the gurney. She had looked up at him, unable to speak because of terrible lacerations sustained to her throat, but the look of absolute fear in her eyes as the medical staff had tried to pull her away from him had tugged at Sophie's heart strings. She remembered how he'd talked softly to her, reassuring her that she was safe, and his gentle smile had somehow calmed the girl.

It had struck Sophie for the first time that this man had been there from the very first moment, talking her through a horrific experience when she was in tremendous pain and shock. Their bond, created through a violent tragedy, was obvious, and Sophie had been incredibly moved.

That's when she realised what she wanted to do. She wanted to help people—really help them. She wanted to comfort people in their most dire moments. She wanted to make a difference—and she had, until lately. Until the day someone had almost ended her life and stolen everything that had made her who she was. She pushed away the gloom that threatened and reached for her phone instead.

'Mitcham,' the gruff voice answered on the third ring.

'Where the hell have you sent me, Darrell?'

'You made it, I take it?' Sophie heard the slight amusement in his tone and could picture the twitch of his lips that he considered a smile.

She looked around the room and gave a small grunt. 'I drove on dirt for part of the trip, Darrell. *Dirt!* I didn't even know there *were* dirt roads anywhere nowadays.'

'It's upgraded since I was there then—used to be *all* dirt road.'

'What were you thinking? The last place that sold petrol was, like, two hours before I reached this place.' Well, maybe not exactly two hours, but it felt damn near that far away.

'I told you it was a bit remote,' he said without any kind of remorse in his voice.

'A bit! It's like, *literally,* the sticks.'

'You wanted something quieter,' he pointed out. 'Trust me, the place will grow on you.'

'Well, if it's so great, why did *you* leave?'

'For a woman—what else? I had the perfect life there, laid-back lifestyle, great pub, great people, and then I went to Sydney for a training seminar and that was the end of that.'

Sophie couldn't help the reluctant grin that followed this disgruntled admission, especially when she knew just how much her big tough boss loved his wife. 'Terri's a lucky woman having an old romantic like you,' she replied drolly.

'Just give it a chance, Soph,' he said, suddenly serious. 'The place will be good for you.'

After Sophie said goodbye, she sat on the end of the bed and battled a wave of homesickness brought on by hearing Darrell's voice. She'd left everything she'd ever known behind in Sydney—her friends, her job, everything familiar—to come out here . . . to what? What the hell had she been thinking?

Give it a chance. It was something that Garth would have said, and she squeezed her eyes tightly shut and lowered her head.

It'll be alright.

She opened her eyes, half-thinking that he'd be standing in front of her, but the small room was empty, just like it always was. Sometimes she could almost feel him there with her. She'd never tell anyone or they'd think she was crazy, but since her husband's death there had been times when she could feel his presence—not literally, but in a strange, calming kind of way.

A natural sceptic, she'd never had much time for ghost stories and fortune tellers, but over the years she'd encountered certain situations that she couldn't find a logical explanation for—people who'd been pulled from car wrecks by mysterious bystanders on dark, lonely nights, who had disappeared without a trace afterwards. Dying patients who reach out and talk to people who aren't there. Before losing Garth she may have brushed these things off as trauma-induced apparitions, but now she wasn't so fast to dismiss them. Maybe these feelings *were* just grief messing with her emotions, but whatever it was often helped her put things into perspective. Garth had always been the calm, rational one.

'I miss you,' she whispered to the empty room. The only response was the bar fridge humming quietly in the corner.

Three

Sophie felt better after a quick shower, changing into a white top and clean denim jeans. She'd taken out the pony-tail she'd worn earlier, deciding to wear her hair down for the occasion. She was glad she'd treated herself to a haircut before she left. Truth be told, she was a little worried it may be the last time she'd have the chance—who knew if this place had one. Her poetically inclined hairdresser had called her brown shoulder-length hair burnt toffee; eyeing it in the salon mirror she had thought that something like maple syrup or caramel sounded better.

She pulled on long suede boots and gave herself a mental pep talk. Crowds put her on edge these days, so she avoided large gatherings as much as she could. She also hated being in the spotlight, and seeing Sophie was the whole reason these people were hosting a dinner downstairs, she could pretty much guarantee she wouldn't be able to hide in any corners tonight.

Her mind flashed briefly to the pills in her toiletry bag before pushing the thought away. She hadn't taken any in the past two weeks, worrying that she was depending on them a little too much to get her through the day. She didn't want to be propped up by medication in order to function. In all fairness, she probably wouldn't be judged too harshly if she did take a pill tonight. They were to help lower her anxiety, and meeting a town full of strangers was pretty damn stressful. She was tired of feeling like this. She just wanted to get back to normal . . . whatever the hell *that* was nowadays.

Sophie got to her feet, slipping phone and room key into her pocket and heading for the door before she could talk herself into taking a pill. She could do this—without any drugs. She *would* do it. This was a new beginning, a fresh start. This was going to be good for her . . .

Heading downstairs, the sounds of a country pub floated all around her. The monotonous computerised bells, chimes and whistles from poker machines in all corners of the room bombarded her senses. In the background a commentator excitedly called a horse race, while on another large screen a football game played to yelling patrons. The smells of beer, hot chips and carpet shampoo mixed in an odd combination as she made her way across the room to the bar. The bartender, a short, stocky man with grey hair, came over to her with a wide smile. 'You must be the new ambo—how you doing? I'm Joe. I own the pub. Sorry I wasn't here earlier to show you around.'

She stopped herself automatically correcting him over the ambo title. They were paramedics now, had been since the nineties, really, but there was still a large proportion of the community who were unaware of the hard-earned title change. 'No worries, I found everything. The room's lovely.'

'Yeah, we gave the old girl a bit of a facelift not too long ago. I reckon we could give some of them city places a run for their money now,' he grinned. 'You'd be looking for the shindig to welcome you to town, I'm guessing?'

Sophie smiled and nodded. 'I would.'

'Head through those two doors on your left. You better take a drink. You'll probably need it. What'll you have?'

Sophie liked this man. 'White wine—whatever you have open is fine.'

'Ah, an indiscriminate drinker, I see. I like it.' He selected a bottle from the fridge behind him and poured her a glass, handing it across. 'On the house. Welcome to Hilsons Ridge.'

'Thanks, Joe.'

He waved her off with a smile before serving the next customer and Sophie's spirits lifted slightly.

She walked into the large room and was immediately greeted by a dozen or so smiling faces.

'Here she is.' Janice's voice sang out as she crossed to Sophie's side, arms open for another hug. This woman clearly had the nurturing thing down pat, but she really needed to ease off on the hugs a little. 'Come and meet everyone,' she said, latching on to Sophie's hand and tugging her forward.

A smartly dressed couple in their late fifties smiled as Janice stopped before them. 'Sophie, meet Jeff and Anne Harding. Jeff's one of our local councillors and Anne's on the town's progress committee.'

'It's so nice to meet you, Sophie,' Anne Harding said, clasping Sophie's hand warmly.

'I guess it would be you I have to thank for having a station to come to?'

'Oh, not just me. It took a mighty effort from a lot of wonderful people to do that,' she said, smiling as she gestured with her hand to everyone else in the room before leading her forward to meet another nearby couple.

'This is Dave Spicer and his wife, Shelly.'

'I believe you came to us from Sydney?' Dave asked.

'That's right.'

'You were given a glowing reference by Darrell Mitcham—I remember him from many years ago.'

'Yes, he often talked about his time out here,' Sophie smiled, feeling a pang of homesickness at the mention of her old boss's name. Darrell was a big, gruff teddy bear of a man. For all his outwardly grouchy exterior, he was a kind-hearted, generous man who Sophie had come to admire and respect both professionally and personally in her years working under him. Darrell and his wife, Terri, were like family to her, having supported her through some of the toughest days of her life after losing Garth.

'I hope you like your time out here with us just as much,' Dave said.

'What do you enjoy doing, Sophie?' Anne asked. She reminded Sophie of an inquisitive sparrow with her head tilted sideways, listening intently.

'Doing?'

'In your spare time,' Anne prompted with a smile. 'We have lots of sporting groups, tennis courts, squash courts, a beautiful golf course, lots of social activities.'

'Oh. I'm not much of a sportsperson. I tend to keep to myself a bit.'

'Well, not too much, I hope.'

Sophie managed a weak smile at the woman but could feel a cold sweat start to break out on her back at the thought of being bombarded with offers to join every conceivable sporting group known to Hilsons Ridge. What she craved was some peace and quiet—that's why she'd allowed Darrell to talk her into coming out here. That and the nervous breakdown he was convinced she was about to have coming back to work so soon after being released from hospital.

As loudly as she'd protested that Darrell had been exaggerating about her health, part of her knew that maybe he was right. She loved her job—it was her life. After Garth's death it had given her something to focus on. Her work colleagues were like family, and surrounding herself with them had lessened the gaping hole he'd left in her life so unexpectedly. But after the shooting, everything had changed. She'd lost her confidence, she felt scared and on edge all the time and, worst of all, going back to work, something that had always helped her cope with problems in the past, only added to her anxiety now.

For a while her family had encouraged her to find a different line of work after Garth's death; they'd always worried about her safety on the job, having heard of the not so nice side of ambulance work for too many years. The drunken abuse, the drug-fuelled violence of people you were sent in to try to help wasn't pleasant, but it came with the job and she'd always taken the good with the bad. After Garth's accident, her parents had been an amazing support. They'd stayed with her and helped to take care of everything. Her mother had wanted her to move back in with them after the funeral, but Sophie had needed to get her life back together, and as tempting as it was to allow her parents to mollycoddle her, the longer she put off learning to live without Garth, the harder it would be to do.

Garth's accident was bad enough, but after the attack they'd become even more vocal about leaving to find safer employment. She knew they worried about her and she was worried herself, but she knew deep down she couldn't give up her job. She hated that someone had taken away the contentment of the career she'd loved so much, but she wasn't ready to give up either. Sophie wanted to fight for her job, to push past the fear that seemed to hang over her all the time now. She didn't want to give into it—to let it win. But she also knew that if she didn't make some kind of radical change soon, the decision to stay or not might be taken out of her hands. *You couldn't get any more radical than this,* she thought.

'I take it you've met Ado already?' Anne said, smiling as the doctor approached them. He was dressed in the same caramel cargo pants and pinstriped long-sleeve shirt he'd been wearing earlier, minus the stethoscope around his neck.

'Yes, we've met,' Sophie said, giving a small nod.

'You're still here,' he smiled.

'Yes, still here.'

'Then that is a good start. We haven't frightened you away?' Ado enquired warmly.

'Not yet.'

'Good, good,' he nodded, and Sophie realised he was kind of attractive when he smiled. His dark eyes were on her now, seeming to look right through the bravado she was trying to hide behind tonight. It unnerved her slightly.

'Am I right in detecting a slight accent?' Sophie asked, trying to make conversation.

'My family came to Australia as refugees from Bosnia twenty-six years ago.'

'How did you end up here in Hilsons Ridge?'

'I did my training in Sydney but, like you, I responded to an advertisement for a position as local GP. The town needed a doctor.'

'I'll leave you two to chat so you can talk about the locals in private,' Anne said with a wry twist of her lips.

'How are you *really* finding it?' he asked leaning in slightly, his eyes twinkling.

Sophie chuckled despite herself. 'I'm wondering what I got myself into,' she admitted.

Ado nodded slightly. 'It can take a bit of getting used to but, I promise, you will grow to love this place. They are good people,' he said as his gaze wandered around the room. 'And they need us,' he said, his eyes fixing upon her face once more.

Sophie took a sip of her drink. The man had the most unnerving eyes—so dark and brooding. His short-cut, dusty brown hair and dark eyebrows only added to the overall mysterious appeal of his features. He wasn't handsome in the traditional sense, despite the fact that chiselled jawlines were almost always associated with model types, but he certainly wasn't unattractive, either. He wore a European kind of sophistication without even trying, which seemed completely out of place in this rural Australian landscape.

'I shall very much look forward to working with you, Sophie,' he said, tapping his glass against hers gently before giving her a small nod and walking away.

'He's single.'

Sophie turned to find Anne had drifted back to her side and was staring after the slender form of the doctor as he crossed the room.

'So I've heard,' Sophie said drolly. What *was* it with this place? She'd been here less than twenty-four hours and this was the second time someone had tried to set her up with the local doctor.

'It's a good lifestyle out here. I know it seems pretty remote, but we've tried to provide everything the community needs—as much as we can, at least,' Anne added.

'You've all done a great job. I was surprised and a little relieved when I arrived to find an actual town.'

Anne gave a chuckle. 'Hilsons Ridge was once quite a busy place. It was a major stop-off point for travellers.'

'Really?' Sophie asked doubtfully, thinking about how isolated the little place was.

'A man by the name of Raymond Hilson discovered gold here back in the 1880s and kicked things off. In the early days the road through here was the only way to link the New England towns to the coast, right up until they built the Gwydir Highway in the sixties. During the gold rush there were thirteen hotels here. After that farming became the main industry, and more recently we've turned to tourism with four-wheel driving and camping enthusiasts.'

'I can see why—the scenery driving up here was breathtaking.'

'It's lovely to have you here. You let me know if you need anything,' Anne said, lightly touching Sophie's arm and giving a gentle squeeze before moving away.

Well, I'm here now, she thought. *May as well give the place a go and see what happens.* It couldn't be any worse than the half-life she'd been living for the past few months, surely?

Four

Sophie's first day on the new job came with a blue sky and cold nip to the morning air. The coffee she cradled in her hands protectively wasn't even touching the sides of her exhaustion yet, but she was hoping it would kick in soon.

It had been a long night of tossing and turning to get to sleep, adjusting to all the new sounds of the town and the creaking old pub as it settled itself in for the night. She'd awoken with a start around dawn, heart racing and a cold sweat running down her back. That ended any hope of ever getting back to sleep, unless she used her medication, but she didn't want to. She just wanted to get back to feeling normal again.

Some things never changed—when she could have used a slow morning to ease into things, a job came in and she and Garry were making a transfer to Grafton.

'And this is all still our area?' Sophie asked as Garry negotiated the narrow, pot-holed road. She tried to keep the astonishment from her voice but apparently failed as he sent her an amused look.

'Yep,' Garry said in his dry as dust drawl. 'Bit bigger than you're used to, I take it?'

'Just a tad,' she said weakly, staring out across the paddocks of grazing cattle and sheep. 'Everything looks so dry. Is it always like this?'

'Well, it's been a bit of a dry winter, but what you're seeing here is quality feed. Our hay gets top price and farmers on the coast often send their cattle up here to fatten up. It doesn't look like much but it's good tucker for livestock.'

'Oh.' Maybe she'd just keep her questions to herself from now on before these people thought she was any more naïve than they already considered her to be.

'How you finding the place?'

'Well, it's a little different to what I'm used to, but I'm really liking it.'

'Not too quiet for you?'

'Quiet's good,' she said with a lopsided grin. She needed some quiet in her life.

'We're all mighty pleased you're here,' Garry said with a smile.

His friendly words filled her chest with a ridiculously warm emotion she hadn't felt in quite a long time. She hadn't even done anything to deserve their gratitude, just turned up, but it still felt good to feel wanted.

'How'd you get into this work, Garry?' she asked after a few moments of silence, watching the scenery passing outside her window.

'I was in the bushfire brigade for years. Still am,' he added. 'When they threatened to close down the ambulance station, the committee came up with the idea of supplying volunteers, so anyone with some kind of background in first aid put up their hand for the training. I already had a bit under my belt with the RFS, so I figured, why not?'

'It's just amazing how you've all pulled together for this.' It still astounded her whenever she thought about it. She'd never been part of a community that worked so hard as one in order to secure something so vital for them all.

'We kind of had to.'

'It's a real credit to you all.'

A self-satisfied grin touched Garry's lips as he kept his eyes on the road ahead and Sophie went back to looking out the window. Up ahead a little house with a wraparound verandah sat back from the road. There were no cattle grazing in the surrounding paddocks; in fact, the place looked deserted. It was the kind of image you'd find on a calendar featuring rustic photos of rural Australia. *That would be stunning with a sunset behind it,* she thought as they passed by. It really was gorgeous out here; there was a rugged, wild kind of beauty that appealed to her. Who would have thought? Garth had always wanted to move to the country. That had always been their plan: to move from the city and raise their family. Only they'd never managed to decide on a time for all that to happen and then suddenly it was too late.

She forced the thought away and asked Garry another question. 'So how long does it take to get to Grafton?'

'About ninety minutes. The road's pretty narrow and windy. If it's serious or we're short-staffed, we get them to meet us at a rest stop that's about halfway.'

It wasn't just the new station she had to get used to it was also the vehicle. Out here they had a fleet of four-wheel drives in order to access the kind of places they may need to get to. The four-wheel drive, although well stocked with equipment, wasn't as roomy in the back as the big Mercedes van she was used to in the city. She was going to have to learn pretty fast how to adjust to the cramped working space, not to mention the driving conditions. They'd hit dirt road once again and it narrowed in parts to barely one car width across. In the city the biggest concern had been negotiating traffic, but out here it was the terrain. The roads may be fairly quiet but they were full of potholes and loose gravel, which would slow down travel times when you had to be mindful of patients in the back. The scattering of roadkill along the roadside also reminded her of other potential hazards—wildlife jumping out in front of you.

Garry glanced across as though reading her mind. 'Yeah, you gotta watch the roos. They can make a bit of a mess.'

Great.

'But the cattle are worse. Don't hit a cow.'

'Don't hit a cow' was not exactly the kind of advice you got when going out on a call in the city, but clearly something she would try *not* to do out here. Oh dear lord, what had she got herself into?

❧

Next shift Sophie found herself rostered on with John, and while the majority of the day she worked alone, until a call came in, it was comforting to know she had company for the evening, especially seeing it was a Friday night and the pub had looked extra busy. It wasn't long before they got their first call for the evening.

Sophie climbed into the passenger side of the ambulance and read out the info she'd received. 'Nineteen-year-old male, sustained lacerations to the hand.'

'Well, it wouldn't be a Friday night at the pub unless someone got into a fight,' John said matter-of-factly. 'Probably a good thing we get it over sooner rather than later.'

As the ambulance pulled up, Sophie searched for the police, frowning when she couldn't spot them. 'No police?'

'The local station is pretty much closed down. They run everything from Grafton or Inverell. Most of the time we get to a call before they do, unless they contact us later.'

Sophie did a quick assessment of the gathered crowd. She wouldn't set foot out of the ambulance unless they had police backup in the city. 'We're not in Kansas anymore, Toto,' she muttered quietly under her breath as she followed John's lead and exited the vehicle.

The lacerations thankfully hadn't been as severe as they'd been expecting, and after cleaning and dressing the small wound they were back on the road again.

'At least it's not a footy grand final,' John commented later as they drove down the main street back to the station from a call to an elderly woman's fall. 'Those nights are crazy.'

'Do we get many footy grand finals?'

John gave a small grunt. 'Not in the last few seasons. Useless pack of bastards,' he muttered. 'Our first-grade side used to be unbeatable, but they lost their coach and, since then, they're a different team.'

'I take it you're a football fan?'

'Yeah. Love me footy. I was training the local under-eighteen side until I took this job on,' he said, eyes on the front windscreen as he drove.

'So you have a background in the military?' Sophie asked when the conversation ebbed.

'Yeah. I did a few years—long time ago now.'

'I guess some of the medical training was fairly similar?'

'To a certain degree,' he agreed. 'I was considering switching to the medics, but it never eventuated.'

'Why's that?'

He sent Sophie a quick sideways glance before taking his attention back to the road. 'I was deployed on a number of peacekeeping tours, all over the place, but I got out after Rwanda. I'd seen some pretty messed up stuff during my time overseas, but that place . . .' His words trailed off and he shook his head slightly. 'After that, I came back to the family farm and this is what I've been doing ever since.'

Sophie let her gaze drift back out her window, not wanting to push the conversation about John's past any further. Knowing he had his own demons to bear cemented an affiliation of sorts with the man beside her. Her memories weren't of a war-torn country and untold human atrocities, but she too had faced violence, fear and death, and sometimes finding an ally—a fellow survivor of trauma—went a long way to reassure her that she wasn't as alone as she sometimes felt.

෴

The jukebox in the main bar belted out another James Blundell song and Sophie buried her head beneath the pillow, trying to drown out the noise. She had nothing against James Blundell personally, but at midnight, after a restless few nights of sleep, Sophie was about ready to rip the plug out of the wall.

She'd already enquired about the renovation progress on her accommodation, but so far she hadn't been able to pin down anyone who could give her a firm answer about how much longer it was going to take to finish. Apparently the job was turning into a bit of a nightmare, with more problems being discovered the further along they got. Sophie had even heard a rumour that it wouldn't be worthwhile continuing with the renovations. What they planned on doing with a half-finished bathroom she had no idea; she was more concerned about where she was going to live. All Sophie knew was she couldn't do the pub for much longer—she'd go crazy. She'd already taken a very brief look at the two houses available for lease through the local real estate office, but had decided she probably wasn't vaccinated anywhere near enough to consider moving into either of them. The little house she had noticed out of town often popped up in her mind from time to time, but she dismissed it. It was completely impractical . . . and yet at times like this when everywhere else was just too *peopley,* the solitude of the old house seemed to call her.

The phone rang and she gave a low moan before reaching for it on the bedside table. 'Bryant speaking.' Sophie listened to the dispatcher as she gave details of a call that had just come in and was instantly awake, grabbing the pen and pad to jot it down.

'I'm sorry, can you repeat that last bit?' Sophie said, certain she'd misheard the dispatcher. 'Okay. Thanks.' Sophie was still shaking her head as she pulled on her uniform and headed out to the ambulance to meet up with John en route. She really shouldn't be surprised by anything anyone did after all this time, and yet there were still times when she was.

⌘

'Thank God you're here.' The woman motioned for Sophie and John to follow her from the front through a set of double gates into the backyard.

A small crowd of people were gathered around a man sitting on the ground. The remnants of a party lingered, a fire burning in a large drum and James Blundell belting out of a stereo system. *Again with the Blundell?* Sophie thought.

Two police officers, who were talking to the crowd and taking notes, glanced up as Sophie stopped in front of them, placing her bag on the ground to take stock of the situation.

'Hi, you must be the new paramedic. I'm Cathy Borne,' the female police officer said with a smile. Sophie guessed her to be mid-forties. Blonde hair pulled back in a short ponytail, Cathy's eyes rolled slightly as she gave Sophie a brief rundown of the events. 'This is Gura,' she started. 'He was in an altercation with another male who fled the scene, and during the altercation the perpetrator has bitten Gura's ear,' she said, indicating the man on the ground holding a cloth to one side of his head.

'Hi, Gura. My name's Sophie. Can I take a look at your ear?' She gently removed the cloth he was holding and immediately heard a woman scream and someone else begin to dry heave in the crowd behind her. The top half of the ear was missing completely, and blood streamed down the man's face and neck once the pressure was removed.

Sophie turned to look at the two police officers. 'Do you think we could move everyone away?'

'Come on, let's give them some room to work here,' the male officer said, shooing the crowd back.

'Any idea where the missing part of the ear went?' Sophie asked.

'No,' the female officer said gravely. 'We searched the area where the fight broke out and there's no sign of it. We're trying not to make any assumptions, but . . .'

Sophie followed her glance across at a couple of dogs wandering around the yard sniffing at rubbish and exchanged a look with the two police officers. Gross.

Reattaching the missing part of the ear wasn't going to be possible then. Plan B would mean reconstructive surgery that was both a long and expensive ordeal and one that a lot of people didn't elect to go on and have.

'I'm going to clean this up as much as I can and dress it, and then I'm going to take you to the hospital so they can stitch you up, okay?'

'Can I have a drink now?' Gura asked, his words slurring slightly. 'They took mine off me,' he said, glaring at the police officers.

'No, sorry, not yet. We need to get you fixed up first.' Sophie put the lack of agonised screaming down to an enormous amount of alcohol consumed beforehand, and he certainly didn't need any more. It was probably a good thing as the wound looked excruciatingly painful.

The police took a few more statements before John helped load the injured man into the ambulance. Nope, it seemed life out here certainly wasn't going to be dull.

Five

A scream and a gunshot reverberated through the room as Sophie sat up in her bed, breathing heavily as she frantically scanned the room, disorientated. With a shaky hand she reached out and switched on her bedside lamp, rubbing her hands across her face before getting up to splash it with water at the small basin across the room.

It was always the same. The end of the gun pointing at her, the cold empty eyes of the man staring at her, and blood . . . everywhere. She could still smell the blood, its metallic-like scent heavy in the air.

Sophie stared into the mirror above the basin and blinked away the image of a dead woman in the bloody hallway of a rundown house. She eyed the box of tablets she saw inside her toiletry bag and turned away, taking a long, deep

breath instead before settling into a chair by the window
to wait for the sun to peek over the horizon.

✍

Sophie sat down at the desk and looked around the office.
There was so much that was familiar despite the different
location. She took out her iPad and went through case
clinical records, chasing up anything that still needed attention and going over details she may need to know for the
coming day. By seven she'd moved on to checking through
the vehicle's equipment and medication. Katie called out a
hello as she came into the office just as Sophie was about
to make a coffee.

The first of her meagre possessions she'd packed in her
car before driving out was her espresso machine, and seeing
she was staying in the pub and had nowhere to use it, she'd
brought it into work. There was no way she was sacrificing
decent coffee.

'Wow, this is a bit fancy,' Katie said, happily accepting
the cup Sophie offered. 'Looks like you need a day's training
to work it.'

'It's not as complicated as it looks.' Sophie patted the
silver machine lovingly.

'If you say so, but I think I'll stick to takeaway from
Betsy's down the street when you're not on shift.'

Katie took out the packet of Tim Tams from the fridge
and they sat down at the table. She slid the packet across
to Sophie then proceeded to bite each end off a chocolate
biscuit and lean over her mug to slurp her coffee through

the biscuit like a straw, before popping the entire thing in her mouth with a satisfied grin.

'What are you doing?' Sophie asked with a puzzled frown.

'What? You've never done a Tim Tam slam before?'

'A what?'

'Oh my God, what do you people *do* down there? You can't eat a Tim Tam and not slam it. It's just . . . unnatural.'

Sophie eyed Katie hesitantly but took one of the chocolate biscuits from the packet as she was instructed.

'You bite off the ends and suck it up, but you have to be quick, before it melts,' she warned. 'Then you slam the rest of the biscuit into your mouth and wait for the magic to happen.'

'Alright,' Sophie said, already doubtful that this would be the life-changing event Katie clearly thought it was going to be. Sophie leaned over her cup, feeling like an idiot as she attempted to suck through the rather odd kind of straw. It took a few seconds before the coffee came through.

'Take it out now, quick! Before it falls apart!' Katie cried, leaning across the table like an over-eager coach. 'Slam it!'

Sophie quickly removed the now alarmingly soggy biscuit and shoved it in her mouth, then closed her eyes as a sudden explosion of gooey chocolate filled her mouth. 'Sweet baby Jesus,' she murmured before opening her eyes.

'Right?' Katie said with a smug grin as she sat back in her chair.

Sophie reached across and took another biscuit, repeating the steps and staring at her cup with a disbelieving shake of her head.

An hour later the first job of the morning came through and Katie and Sophie went out on a priority-three call to a thirty-four-year-old woman with a swollen knee.

Nowhere in town was very far to drive. There was no traffic to dodge and no need to run red lights, considering there were no traffic lights in Hilsons Ridge at all. They were at the address within two minutes of leaving the station. The response time out here would certainly impress all the politicians back in the city.

'You'll probably get to know Isabelle Sutton fairly well. She's one of our semi regulars.'

Sophie figured there'd be patients like that here too. She had her fair share of regulars in the city and you soon got to know them. Katie gave Sophie the rundown on her history, but every call-out needed to be investigated and a thorough examination done before any decision on treatment was offered—even if you knew the patient might have a dubious history.

Sophie knocked on the door. 'Hello? It's the ambulance,' she called out, waiting for a response. From inside the small house she heard a voice telling her to come in, and she and Katie followed the sound to the tiny kitchen out the back. The old fibro cottage still had the original brick fireplace where once an old Aga stove probably had taken pride of place. There was a heavy smell of cigarette smoke hanging in the air. Sophie crossed the room to a gaunt-looking woman slumped at the kitchen table, groaning with half a cigarette in her hand and an almost full ashtray beside her arm.

'Hi there, I'm Sophie—you must be Isabelle. I think you already know Katie?' Sophie made the brief introduction before getting down to business. 'What have you done to yourself?'

The woman looked up at Sophie, eyes slightly bloodshot as she squinted through the puff of smoke she'd just exhaled. 'I tripped over and hurt my knee,' she moaned, pulling up the leg of her tracksuit pants to reveal a thin leg.

'So on a scale of one to ten, with ten being the highest, what would you rate your pain level at right now?' Sophie asked as she assessed the knee, which didn't look terribly swollen at the moment.

'Definitely a ten,' Isabelle replied without hesitation.

Sophie gently pressed around the knee amidst loud protests of pain. Feeling that something was not quite right about the situation, and with Katie's previous rundown of the woman's history still fresh in her memory, she decided to probe a little deeper with her questions. 'Are you taking any kind of medication at the moment, Isabelle?'

'No, nothing.'

'No blood pressure, cholesterol medication?' The woman shook her head for each. 'What about things like antidepressants?'

'Nah, not anymore. I haven't taken any of them for months. I just need something for the pain.'

Sophie still wasn't convinced the level of pain was consistent with the injury as it presented and pressed Isabelle a little further on her previous health issues, finally revealing that the woman was currently in a methadone program.

There was no doubt Isabelle had probably tripped and hurt her knee as she'd stated, but the absence of any significant swelling and bruising wasn't quite meshing with the level of pain indicated and the administration of morphine without being aware of the woman's previous drug issue could have had disastrous effects. Sophie adjusted her pain relief strategy, giving methoxyflurane to the patient in a green whistle instead of morphine, before suggesting a trip to the hospital to rule out anything not obvious, but the woman declined. After finalising the paperwork, Katie and Sophie packed up their gear and left.

It wasn't long before the next call came through—to attend an elderly woman experiencing chest pain. It was a busier morning than Sophie had been expecting, but she was enjoying the pleasant change of pace from a typical city shift.

They pulled up outside a neat little home with a beautifully maintained garden out the front. Sophie headed up the path, bordered with a rainbow of delicate flowers that she couldn't name. She'd never really been a gardener, that had been Garth's domain, and her heart gave a small catch at the unexpected memory.

A woman met them at the door, holding the screen open and ushering them inside. 'Hello, Katie, dear,' she said, sending a relieved smile.

'Shirl, this is Sophie. Shirl is Ethel's next-door neighbour.' Katie turned to introduce her.

'I'm so glad you're both here,' the woman said over her shoulder as she bustled ahead, leading the way to a bedroom at the rear of the house. 'I usually pop over each morning to check on her, but when I arrived today she was finding it hard to catch her breath and she tells me her chest hurts.'

Sophie entered the bedroom and saw a fragile-looking woman, well into her late eighties, tucked up beneath her lace quilt. 'Hello, Ethel. My name's Sophie. I'm guessing you already know Katie?' The woman gave a faint nod. 'You're not feeling too good?'

Ethel shook her head, and even this small action seemed to take a toll on her. Her hands were cold as Sophie took her pulse, which was a little unsteady.

'I'm sorry to cause all this trouble, dear,' Ethel said weakly.

'It's no trouble at all,' Sophie replied, glancing up and smiling warmly. Most of the oldies she attended from this era were the same, never wanting to cause a fuss or put anyone out. It was a nice change from certain other members of the community who tended to treat the Ambulance Service like a personal chauffeur, but it was also frustrating because often, by the time an ambulance was called, their condition had worsened or it was too late. 'This is what we're here for—to help. It's better to find out it's nothing than to ignore it and have it be something serious.'

She noticed that Ethel's breathing was quite shallow and pulled out an oxygen mask, placing it gently over the elderly woman's nose and mouth and instructing her to breathe in and out slowly. 'We're going to do an ECG and check out what's going on, alright?'

Ethel gave a weak nod and Sophie suspected if the mask wasn't on her face she would have probably continued to protest about being a bother.

With Katie working alongside her, they quickly and calmly went through the procedure, attaching the electrodes and leads, and putting the patient data into the device, before taking the ECG recording. 'So we're just going to send this through to the doctor and let him have a look at it,' Sophie said, as she finalised the procedure by selecting the various options on the menu screen to complete the transmission.

'Oh my,' Shirl said, shaking her head as she watched on from her neighbour's bedside. 'Isn't technology wonderful?'

Sophie smiled and murmured her agreement as she transmitted the ECG results to the hospital. Ado would take a look and advise if this was an AMI—an acute myocardial infarction, more commonly known as a heart attack—in order to figure out how to proceed.

Sophie wasn't liking the blood pressure reading she got; while not below what was considered safe, it had dropped since the very first reading she'd taken. 'Katie's going to give you some aspirin. You're not allergic or have any bleeding problems?' she asked as Katie prepared the medication.

Her phone rang and Sophie immediately answered, hearing Ado's calm voice on the other end relaying that he suspected this was an AMI.

After hanging up, Sophie and Katie quickly ran through their checklist and Sophie was once again impressed by the professionalism of her volunteer. Sophie administered the clot-busting drugs, hoping that they'd do their job and, if not stabilise Ethel's condition, then at least hold things at bay until they got her to hospital.

Sophie and Katie transferred Ethel onto the stretcher and strapped her in carefully before wheeling the trolley out of the house and into the back of the ambulance. After calling their departure in, she was referred to the larger hospital at Grafton. A crew had already been dispatched to meet them en route, which would save time and mean Sophie and Katie wouldn't be tied up for the entire three-hour round trip in case another emergency came in which required them.

'How long have you lived in the area, Katie?' Sophie asked on the drive back home after handing over Ethel to the other ambulance.

'Must be about ten years now.'

'What brought you out here?'

'Love,' she said with a smile. 'What else? I met Tim in Tamworth at a friend's wedding. A year later we were married and I became a farmer's wife.'

'So what made you want to be a volly?'

'As you may have noticed, we might not be in the middle of the Never Never here, but we are still over an hour and a half drive to the nearest big hospital. That's a long time when you have an emergency on your hands. When they tried to close the station down, I was at home with three children on a property out of town. When the town called out for volunteers, I just figured it was a great opportunity to learn some skills that might one day save my child's or a neighbour's life.'

Sophie was impressed by the woman's reasoning. Out here it *was* remote. In an emergency when every second counts, an hour and a half away from help was quite literally a death sentence in some cases.

'Plus, they give you a uniform,' she added, waving her hand up and down her blue-clad body with all the flamboyance of a game show hostess. 'And what's not to love about that?' In an occupation where the one style of uniform was not always flattering to every employee's body shape, it was a constant source of irritation.

'Well, you wear it fabulously,' Sophie told her, smiling. It was nice to have a female partner for a change.

'I think we're going to get along just fine,' Katie said. 'I'll just fatten you up a bit on Tim Tams and then I won't have to hate you for looking so much hotter in uniform than me.'

Sophie scoffed. Considering the woman had been through three pregnancies, she'd kind of earned the right to carry a few extra kilos, but she was not obviously overweight.

'I think we've earned our Tim Tams today,' Katie said after they unpacked the ambulance, replaced the sheets on the stretcher and cleaned up. 'Time to fire up that monstrosity of a coffee machine again.'

I'm definitely going to have to take up some kind of exercise if I work too many shifts in a row with Katie, Sophie thought, following her inside. She was becoming a very bad influence.

Six

Sophie was too restless to head back to the pub at the end of her shift and decided to go for a drive instead. Passing by the picturesque house she'd noticed the other day when out with Garry, she pulled the car over to the side of the road and stared at the lopsided *For Sale* sign hanging off the fence post. What was it about this place? Why did she keep thinking about it?

An ocean of whisky-coloured grass swayed like a wave in the gentle breeze, sweeping from the roadside to the small house in the centre of the paddock, with the mountains in the distance behind it.

Sophie glanced quickly both ways before turning the car into the driveway and climbing out to inspect the gate. There was no padlock, just a simple hook and chain. She

shaded her eyes and squinted, trying to gauge if anyone
was home in the farmhouse, a good five hundred metres
from the front gate.

There was no movement, no sound of anything other
than the birds and the breeze through the grass. Before she
could talk herself out of it, Sophie reached over the gate and
unhooked the chain. There was a protesting creak of rust
and infrequent use as she pushed it open before heading
back to the car and driving along the dirt drive towards
the house. In the silence she heard her mother's voice in
her head, asking, *What are you doing?* She had no idea.
There was no logical reason she should be driving up to
take a closer look at this house.

It looked as though it hadn't been lived in for quite
some time, judging by the dusty windows and accumulated
pile of leaves the wind had blown up against the front
of the house. She walked up the two steps and onto the
old, weathered verandah, crossing to the timber door and
giving three sharp raps before standing back to listen for
any sound of stirring inside.

'Hello?' she called out. 'Anyone home?' Silence greeted
her. Sophie walked around the corner of the verandah and
saw that all the windows on that side, like the two at the
front, were covered by curtains.

Sophie shaded her eyes as she scanned the vicinity to see
if the occupants were somewhere outside. A short distance
from the house sat a large tin shed, which was the size of
a double garage, and behind that was an empty fenced

chook pen, its residents long gone. It was all very quiet and seemed to be abandoned.

She walked the rest of the way around the verandah back to the front steps and looked out across the empty paddocks, listening to the loud, lonely cry of a crow somewhere in the distance. For a moment Sophie closed her eyes and listened to the breeze whispering through the trees nearby and felt . . . peace. The tension she'd grown used to carrying on her shoulders lifted and the tightness that had clenched her insides for an age was suddenly gone. For the first time in too long to remember, she felt completely and utterly at peace.

When she opened her eyes, she knew why she'd come back here. Sophie gave the view before her one last look before heading back to the car to grab her phone.

The agent pulled up beside Sophie half an hour later and climbed out of his dusty four-wheel drive, leaning back inside the cabin briefly to grab his Akubra and put it on before extending his hand. 'Bruce Lovell, and you must be our new ambo.'

She caught the faint whiff of tobacco on him as he gave her a hearty handshake. 'Sophie Bryant,' Sophie said with a smile.

'So you want to take a look at the old place then?' he said, turning around to look at the house in front of them.

'I do. There wasn't any information on the sign. How many hectares does it come with?'

'The land is 883.8 hectares, or 2183 acres in the old language. There're two permanent creeks and a mountain boundary that forms a basin,' he told her. 'It hasn't been used in a number of years, as you can probably tell. It got a bit too much for old Archie in the end and he let it go. There's about a hundred hectares of cleared land and the rest is uncleared bush out the back.'

It was considerably more land than she'd been expecting, but as she looked across at the old house her doubts settled. There was just something about this place, something that called to her. 'Would you be able to take me for a bit of a tour?'

'Are you sure you're looking for something this size?' he asked, adjusting his hat before settling it back in place once more. 'I can probably have a look around and find you something a little better suited.'

'I'd like to see this one,' she said, calmly but firmly. She couldn't blame him for thinking her request was a bit strange—after all, why would a single woman who'd only just arrived in town want to buy a property like this in the middle of nowhere? She wasn't even sure *she* could explain it. All she knew was there was something about this place that felt . . . right.

Bruce gave a small shrug of his wide shoulders and waved a hand towards the house. 'Alright, let's take a look inside,' he said, leading the way.

Bruce inserted a key into the lock of the heavy timber door and pushed it open, walking in ahead of her. 'Haven't been out here for a while. I better go first,' he said with a grin. 'Never know what might have taken up residence.'

Sophie wasn't entirely sure he was joking and, judging by the fact there was still furniture inside, she was beginning to wonder if maybe someone still lived here after all. Sophie looked around, taking in the faded carpet and heavy curtains, already picturing something lighter in the windows, maybe lace, so that the sunlight could filter through. A strong old-house aroma filled the air—the kind of smell you get around museums and aged books.

'So the property belonged to an old bloke named Archie Gilbert. I have to tell you up front, Archie passed away out here. I feel obliged to let you know that, but you'd hear about it soon enough in town anyway. He was a bit of a loner, but pretty well known and respected around the district. This place was in the Gilbert family for a couple of generations. The Spicers next door kept an eye on him, brought him meals and checked up on him regularly. They were the ones who found Archie when he passed away.'

'What happened to him?'

'His heart apparently. Died where he fell out in the paddock, over there,' he said, pointing out the lounge-room window.

'How long ago?'

'Going on three years now.'

Sophie did a double take at that, staring at the real estate agent in surprise. 'All this has been sitting here for three years?'

'Just the furniture,' he explained. 'You see, Archie's sister, Elizabeth, moved overseas years ago, and when she passed away Archie's estate went to her children. Neither of them wanted to fly over here to clean out the house, so they gave Archie's solicitor instructions to put this place on the market and give away whatever could be used to charity. The local church ladies came and cleaned out the kitchen and pantry and donated what they could. The furniture was left in case the eventual buyer wanted it.'

As they walked through the rest of the house, Sophie was mentally stripping back walls and repainting, picturing in her head what a fresh coat of paint and a few new tiles would do to freshen up the old place. The house was essentially square-shaped with a timber verandah that wrapped completely around it. Each of the bedrooms and the lounge room opened up onto the verandah via a set of antique French doors, which Sophie loved.

Driving as far as they could by vehicle to take a look around the property, Sophie now understood what Bruce meant by uncleared bushland. The wilderness at the rear of the property seemed to have encroached onto once cleared farming land, reclaiming whatever had been in its path. Steep mountains rose on either side creating gullies and valleys, and the views of the mountain ranges in the distance from atop one of the ridges they managed to drive up were absolutely breathtaking.

'It *is* a lot of land,' Sophie said out loud as Bruce pointed out a fence line in the distance to indicate the boundary. What the hell would she do with it all? But Sophie already knew that she desperately wanted the house, and a large part of that urge was because of the land surrounding it and the quiet and peaceful feeling it exuded. But it also felt like a waste of good farming land for it all to just sit here unused.

'I suppose you could always lease out the land. You might get a few local farmers interested; maybe not at the moment, but once we get some rain and the stock prices and such go up. You won't have much luck until then. Everyone's already flogged off most of their stock.'

'Why's that?'

'Bad prices. Dry winter. You can't afford to keep buying in feed to maintain stock forever, so it's best to cut your losses and sell 'em off when you can, then restock down the track when there's more feed and prices get better.'

Sophie let her gaze wander across the flat land to the mountain range that marked the boundary in the distance. A gentle breeze picked up out of nowhere and toyed with the ends of her hair; the wind smelled warm and sweet, with a slight tinge of lemony eucalypt from the nearby tall trees. She had to buy this place. It was insane, but it was what she knew she had to do.

On their drive back to the house, Bruce explained the terms of the sale. The property would be sold as is, which meant furniture and all. A long settlement wouldn't be necessary seeing she had the funds from the sale of her previous house in Sydney, and the niece and nephew of Archie were eager to secure a sale.

There was something sad about the fact that two people on the other side of the world weren't interested enough in their uncle to even bother coming over to go through his belongings. Surely they would be a tiny bit curious about the man's life and what he'd left behind? Still, she shouldn't judge—who knew what their own circumstances were and whether heading off to the other side of the world out of curiosity was an option for them. And she'd seen enough dysfunctional situations in her line of work to know that when it came to family, being related to someone didn't mean you necessarily had to like them.

There'd been so many elderly people, injured or left alone in homes without any close family to call for help, and sadly she'd been to more than her fair share of call-outs to deceased elderly who hadn't even been missed until the smell of decaying bodies alerted nearby neighbours. Sophie couldn't think of anything more depressing than to not even be missed by someone.

Poor Archie.

The sound of the real estate agent's vehicle eventually faded and Sophie smiled to herself as silence floated back into place. She couldn't explain the sensation that filled her being as she stood there hearing only the wind gently touching the long grass and treetops; she only felt peace.

'You're doing *what?*' her sister said on the other end of the phone, loudly.

'I'm buying a farm.'

'I'm coming out there.'

Sophie rolled her eyes at her sister's typical overreaction. 'Great, Monique! You can help me clean the place up.'

'What on earth are you going to do with a farm?'

'I don't know,' Sophie admitted. She wasn't unaware that this was completely out of character for her, but once she'd made the decision, it had felt right. 'Yet.'

'No one buys a farm in a town they've just moved to, in the middle of nowhere. What happens when you want to leave? How are you going to sell it? I cannot *believe* you jumped into this kind of massive decision without running it past me first!'

'Because as a twenty-nine-year-old woman, I need to get permission from my older sister before I make any major decisions in my life?' Sophie asked drolly.

'Clearly you do if this is the kind of insane decision you're making. I'm a finance graduate, for God's sake, you should have come to me with this before rushing into anything.'

Her sister had what Sophie considered the most boring job in the world, working as a credit analyst in a government finance department. 'You would have only talked me out of it,' Sophie said dryly.

'Of course I would have!' Monique yelled. 'That's what a *normal* person would have done.'

'Mon, I know you're only looking out for me, but I *want* this. I can't explain it, but I really want this place.'

There was a silence on the other end of the line and Sophie could picture Monique rubbing her forehead with her fingertips and mentally counting to ten. She loved her sister, but they were like chalk and cheese. Monique was what people referred to as high maintenance. She liked things a certain way—*her* way—and needed an orderly, calm environment to work in, preferably one that she had complete control of. Sophie on the other hand was used to a more controlled-chaos work environment. She had to make split-second decisions under enormous pressure. Or rather, she used to, in her old life.

'I'm just not sure this decision is about *you*.'

'What are you talking about?' Sophie asked, frowning.

'Are you doing this because it's what Garth wanted?' Mon asked softly.

Her sister's question surprised her and for a moment she was unable to respond.

'Do you think maybe you're trying to live out Garth's wishes instead of your own because you feel guilty?'

'No,' Sophie cut her sister off abruptly, 'I don't.'

'Soph, I know—'

'You don't know anything, Mon,' Sophie said around a tightening throat. She hadn't expected her sister to use what she'd once told her in private to bust her bubble of happiness. 'I've gotta go. Say hi to Mum and Dad. I'll call them later.' She disconnected the call before her sister could protest and put the phone down on the bed. It rang almost immediately, her sister's name flashing on the screen but Sophie ignored it.

She was angry, but not at Mon, she conceded as her head drooped and she closed her eyes. Maybe part of her was trying not to acknowledge the truth behind her sister's words. She hadn't been thinking about it though when she'd decided to buy the property—that had been solely about a connection she'd felt with the place. But part of her *did* feel guilty, and had done ever since Garth's death.

Garth would have had kids years ago if she'd agreed. But Sophie loved her job, she loved living in the city, and their life had been perfect the way it was—just the two of them. And then one day Garth had gone off to work and never come home. A truck had slammed into his ambulance at an intersection and he'd been killed. Guilt had weighed her down for a long time. If only she'd agreed to have kids he would have been a father—even for a little while. He'd never had the chance to have the family he wanted, and he'd never moved to the country. But then there were a lot of things he'd never got to do. They'd never grown old together like they were supposed to either. Everything had been cut short—way too short.

Seven

Standing in the doorway of the old house she was now the proud owner of, Sophie could hear her sister's warnings echoing in her mind once again. She stepped inside and inhaled the heavy, musty scent of ageing carpet and dusty furniture.

Surveying the room, Sophie began a mental list of things that would need to be done. The first was giving the place a good clean. She'd already arranged for the local charity shop to come out this morning and take most of the furniture, making room for her own that had been sitting in storage for the past twelve months.

They'd bought a house as a compromise to starting a family. She hadn't been ready to give up her career just then, but she could see that buying a house was a smart decision—their apartment wouldn't be big enough for a family and Garth had wanted his own space: a yard to have barbecues and a garage to do manly stuff like pull car engines apart and put them back together again.

After Garth died, the three-bedroom house and yard had become far too big for her to maintain. With the extra shifts Sophie had taken on after he'd passed away to keep busy, there was just no time to mow lawns and clean out gutters so she'd sold the house.

That time she'd taken Monique's advice and invested the rather substantial amount she'd got for the house, renting a small furnished apartment closer to work for herself.

It'd be nice to have her own things back. There was a time when she was happy not to surround herself with memories of Garth and their life together. But that was before, when everything was still too raw and painful to deal with. She'd tried to go on with her life and take comfort from the familiar things around her, their home, their photos and memories of a life together cut brutally short, but it had only served to remind her of just how much she had lost. But now she was ready.

'Standing around isn't going to get anything done,' she said, forcing her thoughts away from the past. The sound of an approaching truck was a welcome distraction, and within an hour the two men had loaded all the furniture and were heading back down the driveway, leaving Sophie with an empty house ready to be scrubbed clean of about a century's worth of grime.

Late that night, streaked with dust and sweat, Sophie eased her tired body down onto the top step of the front verandah and leaned back against the post with a weary sigh. Next week the floor guy would be coming to rip out the ancient carpet and restore the beautiful old floorboards she'd found hidden underneath. Until then she'd just have to live with the dusty grey pile and its faded pink rose pattern. Once it was probably someone's pride and joy, but after decades of use it was worn, stained and smelled of years of acquired smoke and mildew.

All around her the sound of crickets and frogs filled the early evening air, and a calmness not unlike the one she'd felt on that very first day she'd stood in this spot enveloped her once again.

As far as she looked in every direction there was nothing: no lights, no traffic, just endless plains of shadows dotting the landscape as far as the eye could see. For a city girl born and bred, she probably should have felt lonely with all this space stretching out around her, but she didn't. For the first time in a very long while, she felt free. It was almost as though she'd been confined to a small space, and now she could breathe. She wasn't sure how else to describe this feeling she had. She could finally just *be*.

As the sun faded away Sophie knew it was time to head back into town, but she hated leaving. There was nothing to sleep on since she'd got rid of all the mattresses, but maybe she could borrow a spare one from the pub for a few days before her furniture arrived. She made a note to ask Joe. The thought of camping out in her new house was exciting, and she got to her feet with a new burst of energy. She'd get together some supplies—enough to make do until her stuff arrived.

She couldn't wait to wake up here every morning, to sit out on her verandah and drink her coffee as the sun came up. As she locked up, a smile spread across her face at the thought. She said a silent goodnight to her old house and pulled herself into the car, feeling exhausted but happy. The emotion caught her unexpectedly. When was the last time she'd felt happy? Too long, it seemed, as she felt the happiness slowly subside and that familiar greyness began to seep back in its place. *No,* she thought firmly. *I've mourned and I've grieved and I've denied myself happiness for far too long. It's time I was allowed to feel things again.* The small pep talk held off the complete submersion of sadness that had been trying to get inside her, but some of the previous joy had dimmed a little.

As Sophie drove back into town, her mind went over the strange effect the place she'd just left behind had on her. Maybe this was what people meant when they talked about going to your happy place, except hers was a real place, not just somewhere in her head . . . at least, she thought it was real. Maybe this new-found tranquillity *was* all in her mind. Maybe it had nothing to do with the actual place. But if that were true, why didn't she feel the same anywhere else? She was too tired to try to dissect this all now. Maybe she'd figure it out tomorrow after she'd had a good night's sleep.

Eight

Unsurprisingly, news apparently travelled fast in Hilsons Ridge. Everyone she bumped into had an opinion on her decision to buy the old Gilbert place. Some were politely curious, trying to sound positive about what appeared to be a mini lapse of sanity, others took it as a commitment to put down roots and started suggesting names of eligible men who they thought she should consider.

She supposed it was a logical conclusion for them to make—after all, it wasn't as though selling a property in this place would happen as quickly as in the Sydney real estate market. Yes, she could see why her family were stressing on her behalf, but she didn't care. For the first time in too long she felt happy. There was no lingering sense of having made a mistake. She was completely comfortable with her decision but she certainly hadn't bought the place with any intention to start a relationship and family. All she was thinking about was that she'd managed to find a place where her heart stopped hurting and she could feel herself beginning to heal. What would happen in the future she had no idea. She hadn't been thinking that far ahead.

As Sophie reached for a carton of milk, she looked up at her name being called and smiled at the woman walking towards her in the supermarket.

'Sophie! I've just heard the news. You bought Archie Gilbert's place?'

'I did,' she answered, feeling a little apprehensive after the reception her family had given her. She hadn't seen Anne Harding since the welcome party, but her hair and makeup were once again impeccable, as were her tailored trousers and blouse. Sophie had a feeling you wouldn't want to ever make the mistake of thinking her conservative, middle-aged looks made her some kind of pushover.

'Now that's the kind of juicy gossip that'll have you fast-tracked into becoming a local in no time.'

'Have I actually ever been *out* of the gossip mill since I arrived?' Sophie asked doubtfully.

'Technically, you weren't gossip. You were an interesting new person in town,' she smiled.

'As opposed to being uninteresting now?' Sophie could only hope.

'Oh no, *now* you're being gossiped about,' she informed Sophie quite cheerfully.

Excellent.

'So do you have a project in mind? For the land,' she explained at Sophie's confused expression.

'Oh. No. Not really. I'm focusing on renovating the house first. It was the house that made me buy the property in the first place.'

'Ah yes, there's something about those old places, isn't there? I'm sure you'll bring it back to its former glory.'

'Do you know much about it? About the history of the house?'

Anne tilted her head, tapping a finger against her lips, as though trying to search some kind of internal databank for information. 'Well, originally the land was part of the Spicers' property. I'm pretty sure the house itself was one of the original homesteads.'

Sophie had heard of the Spicers; it was hard to miss them as they seemed to own a lot of the stores in town. She'd noticed Spicer's Hardware and Spicer's Butchery, as well as a rather impressive store that sold a mixture of clothing, homewares and gifts.

'Then the family split the property up into four. Danny Spicer was given your place but he wasn't there long, and he sold it to the Gilberts and left the district after losing his wife. That was a sad story,' she said, shaking her head slowly. 'Their little girl died, and the wife, Edith, who I believe was always a little bit nervy to start with, killed herself a few months later. Just terrible. Anyway, apparently there was some kind of falling out between Danny and the rest of the Spicer family and he sold it to the Gilberts instead of offering the property to any of his other brothers. It caused quite a stir at the time.'

Sophie was still trying to wrap her head around the entire history lesson that Anne had somehow crammed into fifteen seconds of conversation. 'Does everyone know this much about the Spicers?'

Anne gave a light laugh. 'When you grow up as fifth generation in a town this size, you know everything about every family,' she shrugged. 'The Spicers were always a colourful family and, when you have a love of local history like I do, you tend to come across lots of interesting titbits.'

Well, that was comforting. She was kind of glad she had no family history out here for anyone to go digging through.

'So, anyway, Archie took the farm over from his father and was there until he died. You did know he died out there, didn't you?' Anne asked, sending Sophie a somewhat alarmed glance.

'Yes, I knew.'

'Some people are a little bit strange about living where someone's died.'

'He was in his nineties, wasn't he?'

'Oh yes,' she assured her. 'He lived to a ripe old age.'

Sophie smiled, 'Well, I don't think he'll be giving me too much trouble. Although it's a wonder none of the Spicers wanted to buy it back now, while it was on the market.'

'That was a long time ago,' she replied, flipping a hand briefly. 'No one's really in a financial position to be buying much of anything nowadays.' Anne shook her head. 'I think the Spicers are busy enough trying to take care of the land they've already got.'

That seemed to be the sad truth. It's what she'd been hearing ever since she'd arrived out here. But for all the gloom, there always seemed to be hope in the conversation: when the rain came; when stock prices went up. Sophie was pretty sure you didn't stay out here as long as some of these families had and not build up a bit of resilience. They always seemed resigned to the weather, but never defeated by it.

'I'd better keep moving, but I'm very happy that you've decided to buy a place and, who knows, maybe you'll come up with some wonderful new venture and surprise yourself.'

'I'm not sure I can handle any more surprises. Deciding to buy a house was pretty much the mother of all spontaneous decisions,' Sophie assured her with a grin as they waved goodbye. Thanks to Anne, she now had some more interesting information to mull over about her property. She was enjoying learning about the local history attached to the place. She had no idea it would all be so interesting. Maybe she should see if she could track down some books in the library to do some more reading. At least it would give her something to do when she couldn't sleep.

cn

Sophie walked across the paddock, keeping one eye on the ground for snakes. She'd been itching to go for a walk but hadn't intended to go quite this far. When she reached the closest fence line, resting her folded arms on the top of the post to take in the scenery, something caught her attention further across the paddock. It was too far to see clearly, but there was definitely something over near the edge of the bushland.

Easing through the barbed wire fence, she cautiously made her way across the paddock. As she drew closer the blob took on a shape: four legs, a long body and a wide head. Sophie frowned. A horse? It must have got through one of the boundary fences somehow. She hesitated briefly before deciding to approach it. If it had broken through a fence then maybe it had hurt itself, since they were all barbed wire as far as she knew. She couldn't leave it if it was injured.

Sophie knew next to nothing about horses. She'd never even ridden one, despite begging her mother to when she was about five or six years old and saw a children's pony ride at the show.

She wasn't entirely sure what she was going to do with it if she got close enough to discover it had hurt itself, but she'd come too far now to turn back without checking.

The animal had been grazing quite happily as she'd stealthily made her approach, but it must have heard something and suddenly lifted its huge head in the air and stared straight at her.

Sophie froze—she wasn't sure if it was from fear or so as not to startle the animal any further—but in that moment human and horse eyed each other warily from across the short distance.

He was magnificent. Sophie wasn't even sure it was a he, but something about the way it held its head, and the

72

confident, almost arrogant way it eyed her, instantly made her think it was male. Its coat was black but he had a white mark on his forehead, like a paintball had hit him and dribbled down his face. His long tail and mane gleamed like black silk.

He was dusty and clearly hadn't seen a bath in a long time, but he looked to be in pretty good condition. She moved forward slowly and saw his ears twitch and his head bob. Did horses charge like bulls? He certainly had an alert uneasiness about him now, and Sophie realised she really didn't have anywhere to run if he did decide to chase her and stomp her into the ground. Then suddenly he gave a loud whinny and pivoted, galloping back into the scrub behind him with a crash of snapping branches and undergrowth.

Maybe he was returning home, she thought, making a note to track down whoever lived behind her property and check the fences. She gave a small sigh as she realised this would be the first of many ongoing expenses she'd be facing now that she was responsible for a property. She didn't want to hear her sister's voice in her head right now saying, *I told you so.*

Nine

Sophie stood back and eyed the lounge room critically. This was the third time she'd moved the armchair and it was now back in the very first place she'd tried it. She'd missed her furniture. After Garth's death she'd downsized but hadn't had the heart to sell all her stuff, despite the fact that it was silly to pay for a storage unit to keep it, but she was glad now that she had. It reminded her of happier times. The memories were still bittersweet, tinged with the familiar ache of grief, but it was getting easier. She and Garth had picked out most of the pieces when they'd bought their apartment together shortly before their wedding, upgrading from the well-used second-hand furniture that today would be trendy but back then was 'student poor'. When they bought their house, Sophie had put her foot down and they'd invested in brand-new furniture. Each piece had been lovingly chosen and sometimes argued over, but all of it had helped to make their house a home.

And now it was making a new home.

The restored floorboards had come up beautifully, giving it a rustic style that Sophie loved. The house hardly looked like the same place she'd moved into three weeks ago. While she'd been spending every spare minute she had on the house, there was still the old shed outside that needed going through, and Sophie knew she couldn't put it off for much longer. Her car needed a home, and until she cleaned out all the rubbish stored inside, there was no room for it.

The old timber doors made a groaning noise as she opened them up wide, letting in as much sunlight as possible. *Rats hated sunlight, didn't they? Or was that just vampires?* She really wasn't keen on moving the neatly stacked piles of boxes from where they looked as though they'd been sitting for a number of decades. God only knew what had decided to make a home inside them. A scurry of tiny feet and then some not so tiny feet had her letting out a squeak of disgust as she tentatively shook a box and jumped back.

Maybe I should burn the whole shed? She briefly wondered how expensive it would be to build a brand new one, until she remembered the rapidly depleting amount she had left in her savings account. She'd just have to toughen up and get on with it. 'They're only rats,' she reasoned, hoping she could convince herself if she said it out loud. 'They're probably more afraid of you than you are of them.'

Bracing herself, she reached over as far as she could go without getting too close to the nearest box and pulled it outside, clear of the shed. When nothing jumped out and attacked her, she picked up a stick on the ground nearby and gingerly poked open the top flaps of the cardboard box. 'So far so good,' she murmured. 'Come on, Bryant, you can do this.'

She inched closer and peeped inside, letting out a long breath when she found only old magazines.

Archie was clearly a bit of a hoarder, she thought as she pulled yet another box from the pile. There were bits and pieces of machinery and boxes of old clothing that had been inadequately stored, now well and truly out of date and moth-eaten. A somewhat newer box had been placed at the front of the shed, and when Sophie got to it she found a scribbled note on top saying, *Personal belongings of Archie Gilbert.*

One box of personal items. It didn't seem much to show for such a long life. Sophie recalled the real estate agent mentioning that the ladies' church group had made a sweep of the house after Archie's death, and these must be the things they couldn't use as donations. She had a quick peek but there wasn't much inside: a few frayed notebooks with scribble marks on the front, the kind you make when testing a pen, perhaps; some shoe boxes with receipts and paper-work haphazardly tossed inside; and an old photo album.

She opened it and immediately two of the yellowing pages fell out into the bottom of the box. Sophie turned her nose up at the musty smell and dropped the album back in, closing the lid of the box and putting it to one side. She had no use for any of it but they were the belongings of a dead man, and it didn't feel right to simply toss them in the rubbish pile. The church ladies had obviously had the same thoughts and left them out here for someone else to deal with. Maybe she could try the family again later to see if she could send the box to them.

She made one pile of things to take to the tip and another for someone to look at and see if there was anything worth selling for scrap or spare parts. After two solid days of sorting, the throw-out pile was growing at an alarming rate. By the end of the third day she'd almost cleared the entire shed and could finally see the back wall. She was surprised at how much space there was now that all the rubbish had been dragged outside.

Underneath the last box she found a heavy metal case about the size of a coffee table. Her curiosity was immediately piqued—unlike most of the other stuff she'd uncovered in plastic bags and rotting cardboard boxes, whatever was inside this had been stored in something far sturdier. The top of the chest-like object was discoloured in sections, and rust had formed along the edges. Sophie knelt down to flip open the stiffened latches and lifted the lid cautiously, hearing it groan in protest.

A musty whiff of camphor and leather rushed up to greet her as daylight hit the contents of the old trunk for the first time in probably many years. Sophie tentatively reached inside and lifted out what appeared to be a folded woollen blanket, only to discover that it wasn't a blanket at all but a uniform of some sort. It looked incredibly old; she felt sure hadn't seen anything lately made from this kind of thick, stiff woollen material.

There was also a hat that she recognised instantly by the long feather that had been placed on top of it. This was a light horseman's uniform. She didn't know much about military history, but she knew that much from watching the odd documentary and movie over the years.

A tingle of excitement ran through her as she carefully placed the folded uniform and hat on top of a nearby hastily dusted box and then peered back into the trunk to see what else had been stored in there.

She picked up a semi-circular leather case with straps attached and inside found a horseshoe and some rusty nails. There were a few other bits and pieces of clothing and, as she picked up a neatly folded shirt, something fell from inside it, landing on the ground.

Sophie bent down and picked up the small red book, which had *Collins Gentleman's Diary* printed in faded gold lettering on the cover, and carefully opened it.

On the inside page was written *Clarrie Gilbert, 7th Light Horse Regiment.* The words were scrawling but easy enough to read as Sophie turned the page and looked at the first date written at the top: *October 25th, 1914.*

The diary was over a century old.

The bulge in the back made her curious and she gingerly opened the last page to find a small stack of photos and postcards. One showed a man on a horse, another a small group of men on camels in front of the Sphinx, and another was of two Australian men in uniform, one of which looked to be Aboriginal, posing beside a pyramid.

Sophie peered back into the trunk and found a small pouch which she unfolded, discovering to her amazement a collection of medals on brightly coloured ribbons. Laying them gently on the ground, Sophie stared at the contents of the trunk and felt somewhat dazed. Why had these personal possessions been left to rot in a shed for all these years?

Sophie knew she was staring at a time capsule of history, and a mixture of excitement and sadness filled her. She'd never had a particular interest in military history, but she remembered an old photograph in a wrought-iron frame, which had sat for years on her grandfather's mantelpiece, some great-uncle of her pop's who'd died in the war. He'd been dressed in a similar uniform to the one the man in the photo wore. She wished she'd asked more questions back then; now it was too late to hear the stories her grandparents would have grown up with. But her grandparents had installed in her a deep respect for past generations and what they'd sacrificed, and again she wondered why a family wouldn't have treasured these items. The weight of responsibility rested heavily on her shoulders as she carefully packed everything back into the trunk. She wanted to find out more about who this Clarrie was and why his belongings were stored in the back of a shed, all but forgotten.

She lifted the trunk by its handles and shuffled her way across to the house, depositing it inside the back door, then returned to the shed to finish the sorting. Sophie renewed her efforts to get through the junk, but now kept a wary eye out for anything else that may have been stored in there and forgotten. By the end of the day she had a trailer filled ready for the tip, and a pile of unknown farming-type bits and pieces she figured she'd ask someone to look at later. The shed was now cleared and there was finally enough room to house her car. Exhausted but still feeling excited, she headed inside for a shower before going through the trunk she'd discovered earlier as her reward.

⁓

October 25th, 1914
Can't say I've ever been one for keeping a journal, but seeing as I don't have too many people to write home to, I may as well write to myself. Who knows, maybe some day when I'm old and grey (all going well) I might feel a need to sit in my rocking chair and read back over my grand adventure.

They let us bring our own horses as long as they passed the requirements—which of course Cobber did, seeing as he came from the same place most of these brumbies were being brought from. I was glad I brought Cobber with me. I feel like I've still got a piece of home here with him by my side.

Since joining up, I've met quite a few decent fellows. We were all a bit wary of this riding test that was set to sort out the 'boys from the men'. We had to clear a water jump bareback and then jump some logs . . . and that was it.

The good news is that I passed the test.

October 28th, 1914
Lots of horse work today, and drills. Flamin' drills! Was
on sentry with a bloke named Henry Baker, a dark fella.
He's a good sort, bit of a larrikin, which is a nice change
from some of the officers you see walkin' around this place
like they've got a stick up their backsides.

There were more pages of daily life in training camp that
Sophie found fascinating to read through. She could picture
the sights and sounds as Clarrie described the camp, with
rows of tents as far as the eye could see housing twenty
thousand men. It must have been an exciting experience for
a young man who it seemed up until this point in his life
had barely ventured outside the New England highlands.
Sophie had a very limited knowledge of the Light Horse
regiment, only what she vaguely recalled from movies and
the odd war documentary, but reading about it firsthand
made it suddenly come to life. This was a real man experiencing a real war and she couldn't put the diary down.

Clarrie seemed to have taken to his journal writing
initially. He wrote daily for the first few pages, documenting
in vivid detail everything he saw around him: sometimes
long, humorous recounts of his day as he and his fellow
comrades were turned from farmers, bank tellers and office
clerks into lethal fighting machines; sometimes barely a
few lines to note his displeasure at whatever the officers
were doing to make their life a misery. The training seemed
intense and somewhat rushed, Sophie thought as she did a

quick calculation. From the date when he'd started going through the preliminary enlistment process to the entry when he was on board the ship to depart Australia was only a little over two months.

He wrote often about his new friend Henry Baker. In an era where Indigenous Australians had limited basic rights, it came as a surprise to Sophie to discover Henry had been enlisted. Although she sensed through a few of the entries that fighting for his country didn't shield Henry from prejudice.

December 23rd, 1914
We embarked from Sydney on December 20th.

I haven't been up to writing much lately. For the past few days I've been feeding the fish on a regular schedule. Henry, it seems, has found his sea legs and couldn't be happier. We're kept pretty busy even stuck on a boat. We're up at 6am to feed and water the horses. 8am is breakfast, then parade at 9. Stables at 9.15, cleaning and exercising horses. Feed horses and have lunch. Horses again in the afternoon. Lights out at 9.15.

Think I'm coming back as a horse.

December 25th, 1914
Merry Christmas.

It was a strange feeling to be out at sea for Christmas. We had a fine feast, for those who could keep it down. I'm glad my stomach has settled—some of the other poor blighters are still hangin' over the side of the boat every hour on the hour.

Sighted land at Aden, the hills in the distance were not like home. They were dry and rough looking. We pulled into harbour and swarms of natives circled the ship trying to sell their wares.

Sophie counted the voyage as lasting forty-two days and her mind boggled at trying to remain sane after that long at sea in such cramped conditions.

She tried to imagine herself in Clarrie's situation, back before they had television and the internet, finding himself, a kid from the bush, suddenly in some exotic, far-off land. She could almost hear the strange new music and the noise of a busy marketplace with shouting in a foreign language, children begging in the streets and tugging at clothes as he moved through the crowded streets of Alexandria and Cairo, places he may only have read about in Bible stories. Her eyes drifted back to the next entry as she imagined the wonder on Clarrie's face.

February 15th, 1915
Arriving in Cairo, I was immediately impressed by how fine it was. We rode for a good hour before we were out of the city, heading for our camp that was somewhere near the pyramids. We rode for another three and a half hours before finally reaching our camp. We were too tired to do anything more than tend our horses and then fall asleep.

The next morning, we got our first look at our surroundings. Sand everywhere. Dusty, fine sand that makes our life a misery. It's too soft to peg in the horse lines and it gets in our clothes and bedrolls, in our eyes and in our food. But the sight before us, looming over the flat landscape, more than makes up for any discomfort. The pyramids are only about four miles away. They stand 450 feet. The base covers 3600 sq feet. Built 3753 BC. Kind of hard to imagine how they built it. It was a bit of a climb but the view of Cairo in the distance was one of the most awe-inspiring things I've ever seen. Getting around is hard work because of all the flamin' sand, but it was worth it.

This place has made me realise how good we have it back home. We never had much of anything, but compared to some of the poor blighters you see in this place, we lived like kings. There's a lot to be said for wide open spaces and plenty of food. I can't imagine living in the kind of squalor and filth of some of these back alleys. Makes you stop and think.

February 19th, 1915
Me, Henry and a few of the others took a camel ride. They're everywhere over here. We've seen the camel corp moving about—but they're a weird lookin' animal and I'm happy to say, after experiencing it once, I'm more than content to stick with old Cobber. Our ride took us around the Sphinx. It is 66 feet high and they haven't uncovered all of it yet.

The fella we paid to be our guide reckons it's got arms and a whole body under all the sand. Imagine that. It must be enormous. From ear to ear it measures 14 feet! It must have been a sight in its heyday. It's missing its nose from cannon fire—not us but Napoleon. Hope it doesn't get hit again. After seeing all this history, it would be damn near heartbreaking if any of these ancient things were destroyed. Standing for over 6000 years only to be blown up in a matter of seconds.

We had a photo taken in front of it. I can imagine the looks on the faces of some of the folks back home when they see this.

⁂

Despite being surprisingly neat for a kid from the bush, the faded pencil and cursive handwriting made for very slow reading, and Sophie often found herself rereading entries multiple times. Before she knew it, two hours had gone by and she'd barely made it through the first few months of entries. But it was so worth it—she felt as though she'd stepped back in time, and the privilege of having this firsthand retelling of such pivotal events in a country's history was at times a little overwhelming. Sophie often found herself quite emotional as she read Clarrie's thoughts.

Sophie picked up the photo from the back of the diary and studied it carefully. It was surreal to hold the image in her hand after reading the story behind it from a diary that was over a hundred years old. The smiling faces of the men in the photo told how happy they all were. They'd already come such a long way and they had no idea how terrible things were about to get. She wondered how many of them came home.

Ten

Sophie pushed open the door and walked inside. The cool darkness of the pub was a stark contrast to the heat outside. In uniform she would have stood out anyway, but she thought maybe the interest she was drawing from the scattering of men inside was partly to do with her being the only female in the building.

She smiled a hello at Joe as he came over to the bar. 'How's farm life going?'

'It's just a little bit quieter than this place,' she grinned.

'I bet you miss us,' Joe said, shaking his head slowly. 'Why on earth would a young thing like you want to move all the way out to the middle of nowhere?'

'I do miss the all-you-can-eat brekky,' she conceded, 'but I like the peace and quiet. Hey, I was actually hoping you might be able to help me with a name.'

'What'd you need?'

'Do you know who owns the property behind mine?'

Joe scrunched his broad face up as though trying to picture a map and scratched his head. 'It'd have to be Lenny Spicer, I reckon. You're pretty much surrounded by Spicers.'

She'd suspected it would be a Spicer who owned it, but wasn't sure which one. She also had no idea how to access it from the road, since only the rear of his property backed onto hers. 'How do I get to his place?'

'Head out of town and then turn onto Lovetts Road and about another, I don't know,' he looked up at the ceiling, roughly calculating the distance, 'maybe five k's? You'll come to a dirt road on your left, Spicers Ridge Road. Take that and Len's place will be the first gate you come to on your left. Place is called Hill Song. Can't miss it.'

Sophie inwardly rolled her eyes at that. After every set of directions anyone gave her, they always ended it with *Can't miss it*. But it turned out you *could* miss it. Like when you're expecting a decent-sized sign with a road or property name, only to discover the signs have faded over the years to become barely legible or have fallen off completely.

As it turned out, Len's place *was* pretty easy to find, which came as a nice surprise. On Spicers Ridge Road she came across a large, engraved timber sign with 'Hill Song' etched into it, which made her smile. Now *that* was a sign. She turned into the driveway, which wound its way through gum trees and other tall natives until it opened out into a wide clearing where a homestead and collection of large silver machinery sheds were clustered.

Sophie could hear dogs barking as she pulled the car to a stop and opened her door. A sprawling sandstone house with a wraparound verandah stood before her, surrounded by a timber fence that enclosed an impressive green lawn and flowerbeds. As Sophie unlatched the gate, a woman who looked to be in her late sixties walked out the front door, shading her eyes against the afternoon glare.

'Hello,' Sophie said shutting the gate behind her. 'Sorry to come around unannounced. I was on my way home and thought I'd call in and introduce myself. I'm Sophie Bryant. I've bought Archie Gilbert's place.'

'The ambulance lady,' the woman said, smiling as Sophie reached the steps.

'That's me.'

'Come on inside. Lennard just came in, he'll be happy to meet you.' The woman led Sophie in through the large front door and down a hallway. 'I'm Julie, by the way,' she said over her shoulder. 'Lennard, we have a guest. Come on out.'

A man came into view who looked freshly showered, dressed in jeans and a button-up shirt, although both were the expensive kind and he looked as though he'd stepped out of an R.M. Williams catalogue, his receding grey hair clipped short.

'This is our new ambulance officer. She's bought old Archie's place.'

'Ah,' he said, his face lighting up into a smile. 'Finally. It's nice to meet you. Sophie, isn't it?' he asked hesitantly.

'Sophie Bryant, yes.'

'Len Spicer.' He shook her hand and indicated that she should take a seat on the sofa nearby. 'So you bought the Gilbert place. Why?'

His question may have seemed blunt had he not been wearing a perplexed smile, and Sophie felt an initial stab of irritation melt quickly away. 'Bit of a tree change,' she said casually.

'Ah, I see. You're not planning on bringing in some exotic kind of wildlife or anything, are you? I hear water buffalo and deer farms are pretty trendy nowadays.'

'No,' she shook her head, 'no plans for any farming. I like it the way it is.'

The phone rang and Julie excused herself, leaving with a 'You two carry on' as she exited the room.

'I see.' He leaned back in his chair, watching her. Sophie got the feeling that Len Spicer was a crafty kind of fella. He had a charming way about him that hid a calculating mind. She could almost hear it turning over the questions as he observed her.

Sophie cleared her throat. 'I actually needed to ask you something too—do you own a horse?'

'A horse? Why? You looking to buy one?'

'No, I came across one on my property the other day. I thought it might have got through a fence somewhere.'

'I keep my fences maintained. No holes on my side. Besides, wouldn't catch me owning a horse. We don't keep anything around here that doesn't earn its keep.'

'Well, that's weird. It ran in this direction so I thought it must be heading home. I don't suppose you know if any of the other neighbours might own a black horse?'

'I'm afraid the only people you share a fence line with are Spicers. Me and my cousin Horrie are on the other side of you, and I can guarantee Horrie doesn't own a horse either. It's hard enough keeping feed up to cattle and sheep. You won't find many people who can afford the luxury of feeding an animal that's only talent is to eat and shit all day. Here,' he said, standing to cross the room to a wall where a large map hung in a frame, 'this is an old family heirloom passed down through the generations starting from my great-great-grandfather, who owned the land before it was divided between my grandfather and his brothers years ago. It shows the original holding the Spicers once owned.'

Sophie walked across and stared at the aged map, its edges browning and ink marks faded. 'Most of this bush surrounding us is now national park, but back when this map was drawn up it was all privately owned.' Len traced a large section of the map in the centre with his finger in the shape of a square. 'This was the original holding. Then it was divided into four allotments.' He traced three non-existent lines across the glass, side by side. and one long one that was narrower and ran the length of the old property line behind the others. 'That's Hill Song,' he pointed to the long narrow one. 'At the far end is my cousin Dave's. The one next door to that is my other cousin, Horrie, and beside him is your place.'

'And none of them are missing a horse?' She saw him shake his head adamantly. 'Where did it come from then?'

Len shrugged, turning away from the map to take his seat once more. 'Like I said, out here we're surrounded by national parks—you share a fence line with it on the far side. Horses have been running wild through this area for centuries. This whole region supplied a lot of the horses for the military in the Boer War and the First World War, you know,' he said with a decisive nod. 'That back country is a natural corridor for all kinds of animals, including brumbies, to this day.'

'A horse, you said?' Julie asked, coming back into the room. 'I've heard them from time to time while I've been out checking water for the livestock. Very rare to see them though.'

'Are you sure it was a horse you saw?' Len asked Sophie doubtfully.

'I may be from the city, but I do know a horse when I see one,' she told him dryly.

Len gave a grunt and shook his head. 'Sounds like you might have some wild horses taken up residence. Not surprising with all that flaming bush the Gilberts let go. Waste of good cattle country if you ask me.'

Sophie frowned at that. Wild horses? She wasn't sure if that was a good thing or a bad thing. 'Maybe I'll check with the others just to make sure no one's missing one. I better get going. It was lovely to meet you both.'

'You can ask, but I'm telling you right now that you won't find any of them throwing away money on a useless damn horse.'

Sophie mulled over Len's parting statement on the drive home. It was beginning to seem likely that this horse could be wild after all. If most farmers had the same opinion about horses as Len did, it seemed unlikely that Archie would have a horse as a pet. And going by the condition of the place, he hadn't been farming in a while so it was quite possible that the fences adjoining the surrounding national park could have been relatively easy to push through and for animals to happily exist without discovery for quite some time.

When she got home she checked the paddocks close to the house, but there was no sign of horse dung anywhere, not even dried-out ones. So either the horse hadn't been on the property long if it got through a fence somehow, or, if it did live here, it never ventured this far from the bush at the back of the property. Maybe it was antisocial. Sophie could understand that all too well. Tomorrow she'd pay a visit to her other neighbours. If she didn't find out anything useful about the mystery horse, at least she'd get the introductions to all her neighbours out of the way.

Tucked up in bed later that evening, Sophie opened the old diary and read through a few more entries. Horses seemed to be everywhere she turned lately. Maybe Clarrie had some words of wisdom she could use.

April, 1915
Word came today that they're sending us to Gallipoli. Apparently the terrain there isn't suitable for the horses

and they are to stay behind here. We're not too happy about leaving the horses, but there's little we can do about it. Not too sure how long we're supposed to be away for. Henry and some of the others are staying back with the horses. He's pretty disappointed that he's missing out on all the action.

May, 1915
We could hear the gunfire and shells from the ship where we were anchored off Anzac Cove on our arrival. The shelling dropped all around us, but fortunately there were no casualties. All night the guns and shelling went on. None of us were looking forward to heading into it. After landing, we were directed towards headquarters and it was a very quick initiation indeed into life at Anzac Cove. Sandbags were piled up alongside the track at short distances, and the safest way to get from one place to another was to run from one spot to the next and stay low to avoid the enemy snipers. One of the squadron leaders in desperate need of a smoke got a right welcome by the locals when he lit a match. He soon learned the hard way not to make himself and everyone else a target for the Turks. He was dropped by a single sniper shot before he could even touch the match to his cigarette. The smell is something terrible, dead bodies lying where they fell in the middle of the Turks' trenches and our own. The beach is scattered with all kinds of equipment: helmets with holes in them, ripped clothing, spent shells and artillery left over from the slaughter that

was the first few days of landing here. The poor wretches had walked into a bloodbath from all accounts. I'm pretty sure this place is what Hell is supposed to look like.

June, 1915
We've been spending most of the days digging communication trenches since our arrival.

It's a constant routine of night post duty, night patrols, day observation, sniping, digging, wiring, ration and water carrying. If digging can be done safely in daylight it is, but mostly it's done under the cover of darkness. Night post duty comes with its own set of difficulties. The terrain in front of our trenches is covered in scrub, giving the enemy plenty of opportunity to blend in with the scenery. Our post is made up of three men and we each take turns to do sentry duty, two hours on and four off. In theory, a man should get at least two nights' sleep to one on night duty but, owing to the shortage of men, it is often a night off to one on.

Where we are posted, the distance between us and the Turks' trench is 22 yards. In the event of an enemy raid, there would be no time to put on boots or clothes so we sleep in them. We are allowed to take our boots off in the daytime if things are quiet. My poor feet are beginning to show the first signs of trench foot. Trying to keep them dry when you live in a trench is near impossible. I've written to Mum and asked if she can send more socks.

My least favourite task is wiring. It's a bastard of a job. We use wooden frames with a mass of barbed wire *wound round them, and push them up in front of the trench with poles as its too dangerous to try to stick your head up. Later, when things are quiet, we crawl out and lash these frames into one long line. It's a dangerous job with the trenches so close and the risk of being exposed by the Turks' constant flares makes you a sitting duck.*

We are about a mile from the landing stages so rations are brought part of the way from the beach to us by mule, and then carried by man the rest of the way. Water isn't easy to come by. A gallon a day per man is the normal issue and has to be used for drinking, cooking and washing. Some days the rations aren't able to be delivered, so we go without. The water quality isn't flash, but when you're this thirsty, you suddenly aren't as picky as you might have once been.

Bloody lice are driving me bonkers. I've been covered in a red rash for the last few days, they get inside your clothes and give you a mighty uncomfortable time. The water rations don't stretch to washing, especially if you've been digging trenches and the like all day—the last thing you want to do is waste water on washing your clothes, so the little blighters are having a field day in these conditions.

Snipers got 17 men today. Shelling has barely stopped in last few days. Heartbreaking to see so many men killed and maimed. Every day we lose more. So many have gone. The rain hasn't stopped and there's barely any timber available for a fire. What I wouldn't give for a nice hot meal and cuppa right about now.

Good news! Just been speaking to the bloke next door and he has a couple of onions and some jam. I have a tin of bully beef and some biscuits. We're going to have a feast tonight!

Sophie found it interesting that Clarrie's mood came through in his writing style. On bad days he wrote very short, almost abrupt entries, usually brief with a more factual aspect to it, simply jotting down points, probably too exhausted to bother with complete sentences. Then at other times his writing was sprawling and untidy, the words falling onto the paper in a huge gush that filled an entire page. The days when he seemed to have more time to write were always a lot more thought-provoking and philosophical.

She could almost picture him huddled in a trench, as the scream of shells flew overhead and shook the ground. Had Clarrie awoken from nightmares through the night, lathered in a cold sweat after this? Had his hands shaken and his heart rate galloped at loud noises? The men were clearly cold, hungry and miserable for a lot of the time while they were stuck in the trenches at Gallipoli, and Sophie couldn't imagine how they survived the conditions that Clarrie's diary skimmed across, mentioning but not dwelling on them. She knew if it had been her she'd have filled page after page with angry ranting. Not enough food or water, inadequate clothing for the weather, lice—was it just the times or were people simply used to going without and learning to deal with things back then? It was hard to envisage today's eighteen- to twenty-somethings coping with the conditions Clarrie and his mates had been forced to live through. It highlighted to her just how materialistic today's society had become. While this generation is so busy being offended by absolutely everything, Clarrie and most of *his* generation were being slaughtered in a foreign land, fighting for their country. It really did put things into perspective.

November, 1915
Been crook last few days with a headache and fever and the doc reckons it's a touch of trench fever, which goes well with the constant Gallipoli Gallop most of us have. Never thought I'd be missing the sand and heat of Egypt.

The shelling has been heavier than it has been in days. I'm holed up in my dugout writing this as best I can while lying on my back. One poor chap nearby just got hit with shrapnel, and his mate next to him got to his knees to help him and a fragment took off the top of his head. Just like that. Only moments before they'd been sharing a good laugh with us. All around me I hear 'Stretcher bearer!' and the screaming of the wounded, mixed with the low moaning of the dying. The shells have been falling for hours and it feels like an eternity.

It snowed last night. Rations of water have been almost non-existent. With no water we can't cook anything to warm our stomachs. If I ever make it home after this, I will never again take a simple cup of tea for granted.

Who would have thought something so simple would come to be one of the most wished for things in my daily life? What I wouldn't give for a nice hot cup of tea right now.

Eleven

Sophie drove across the paddock and back to the place where she'd first seen the black horse, peering into the tree line hopefully. If she could get a photo of it then maybe she could show someone and they'd recognise the animal.

She parked the car and climbed out, listening for any sort of horsey noises, but the only sounds were birds calling and the hum of insects in the air. Staring into the bush she realised how easy it would be for an animal—or anything, for that matter—to remain out of sight if it chose to do so. It was so dense in places she couldn't even see past the first few rows of trees.

It was quiet out here, with no sound of anything other than the leaves of the trees rustling and insects. She could almost be the only person left on the planet. Grabbing a plastic bag off the front seat, she walked a little further on into her own little pocket of bush. She loved the wide open spaces of the cleared paddocks around the front part of the property, but there was something special about these huge trees and the wildness of the landscape. Lizards darted off rocks they'd been sunning themselves on as she walked by, and high in the trees she heard birds calling to each other. A loud snap of branches and the blur of brown fur startled her, and she swore under her breath as she watched the small kangaroo or maybe it was a wallaby, she wasn't sure how to tell the difference, bound off through the trees. These animals had a home here and she realised that either by intent or, more likely, a lack of interest, Archie had provided a wildlife habitat on his property. She walked for a few more minutes before turning around and heading back to the car, disappointed. She'd been hoping she'd see him again.

As she came out of the trees she stopped. Standing at the rear of her car, the big horse was sniffing inquisitively. Sophie held her breath, almost too scared to breathe in case the slightest movement scared him off. He seemed even bigger than before, but this time she was so much closer. She gauged the distance at less than fifteen metres. She heard a low nicker and the soft, breathy sound was accompanied by a bit of head bobbing as he eyed her standing across the small clearing between the trees.

Sophie remembered the bag of bread in her hand and slowly pulled a piece out, inching her foot forward slowly. 'Hi there,' she said, keeping her tone low and gentle. His ears twitched at the sound and she wondered how long it was since he'd heard a human voice, if ever. 'Do you like bread?' She took one step and then another when he didn't move. 'What are you doing all the way out here, hey?' she continued, moving slowly closer and keeping an eye on his body language. She couldn't say she had a great deal of experience with animals but she was hoping she could pick up on any signs of imminent danger. So far he looked extremely wary, but he wasn't moving so that had to be a good sign. Then just as she got to within two car lengths of him, he spun without warning and galloped off into the tree line once more.

'Damn it!' she said, frustrated at how close she'd got. She stared after him but knew he wouldn't be coming back out again today. With a disappointed sigh, she tossed a few pieces of bread on the ground before climbing back into her car.

The road stretched before her, but Sophie's mind was not on it or the scenery outside the window. Her mind was racing with everything she needed to do. The call had come in that a farmer had his leg caught in a fence-post digger on a property a few kilometres out of town and it wasn't sounding good.

Sophie and John pulled up beside a tractor parked in the middle of a paddock. 'What's his name?' Sophie asked as they grabbed their equipment.

'Huey Johnson. They call him Johnno,' John said, as they headed across to the tractor. The nasty spiral-shaped drill hovered menacingly above the man on the ground, while another man knelt beside him holding a blood-soaked shirt to his leg.

Sophie ran an experienced gaze over the patient, searching for signs of shock and noting his pale complexion. 'Hi, Johnno, my name's Sophie. Can I take a look at what you've done?'

The man in his mid-fifties opened his eyes to look at her, and she could see the pain reflected in them at the effort it took to keep them open. 'Sure,' he said faintly.

The other man released his hold on the fabric covering the wound and immediately blood began to soak through the ripped and torn denim of his jeans from deep lacerations. Sophie spotted shards of bone and knew they were dealing with a particularly nasty fracture. 'Okay, we need to control this bleeding,' Sophie said calmly as she looked up at John, who was already moving to hand her the arterial tourniquet. They worked quickly and efficiently. Sophie's next concern was pain relief. As she got herself organised to administer morphine through an IV, John called for a helicopter while helping the man use the painkiller in the green whistle to tide him over until she inserted the cannula.

'What happened?' Sophie asked the other man, who hovered anxiously as she drew up the analgesia and waited for John to crosscheck the dosage.

'The auger hit a rock or something and it jumped out of the hole and grabbed hold of Johnno's leg. I managed to shut it off and then I had to pull him away from it.'

Sophie noticed the roll of fencing wire laid out on the ground near where the men had been digging post holes. Judging from the ripped work pants, she suspected the digger had caught hold of Johnno's jeans and dragged his leg into the spinning shaft.

Now that they had some pain relief in the injured man, Sophie and John could splint his leg. The auger had done some pretty nasty damage to the lower part of the limb, and Sophie was more than a little concerned that he may actually lose it. As careful as they tried to be, it was impossible not to cause some pain, despite the morphine, as they applied traction to the injured leg.

'You're doing great, Johnno,' Sophie reassured him as she monitored the analgesia and tried to keep him as comfortable as possible while they waited.

A buzzing sound in the distance soon grew into a droning throb as the helicopter approached. Once it landed, Sophie gave the handover and helped settle the injured farmer inside before running back to the ambulance and watching with the two other men as it lifted up into the sky and swooped off, bound for the major trauma centre in Tamworth.

'I thought you guys said this place was going to be a slower pace than the city?' she said after they'd packed away all their equipment, opening her door and climbing into the four-wheel drive.

'It usually is,' John said with a soft grunt and a smile. 'This is the most action we've had in years.'

Sophie wasn't sure if she should be concerned that her partner seemed almost cheery, and her own heart had been pumping more than a little fast as she'd worked. There was no denying that the adrenaline rush was a pretty exciting part of the job, but the satisfaction of knowing you'd helped to save a man's life was an even bigger high. She wasn't sure what would happen to Johnno in the operating theatre, but she knew that they'd done everything possible to ensure he had a fighting chance of survival.

Twelve

Waiting at the butcher to be served the next day, Sophie overheard a conversation with a customer who looked vaguely familiar.

'Did you hear about poor old Johnno losin' his leg?' the butcher was saying.

'Yeah. Silly bastard should have been watching what he was doin',' the customer replied, leaning a hip on the counter as he watched the butcher weighing out his mince.

'Easy enough to happen. Bloody post hole diggers, dangerous damn things.'

Sophie had followed up on Johnno's progress later that afternoon and heard that they hadn't been able to save the leg. It was a shame, but she couldn't say she'd been surprised. She gave a little shudder at the memory of the damage.

After the man paid for his purchase and turned to leave the shop, the butcher called out, 'See ya, Horrie.' Sophie realised why he'd seemed familiar.

'Excuse me,' she said, stepping in front of him before he reached the door. 'Are you Horrie Spicer, by any chance?'

The man's eyes widened slightly before he gave a grin. 'I am.'

'Hi, I'm Sophie. I bought Archie Gilbert's place.'

'Ahh,' he said nodding sagely. 'Now I know who you are. Lenny said you'd dropped by the other day. He told me about your horse sighting too.'

'So it's not yours then?'

'Not bloody likely,' he chuckled.

Sophie was beginning to feel completely disillusioned with everything she'd firmly believed about country people. Weren't they supposed to like horses? Weren't horses the backbone of farming life?

'Sounds like a brumby. Bloody Archie let that place of his go, so God only knows what's been coming in from the national park. I can come over and get rid of it for you if you want?'

'Take it away, you mean?'

'Shoot it. Make good dog meat if nothing else. You don't want a brumby runnin' wild on your place and breakin' fences. They can be dangerous bloody things.'

Sophie tried not to recoil at the thought of the horse she'd seen chopped up for dog meat. *What was wrong with these people?* 'I haven't seen it again. It's probably long gone by now.' She didn't like lying as a rule, but she didn't particularly like the idea of someone hunting about on her place for a horse either.

'If you see it again, you let me know.'

'Will do,' she said, sending him a brief smile. *Not bloody likely.* There was no way that horse was going to become dog food.

∽

Sophie had been steadily reading through the diary and knew there were only a few more pages with writing on them left. She'd been trying her best to pace herself, but it was inevitable that she had to reach the end sometime, and tonight was as good a time as any.

November 20th, 1915

I'm writing this from on board a hospital ship bound for Alexandria. While out digging trenches I was hit by shrapnel. At first I didn't even realise I'd been hit. The shell dropped almost on top of our position. Three men were killed. I was among three others injured and by the looks of it I was pretty lucky. I just copped a bit of shrapnel in the thigh—the other two lost limbs.

All around me lie men with their heads swathed in blood-seeped bandages. Some have lost eyes, others half of their faces. The devastation of the shrapnel injuries are too horrible to imagine. None of these blokes are ever going to look the same again. Then there are the blokes with missing arms and legs. The doctor I spoke to told me there was going to be hundreds of thousands of them returning home with at least one limb missing by the end of the war. I suppose they're lucky that they get to go home. There's too many to count who are going to be left behind here, buried under crosses in this godforsaken place.

Sophie suspected there was more to Clarrie's bit of shrapnel. It seemed highly unlikely they'd have sent him on such a long journey to a hospital via ship if it hadn't been serious. He didn't go into much detail about his own injury in any of the next few entries but he seemed to take in everything around him during his hospital stay, describing the huge building with row upon row of beds, men who were more mobile shuffling about, visiting with the men who were bedridden to sit and chat or to read them letters from home. She couldn't help imagining the bits he didn't mention, like the smell of infection from wounds and too few dressings. So many men crammed into such closed areas would present difficult challenges for the nursing and medical staff. Many of them wouldn't have washed in who knew how long, and trying to maintain some kind of sterility in a hospital setting must have been a nightmare. She knew they barely had any of the effective pain relief and medications that were available today, and antibiotics hadn't been around back then at all. From a medical point of view, Sophie was astonished that so many men did in fact survive their injuries and return home after the war.

November 25th, 1915
Breakfast was porridge, a slice of bread with jam and a hot
cup of tea, with milk and sugar. I swear I've died and gone
to heaven. It breaks my heart that I can barely manage to
get it all down. Too many days going without food has
shrunk our bellies. Seems hard to remember back to a time
when eating a meal like this was normal.

December 1st, 1915
Received a very welcome delivery from the Red Cross
of a comfort parcel that contained soap, socks, lollies,
tobacco and I even scored some newspapers from back
home. The doctors here do a marvellous job. Can't fault
their dedication—they work until they're about to drop
and then work some more. The line of men waiting to be
tended never seems to diminish. Must be terribly disheart-
ening for the poor chaps. They took out all the shrapnel
from my wound but the infection has taken quite a time
to heal. Looks like it's on the mend though and sounds
like they might be kicking me out of these fancy lodgings
any day now. I can't say I'll miss the pain, but I will
sorely miss this bed and clean sheets and the tea. Oh,
how I'll miss the tea.

Good news. They're sending us back to Cairo. Finally, I'll
get to see Cobber and Henry. I won't be sorry to see the
back of Anzac Cove. Good riddance to it, I say. I hope
never to see that much death and destruction ever again.

February 15th, 1916
Drills and manoeuvres. I've been back three days now and that's all we've been doing.

Henry did a bonza job of taking care of old Cobber. He looks a treat. The rest and exercise in camp over the last few months has done him wonders. The entire regiment, for that matter. The long voyage on board the ship had taken its toll on the horses and they'd all lost a lot of condition despite our best attempts to give them as much exercise as we could in the limited space. It's good to see him again.

March 3rd, 1916
Got my first decent look at a native Bedouin today while we were out on patrol. We came across a small tribe of them where they had set up a camp with goatskin tents. The men wore long robes and head wear. Their black eyes seemed to take us all in, not missing a thing. The women were covered from head to toe so we couldn't get a good look at them. They had a small herd of camels tethered inside their camp and they seemed very wary of us as we rode past in our long columns. There isn't any love lost between the men and the Bedouins. Our camps are always having things stolen and the men have made a number of complaints, which seem to have fallen on deaf ears.

The Bedouins are supposed to be our allies and headquarters is determined to keep them onside. Despite the fact that its widely known that they've happily supplied the Turks with information on things like troop movements and numbers. We need them more than they need us, apparently.

April 4th, 1916

I haven't written in here for a while. Firstly because there was nothing much happening to report, just drills and training—always training—but the officers have had word that something big was coming and we need to be prepared. They were right. We were given only a few hours to move out and we've been on the go ever since. So far we've had only minimal contact with any Turks—mainly just a few hit and run encounters. They've not engaged in any major confrontations as yet, instead keeping close to their main camp in some place named Beersheba.

The horses are handling the desert splendidly. They're tough little buggers and it makes me more than a little bit chuffed to know that they've come from home. They're doing us proud.

August 19th, 1916

I've been too busy to write lately but we've been steadily moving. Reports have been coming in that the Turks are on the move. They were headed to a place called Romani. We've set out to head them off and hold them back. The days are near torture—the heat and hot winds burn our faces like a furnace blast. We take shelter and find a bit of shade by lying under the horses, but even in the shade it's unbearable. I feel for poor old Cobber and the rest of the horses. Water is scarce and we depend on finding waterholes, which consist of small groves of palm trees surrounded by large sand dunes. Our engineers are doing a remarkable job of digging wells but, all too often, these wells run dry before we've watered all the animals. I've been sharing my water ration with Cobber for the last two days.

Still, we're a lot better off than the poor bastards being carried from the battlefield. You hear their groans of agony as they're placed on a sand cart and dragged by horses across the rough terrain, being jostled and thrown about—makes you think they might have been better off dying, I reckon. But the camel cacolet would have to be just as bad. We passed at least twenty of these only the other day. The camel might be fine for carrying supplies, but they were not designed to carry injured men from the front lines. I won't soon forget the woeful sounds of the injured as they lay on stretchers, strapped either side of a camel's hump.

August 27th, 1916
We encountered a German aircraft today, and we were sitting ducks out in the open. The riders had managed to scatter with most of the horses, but we lost 18 horses and 5 men. How we hate that droning sound when we hear it approaching.

Sophie had spent the day deciphering the entries, with her laptop open to type in place names and read up on a little more of the history. Although Clarrie had written detailed accounts of his life during the war, he'd left out a lot of the specifics where the fighting was concerned. It wasn't until she began reading about the battles that the Australian Light Horse were involved in through the various historical pages online that she understood just how dangerous it had been for Clarrie and Cobber out there. She hadn't even realised there'd been aircraft used in the First World War until Clarrie had mentioned it in his diary. With so much open desert, the men in their camps were easy targets for planes dropping bombs. How terrifying that must have been.

The images she pored over online depicting the men and their horses now held a deeper meaning for her. The heat must have been unbearable and yet these men and their horses endured it day after day on limited food and scarcely any water. She couldn't even begin to imagine how she'd cope in those conditions. But it was the mention of the medics and the hospital staff that really hit home for her. They were the pioneers of her profession, stretcher-bearers and medics who ran into gunfire and danger, risking their lives to save men under the most horrific conditions imaginable.

Clarrie had mentioned various primitive forms of transport that the field ambulance had utilised during the war. Sophie knew that many men hadn't survived their injuries, but that anyone could survive not only the initial wounds but also the transport and limited medical assistance on top of that was completely astonishing. She tried to imagine strapping patients with the kinds of injuries sustained from bombings and machine-gun fire onto the side of a camel, or dragging them on a stretcher behind a horse for miles to a field hospital. She couldn't wait to share these details with the next obnoxious patient who complained of a bumpy ride in the back of her ambulance!

Clarrie and his regiment spent the latter part of 1916 and early 1917 doing patrol work, mentioning various places and smaller battles, but notably leaving out much of the detail about these. He did comment on the number of casualties and their ongoing struggle for enough water, and his concern about the horses was a constant strain on him.

There were also some entries that had no date specified and a few that Clarrie often wasn't sure of. This was testament to how long they'd spent out in the desert on patrol and how exhausted they must have been, at times unable to recall how many days had passed and how long they'd been away.

The almost casual tone at times in Clarrie's diary entries was an attempt to downplay how terrifying it must have been, but almost daily they encountered the enemy, and the killing. He never wrote how he felt about that but simply made mention now and again how they sorted them out. It was hard to imagine how confronting it must have been for these men, most of whom had no previous military experience before signing up and many not even old enough to vote. They were farmers and labourers, teachers and bankers, for goodness sake.

Thirteen

Unsure of date, September, 1916
Death is everywhere you look here. It's become part of
our life. Mostly our dead are buried within a day, but
the Turks usually leave theirs. Dead Turks are part of the
landscape. The smell of death isn't as out of place as it once
was. Even the sight of death—rotting flesh and bloated
bodies—it's all so normal to us now. But it's the Bedouins
digging up our dead, stripping them of their clothing and
stealing anything they can find like scavengers that really
riles us men up. They roam through the battlefields like
packs of vultures. They spy for the enemy and they steal
anything they can get their grubby hands on and no one
can do a thing about it. They're off limits because they're
supposed to be our allies, but the Bedouin are only loyal to

their own tribes and are known to swap sides depending on who offers them more gold. There is no great love for the Bedouin by the troops.

Still not sure of date, September, 1916
The desert is brutal. It's hard to imagine how people have survived out here for thousands of years. Our progress centres around water—or rather our ability to get it. Engineers have been busy digging wells as far ahead as they can, but keeping it up to this many men and horses seems like a near impossible task.

The horses are handling the terrain remarkably well. They're a sturdy bunch. Cobber's taking it all in his stride, but I think he's dreaming of the day we head back to the green mountains of home. I'll never complain again about being cold. If I ever see sand again, it'll be far too soon.

September 20th, 1916
We continue to move forward. The Turks have been positioned high up in the hills above us, peppering us with gunfire at every opportunity. We've taken refuge in a dry wadi, but it doesn't offer us a lot of protection. Henry and I, along with a few other boys, were sent up to try to take out the machine gun that had been giving us the most amount of grief. It was a little hairy climbing the steep cliff face; we lost our footing more than once and I'm not sure how Johnny Turk didn't hear us coming from a mile off. Just before sunrise we launched into a surprise attack

and managed to take out the gunner, returning to camp just in time for a breakfast of two sips of water and some stale bread.

Riding at night to avoid the heat of the day and the eyes of the enemy has its merits, but we are beyond exhaustion and the ride is often done with many a rider taking a nap in the saddle and allowing their horse to follow the horse in front of it.

September 29th, 1916
Henry has been pretty crook for the last few days. They've sent him to the field hospital to get checked out. He wasn't looking too good. Think it's malaria.

September 30th, 1916
Just received word that Henry died.

Sophie almost missed this entry as it was so unexpected and brief, but when she went back and re-read it there it was. Henry had died. A tightness in her chest made her frown. She didn't even know these people, but she felt as though she did. Poor Henry. Then her thoughts turned to Clarrie. Poor Clarrie. In the same way that he never put his feelings about killing down on paper, she knew that he probably wouldn't write about how devastating Henry's death would have been for him. In some ways Clarrie wrote from his heart, but regarding experiences that were deeply personal to him, it seemed he couldn't bring himself to write them down at all. Was it because he didn't want anyone else to read about these events, or because once he wrote about them, he would be forced to acknowledge the pain himself?

Sophie turned the page and saw that the diary date had been crossed out and Clarrie had started a new year. Sophie imagined the war had taken its toll on him heavily after his friend had died, given that he seemed to have given up writing regular entries following Henry's death.

October 25th, 1917
We've been camped in this place for two nights now. All around us are graves and crosses of our fallen dead from recent battles. There's a lingering sadness, although we are all too exhausted to grieve for them. I think most of us are accepting that we won't all be making it home and that one day we could be beneath one of those crosses. I think of Henry often. There's a sadness inside me that I can't shake. I've lost so many of the mates I signed up with. They've all gone but for a few. From my dugout I can see the crosses scattered across the top of a nearby sand ridge as though, even in death, they are standing guard over our camp as we sleep.

October 30th, 1917
We travelled 30 miles last night. Both horses and men have now been without water for 36 hours and the horses

were down to 3 handfuls of grain each. The closest water to us is being held in a place called Beersheba. I hate to think what will become of us if we fail to capture it from the Turks.

November 12th, 1917
I haven't been able to write for a while as we've been too busy chasing old Johnny Turk back to where he came from. There has been a lot of waiting around in the most terrible heat, with our horses a whisker away from dying of thirst—and us not too far behind! Just as the afternoon was promising us a measure of relief from the blazing sun, we were told we were going to take Beersheba.

All day we'd been trying to take this fortress, and it was looking dire. Then the order to charge was given and all hell broke loose.

We hit them in waves, starting at a trot before breaking into a full gallop, man and animal as one—streaking across the plains in a wave of yells and thundering of hooves that even deafened the sound of shells which were exploding all around us.

By the time I crossed the trenches, men were already in hand-to-hand combat with the Turks. Others had their hands full with the willing surrender of the enemy, still in shock over the daring attack. The horses were near mad with the scent of water, as were we. The wells had been wired for detonation but thankfully our boys managed to disarm them and we captured them intact.

I wish Henry had been here to see this. He would have got a right kick out of it I reckon.

Clarrie and Cobber had been at Beersheba? Goosebumps broke out across Sophie's arms. She'd heard of it, of course, although she only had a sketchy knowledge of the details— she did know though that it had been one of the most amazing victories in the history of the entire war. The fact Clarrie had written about the lead-up to it without a clue that he and his fellow troopers would soon become part of this legendary battle made it all the more awe-inspiring.

⁂

December 31st, 1917
It's New Year's Eve. Another year away from home. Another new year to wonder if this will be the one where we finally go home. I don't remember the man I was before I joined up. I don't know that person anymore. He's a stranger.

I sometimes can't remember what it feels like to smile or laugh. Of course there's always a few larrikins around camp who brighten your spirits once in a while—it's the Aussie way, after all—but none of us really laugh, not like we would have before the war. Joy and laughter doesn't touch you deep down anymore. How can it? The things we've seen. The mates we've lost. The blood and gore—Christ, the blood.

I'm not sure I can even bear to kill a chook for Mum's Sunday roast anymore. How do I explain that? I can kill a man without a blink of an eye, but the thought of being

121

home and chopping the head off a damn bird sends a chill down my spine and makes me break out in a cold sweat.

February 2nd, 1918
General morale is low, despite the fact we finally seem to be winning. We're on the move, taking towns with hardly any resistance. The Turks are fleeing, leaving a trail of destruction behind them. And they're running scared. It seems everywhere we arrive, they've only just left—leaving behind carts of supplies, and campsites still set up. Clothing and packs on the ground, the scattered contents left where they fell in their hurry to flee. The smell of death is everywhere we go. I can't bring myself to write about it anymore. We just want to see it through to the end and go home.

Sophie noticed as she read the diary how Clarrie's general demeanour deteriorated over the next few pages, as he seemed to struggle to write anything in too much detail. Even with the bare details, she could see that life was hard for the light horsemen. She missed Clarrie's earlier humour and his zest for life. How sad that the grand adventure they'd all been looking forward to had left them world-weary and broken like this.

August 17th, 1918
I think this will be the last time I write in this journal. There doesn't seem much point anymore. Cobber's dead

and I'm here after surviving a trip across the desert on a camel cacolet. I only remember parts of it as I was in a pretty bad way and much of it I'm grateful not to recall. I'll be going home soon. My war's over now.

Sophie's heart plummeted and she turned the page, breathing a sigh of relief when she saw more of the now familiar writing.

November 12th, 1918
I thought I'd finished writing in this damn journal, but it seems old habits die hard. I'm home, but it doesn't feel like the home I left four years ago.

So much of my time away feels like a dream. A bad one at that.

As I lie here in my bed, my head bandaged and my foot barely intact, the reality of the situation has hit me hard.

Thank Christ the war is over, but what did we really achieve? It was sure as hell nothing like the big adventure we all thought we were about to go on. Were all the lives lost worth it? Were all the broken men we sent home worth it? Were all those loyal, brave Australian horses that were killed after we put them through hell worth it?

I haven't heard any argument so far to convince me that it was. We were willing to sacrifice ourselves for king and country . . . and sacrificed we were.

My only solace in the way my war ended was that Cobber and I didn't have to suffer the pain that was to come. We were informed while I was in hospital that the government couldn't justify the expense of bringing the horses back home. Those brave, trusting mates who carried us through hell and back weren't worth bringing home. Instead they were to be handed over to Poms to use as remounts for Egypt and India. Others too old or exhausted from fighting would be destroyed. I know that there will be quite a few who will choose to put their mounts out of their misery themselves, so they won't have to suffer a life of hard labour in some backstreet slum.

I'm almost thankful to that Turk who shot Cobber. It was a clean shot, he was dead before he hit the ground. The same shot that killed him went through me as well, but Cobber took the brunt of the impact—loyal to the bloody end.

I'd rather he died a hero than be left behind to be worked into the ground, starved and mistreated. I am thankful we were both spared the torment of parting like that.

There was a welcome home reception held for the few locals who have returned in the past few months—I couldn't bring myself to go. Unless you were there you can't tell people what it was like and I refuse to engage in idle chitchat with old men who couldn't go and want to hang on your every word as if they can somehow experience it through second-hand stories.

Mum said they called us heroes. Cobber was the hero. All those horses were. They carried us across that flaming desert, took us into places no man had a hope of reaching on foot. If anyone was a hero, it was the horses.

And we left them all behind.

Sophie could feel the emptiness of those last few words on the page—felt it like a punch to her stomach. A hundred years hadn't lessened the impact of them.

Sophie turned the page but there were no more entries. She flipped through the remaining pages with more urgency, but they were all blank, yellowed and faded.

She felt sadder than she'd imagined at the thought of Clarrie's beloved Cobber dying on the battlefield. She'd never thought about what happened to the horses at the end of the war. For some reason she'd assumed that the brumbies in the high country were descendants of the horses released after they'd come home from war. Clearly that was wrong. Did they really just abandon them and shoot their horses so they didn't have to bring them all the way home? Sophie couldn't wrap her head around the heartlessness.

Throughout the diary, one of the most important things she'd gained from Clarrie's writing was the love and devotion between man and horse. How many times had he praised their stamina and courage? The battles those horses enabled the army to win, and then to expect the men to stand by and allow them to be shot? Or handed over to people too poor to feed them and care for them properly? That was beyond cruel.

Sophie pulled her laptop closer and began researching. Clarrie had to be wrong. Maybe he only heard a rumour about the horses. Surely someone stepped in and stopped that from happening.

A couple of hours later, having located a documentary online about Australian horses in the war, Sophie was left sobbing as she watched the final credits roll across the screen.

It was all true. At the end of the war, instead of bringing these brave, loyal animals home, the army made the men lead their hoses to a field where they were shot and skinned, their tail and mane hair first cut off to be sold. She felt ill—but even more than that, she felt angry. How was this atrocity allowed to happen?

Clarrie had been right. Maybe the kindest thing *had* been for Cobber to die in battle. A hero's death—quick, hopefully painless and with a hell of a lot more dignity than the remaining horses were ever given. Sleep that night did not come easily and she lay awake long into the early hours of the morning thinking about Clarrie and his war.

Fourteen

Sophie took a call on her way into town early the next morning: an elderly man had fallen down his front stairs but had been able to call it in himself. The address wasn't far from her house, and was on her way into town, so she decided to call Jackie to meet her there.

Coming up the long driveway to the house, Sophie spotted the injured man immediately—he was sitting on the bottom step, leaning back and looking to be in a fair bit of pain.

'What have you done to yourself, Mr Willoughby?' Sophie asked as she slid her first-aid bag off her shoulder and placed the drug box and cardiac monitor on the ground before kneeling down next to him.

'Bill. Call me Bill,' he said, wincing. 'I took a bit of a tumble down the steps.'

'Okay, Bill. I'm going to check you out and see what's going on.'

'Best offer I've had in a while,' he said, grimacing as he tried to sit up.

'Don't try to move.' Sophie took his wrist in her hand and checked the man's pulse, noting that it was weak and a little fast. 'Are you on any medication, Bill?'

'Oh yeah, just the usual: cholesterol and blood pressure tablets.'

'Did you take them this morning?'

He seemed to hesitate, his forehead scrunching into deep lines. 'Yes, I did take them. I remember standing at the sink.'

'Do you remember what happened before you fell?' His answer had seemed a little vague and Sophie wasn't confident yet that this was simply due to being shaken from a painful fall.

'I don't know—one minute I was about to head out to the shed, the next I was flat on my back at the bottom of the stairs. I'm not sure what happened. I must have lost my footing or something.'

Sophie eyed the four timber steps briefly—they were old, but seemed sturdy enough. She took his hand in hers and gently began probing the wrist joint. It was a little puffy, and extremely tender, but on checking his ankle she saw that it had already swollen to a considerable size. 'I'm going to take you into the hospital, Bill, so they can do some x-rays and make sure there're no broken bones, okay?'

'No, no, there's no need for all that. I'm just a bit battered and bruised, that's all. I don't want to go into hospital.' He tried to stand up and Sophie quickly eased him back down when he drew in a sharp breath, going pale as he tried to put weight on his injured ankle.

'Okay, let's sit back down here. I need to splint that ankle and wrist but, before I do, I've got some pain relief to give you that will help with the discomfort,' she said.

'I don't want it—any of it. I'm not going to the hospital. I can't,' he said irritably.

His sudden change in mood, from quite placid despite being in pain to short-tempered, concerned her. 'Okay, what's going on? Why don't you want to go to hospital?'

'Me cat. Who's going to feed her?'

Sophie looked up at the screen door where a fluffy white cat had been watching them, an almost haughty expression on its face. 'Do you have a neighbour who could call around and feed her a bit later? Or any family?'

'I can't trust just anyone to feed her. She likes things done particular like,' he said stubbornly.

Sophie considered her patient calmly. 'Is there any other reason you don't want to go into hospital, Bill? Is something else worrying you?'

The fact that he wouldn't look her in the eye and seemed to be searching for an excuse made her suspicious that there was more to it than concern for his cat.

'I hate that place,' he finally mumbled.

'The hospital? You've had a bad experience before there? With the staff?'

'No, not them,' he said dismissively, before glancing up at her face briefly. 'The last time I was there was . . . when Mabel died,' he finally admitted.

'Mabel was your wife?' Sophie asked gently. The old man's eyes glistened slightly.

'Yeah. She passed away about two years ago now. In that hospital. I haven't been back since that day. I know you probably think I'm some silly old fool,' he said without looking at her.

'Of course I don't. I understand exactly what you're feeling.' She took a seat next to him on the step. 'I lost my husband about eighteen months ago. I remember the day I had to walk out of the hospital without him too.' Sophie placed her hand gently on top of the leathery old one resting on his knee. 'It's not easy to face those kinds of memories.'

'No, it's not. I'm sorry about your husband,' Bill said softly.

Sophie gave a small smile in acknowledgement as they sat quietly for a few moments. 'I wouldn't ask you to do this if I didn't think it were necessary, Bill. I really need you to get those x-rays and tests done. I'll be there with you if you like?'

After a long pause, Bill let out a resigned sigh and nodded his head. 'Alright then. If you think it's that important.'

'I do. It'll be alright,' she told him gently, preparing some pain medication to help with his discomfort and then pulling out what she'd need to splint his wrist and ankle.

'You bought the Gilbert place, I hear?' he said as he watched her work.

'That's right. Did you know Archie?' Sophie asked as she carefully wrapped his wrist.

'As well as anyone could know Archie,' he said dryly.

'Wasn't much of a socialite then, I take it?'

'Nah, but a lot of them came back like that.'

'Came back? From where?'

'From the war. He was over in Singapore when it fell and wound up in Changi as a prisoner of war for the last few years before coming home.' His words faded off and a deep sadness filled his face. 'Those poor bastards went through things, *saw* things, that no one should have to experience. It was no wonder he came back a different man. He never talked about it,' he said looking up suddenly. 'Never marched on Anzac Day, wouldn't have anything to do with it. I reckon it brought back too many painful memories.'

'How horrible.' That would explain why Clarrie's trunk had remained unopened and forgotten at the back of the shed. Maybe it reminded Archie of too many things he'd rather forget from his own war. While Anzac Day commemorated the noble things about war, like mateship and remembering sacrifice, she supposed for many it would also bring back a lot of the things they tried *not to* remember. It would be very hard to be patriotic if all you wanted to do was forget the nightmares.

Sophie noticed Bill was beginning to get a little agitated again in the silence that followed.

'So what else do you know about him?' she asked, trying to keep his mind off the upcoming trip to hospital.

'I know his only family all live in the UK. How did that come about?'

'His mother was an English bride. His father, Sydney, met and married her over there during the First World War and brought her home. She was a bit of a funny woman, never really liked it out here, never tried to fit in. I think she was expecting something very different when Sydney told her his family owned a big property in Australia. After Sydney died, Archie's mother and sister returned to England and Archie took over the property. When the Second World War broke out, Archie signed up and went off to fight.'

'And he never married?'

'Nope. Came home and went back to farming. Kept to himself mostly, but he liked the odd beer—he'd drop around now and again for a drink and catch up then go back home. He used to say he liked the peace and quiet out there. It was good for his soul.'

Sophie felt a strange sensation pass through her body at the words. That's exactly how the place made her feel. It was the thing that had drawn her to buy it. She pushed the thought to the side for now. 'Do you know anything about Clarrie Gilbert?' she asked.

'Clarrie Gilbert,' he said almost wistfully. 'There's a name I haven't heard in a long time. He was Archie's uncle.'

'He was in the First World War too,' Sophie said.

Bill looked across at her, surprised. 'Yeah, he was. In the Light Horse. Part of the battalion that took Beersheba, I believe. He got a few medals, was wounded at the very end of the war, but survived and then came home, only to get killed in a farm accident.'

'What kind of accident? Do you know?'

'You have a lot of questions about people who died a very long time ago.'

Sophie gave him a lopsided grin. 'I found some old stuff in the shed that belonged to Clarrie. I tried to contact the family to see if they wanted it, but apparently they don't, so I kind of feel like I should know a bit more about the Gilberts. It probably sounds weird.'

'No, not at all. In fact, I think they'd like to be known about. There was never much interest in them from their families. Clarrie didn't get a chance to marry, and Sydney ended up being a miserable old bastard, and then Archie had all his demons to fight . . . I reckon it's nice that someone cares enough to find out who they were.'

Sophie wasn't sure she had much choice in the matter. From the very first moment she'd laid eyes on the place she'd felt an unexplainable connection. It was a bit weird to think there could be something behind it, not to mention she would sound more than a little crazy if she started talking about being drawn to a place by some kind of magnetic-like attraction. She gave herself a mental shake—maybe she *did* need to get out a bit more.

'Well, I feel pretty lucky to have stumbled on a time capsule of sorts. It's so interesting. Maybe I should see if there's a local historical group that would want some of Clarrie's things?'

'I could give you a few names of people to try. Let me know when you're ready to part with them,' Bill said.

Ready to part with them? That made it sound like she was attached to a bunch of old things in a trunk that didn't even belong to her ... The diary flashed through Sophie's mind and she realised that maybe she *had* grown attached to them, just a little. Through reading about Clarrie's life she'd got to know him, despite the fact he'd died close to a century ago.

She glanced up as Jackie arrived, waving a greeting.

'Another one?' asked Bill.

'Now you'll have two women fussing over you,' she grinned as Bill huffed about making too much over a simple fall.

'Okay, so are you ready to go?' She saw weary resignation cross his face and smiled softly. 'It's going to be okay, Bill. They'll just do a few x-rays and you'll be home before you know it.'

'Home before you know it,' he repeated quietly. 'That's what I told Mabel that day as they put her in an ambulance.'

Sophie carefully closed the doors, thinking of Bill's wife watching the house disappear as she was driven away, never expecting that it would be the last time she saw it.

The drive back into town was a sombre one.

∽

The Hilsons Ridge emergency room consisted of an examination area with three beds separated by privacy curtains. Sophie wheeled Bill inside and helped him across onto a bed.

'This is all a waste of everyone's time and effort. There's nothing wrong with me. It was only a tumble down the stairs.'

'The doctor won't be long. He's been expecting you,' the nurse said with a brisk smile. 'Is there anything I can get you, Bill?'

'You can get me outta here,' he mumbled gruffly.

The plump older woman gave a haughty sniff as she straightened the bedding. 'That will happen if and when the doctor says so. Now behave yourself, Bill Willoughby, or you'll have me to deal with.'

'Always was bossy, that one.'

Sophie bit back a smile at Bill's disgruntled mood. 'Let's just wait and see what the doctor has to say.'

A few minutes later, Bill announced, 'He's single, you know.'

'Who?'

'The doc. Not a bad bloke either. You could do worse than a doctor,' he said sagely.

Sophie opened her mouth to protest that she wasn't looking for anyone when Dr Tomovic walked into the room. She hoped he hadn't overhead Bill's words, but judging by his whirlwind entrance, white coat flapping briskly behind him, she doubted he'd had time to stop and listen to idle conversation.

'Hello, Sophie,' Ado said, her name rolling off his tongue with his hint of an accent. For a moment it distracted her, before she noticed Bill watching her with a knowing smirk on his face.

'Doctor,' she acknowledged, a little more formally than she might have if she didn't have an audience watching her every move. She waited as Ado asked Bill a number of questions, checked his eyes, took his blood pressure and examined his wrist and ankle. When Bill was taken away to have his x-rays, Ado sat down on the edge of the bed across from her, his expression concerned. 'Did he seem confused at any point when you got there?'

'No, maybe a little groggy though. He's extremely anxious about hospitals. His wife's death still seems pretty emotional for him.'

Ado nodded his head slowly at her answer. 'I'm going to run a few cognitive tests to rule out anything sinister, but at his age we cannot dismiss them.'

'I think he's worried he won't be able to manage at home alone.'

'It's a concern shared by many of our elderly in town. We have been trying to obtain funding to set up a community assist program to help people remain in their own homes longer. We have a community nurse who does in-house visits, but we need more funding for nursing assistants who can assist with showering and personal care.'

'Well, if anyone can get something up and running it will be you lot,' Sophie smiled tightly. 'After hearing about the fight the town put up to keep the ambulance station, I can't imagine there's anything too hard for this community to achieve.'

Ado looked down at the bed, his expression serious. 'I'm extremely hopeful that we'll be able to find a way to help our elderly. I've seen too many of them forced to move to other places to live out the last years of their lives among strangers in nursing homes, instead of here in the town where many of them have been born and raised their entire lives.'

That *was* sad. 'Does Bill not have any relatives in town?'

'Not in town, no. He has a daughter, but I believe she lives out of state. He's lived his whole life on that property, and I can't see him willingly moving.'

'Hopefully the tests come back clear of anything concerning and there won't be any reason he has to move,' Sophie said.

'He's not going to be happy when I tell him I want him to stay overnight though. I'm not confident that there's not some underlying factor behind his fall. I can't risk him returning alone out there with no one to keep an eye on him before the results come back.'

She didn't envy his job.

'And what about you, Sophie? How are you settling in?'

Sophie was momentarily surprised by the turn of conversation. 'Fine,' she said, hoping she covered her initial reaction.

'You're not at all like the previous paramedics we've had out here.'

'Really? Well, I'm just your average run-of-the-mill paramedic,' she said.

Ado shook his head slowly as he considered her. 'No, there's nothing run of the mill about you. Besides, I've seen your credentials. You're a qualified intensive care paramedic.

There weren't more opportunities available for you in the city?' he asked.

Sophie blinked, caught off guard momentarily by the question, but did her best to recover. 'I was just looking for a change.'

Ado nodded sagely.

'What about you?' Sophie asked in an attempt to deflect any further questions. 'Rural medicine isn't too quiet for you? You don't have any burning desire to try a busier environment?'

A slow smile touched his lips as he shook his head. 'I grew up in a war-torn country. Quiet is something I will never take for granted.'

Sophie thought back to her initial observation of the man on her first day in Hilsons Ridge. That world-weary look in his eyes had clearly been put there from a young age. It saddened her to think that the horrific things he must have witnessed had had such a lasting effect on him still, after all these years.

'I recognise the need for escape in you, Sophie—that is something I've seen in myself. This is a good place to heal.'

The phone on his hip sounded and he lowered his head slightly in a farewell as he walked out of the room to answer it, leaving Sophie to stare thoughtfully after him. Maybe she wasn't the blank canvas she'd tried so desperately to project after all. People out here seemed to be able to see right through her. It was more than a little unnerving.

Later, when Bill came back, Dr Tomovic broke the news to him and had been correct in assuming Bill wouldn't be impressed.

'I can't stay in here all night.'

'I really feel strongly about this, Bill. Just for the night so we can keep you under observation.'

'What about my cat? No. I can't stay here,' he tried to get off the bed, and both Ado and Sophie moved to steady him. He let out a muffled curse when he realised his bandaged wrist and ankle made trying to stand near impossible.

'Bill,' Sophie interjected, coming to stand next to the bed. 'How about I go back out to your place and feed the cat? I have to go past there to go home anyway. We need to make sure you're okay and, besides, you can't manage feeding today with your wrist and ankle so sore. Just stay one night, until the tests come back, and I'll take care of feeding the cat until you're back on your feet again.'

'I can't ask you to do that. You've already put yourself out enough for me today,' he muttered, but allowed her to ease him back onto the bed without protest.

'I'm on call so, unless I'm needed, I can work around whatever has to be done. I don't mind checking in on your cat and feeding it. Honestly.'

'Well . . . I suppose that'd be alright,' he said reluctantly. 'But only one night,' he added more firmly.

'One night,' the doctor agreed, giving Sophie a nod of approval. Sophie didn't have any experience with cats, but it couldn't be rocket science; you opened a tin and tipped it in a bowl. She was fairly sure she could manage that.

Fifteen

Sophie pulled up at the front of Bill's house and climbed out of the ambulance. Being on call, she didn't want to risk being caught without it if a job came in while she was out here playing good Samaritan. She looked around the small enclosed verandah for the red pot that Bill had mentioned. As she tipped it sideways and felt underneath, something dark slithered from behind another pot nearby and Sophie let out a loud shriek and jumped back as the snake disappeared over the side of the verandah. With her heart racing at the unexpected discovery, she took a calming breath before scanning the area to locate the key she'd dropped while throwing her hands in the air like a maniac. Picking it up, she kept a wary eye out for any further slithering movements.

Sophie unlocked the door and pushed it open, only to see a streak of white fur squeeze past her legs and run outside. 'Damn it,' she yelled. Was the cat supposed to go outside? What if the stupid thing ran away? *Now what?* Sophie looked around the small kitchen and massaged her temples with her fingertips. Maybe she could persuade it to come back inside if she found its food.

She crossed the room, noticing an ice-cream container full of medications on the table. She stopped beside it and did a quick flip through the contents, taking in that most of them were Bill's prescriptions but there were a few in there with Mabel's name typed on the outside of the boxes as well. Sophie frowned.

She understood how hard it was to throw things out that belonged to a loved one once they were gone—God knows she found herself holding on to the most ridiculous things of Garth's before she'd found the courage to dispose of them when she'd been packing everything in storage after selling the house. But keeping medications like this mixed in a container with Bill's own medications was an accident waiting to happen. It only took Bill not to have his glasses on one day and take the wrong medication . . . *the wrong medication?* Suddenly everything clicked. Maybe Bill had felt so strange just before his fall because he'd taken the incorrect medication.

She grabbed her phone and called the hospital, asking to be put through to Ado. 'Hey, it's me. I'm at Bill's. I think I know what happened . . .'

After ending the call, Sophie pocketed her phone and gave a relieved sigh. At least they had an avenue to look at now, and although taking the incorrect medication could be extremely dangerous, maybe the side effects Bill was having prior to his fall could be attributed to that rather than anything more sinister, which would ease his mind considerably.

Until he discovers I've gone and lost his cat.

The thought brought her back to the problem at hand. In the fridge she found the open tin of cat food that Bill had told her to look for. She also noticed there wasn't an awful lot of human food in there and hoped it was just that Bill hadn't been shopping this week, making a mental note to make sure he had groceries before he was discharged. With can in hand, Sophie went to the door and peered out cautiously, hoping not to meet the snake again, tapping the can with a spoon. 'Here, kitty, kitty, kitty. Come and get your dinner,' she called in a singsong tone.

Miraculously the cat appeared, jumping over the spilled soil from the pot plant it had tipped over in its earlier charge past her. Darting in-between Sophie's legs and meowing loudly and impatiently, it seemed to be doing its best to try to trip Sophie up as she juggled closing the screen door and holding onto the cat food. The tone of impatient cat talk grew insanely loud for the size of the animal.

It was the ugliest cat she'd ever seen: despite its luscious white long-haired coat, it had a pug-like face that looked like it'd been hit with a door.

'Alright!' Sophie snapped, stepping over the cat, who insistently wound itself between her feet. 'God, just wait. I'm doing the best I can!'

She searched the kitchen for a feed bowl, finally spotting it under the table and crouching down to retrieve it. As she backed out, Sophie bumped her head, dropping the bowl with a loud clatter as she reached up to rub at the painful spot. The cat chose that moment to let out a loud meow in protest and jumped up on the table to get at the tin of food. 'Get down!' Sophie yelled, swiping at the cat and in the process knocking the container of medication to the floor. Boxes went flying, and pills inside plastic bottles that obviously hadn't had their lids screwed on properly scattered and bounced across the floor in every direction.

Sophie's loud expletive doubled in intensity as the cat jumped from the table and ran to the rainbow of tablets now scattered across the floor, sniffing around them.

'Get away from those,' Sophie called, throwing the closest thing at hand, which happened to be the feed bowl. The cat scooted from the room as the tin made a loud bang and spun on its edge before clattering to the ground. Sophie gave a defeated sigh as she searched the kitchen cupboards for a dustpan to sweep up the tablets.

'Could things get any worse?' she muttered as she scanned the floor for any remaining pills. Satisfied she'd got them all, Sophie stowed away the dustpan and tried once again to feed the bloody cat. 'Come on, cat,' she called, banging the cat food tin when there was no sign of it.

'Oh, for goodness sake!' she growled impatiently, heading out of the kitchen in search of the missing feline.

There were touches of Mabel everywhere through the house, from pretty crocheted doilies on the tables to the collection of figurines in a glass display case in the living room. Sophie gave a sad smile thinking of Bill, knowing he found comfort in keeping his wife close by him in the house they'd made a home together.

She looked across and spotted the cat lying on the sofa and frowned. 'What? You're expecting room service or something?' She tapped on the can again and turned away, frowning over her shoulder as the cat showed no interest in following. 'Oh, for the love of God,' she muttered, walking over to the sofa to pick the cat up. It sagged limply, and Sophie had a sudden, terrible sinking feeling. Placing the can on the floor beside her she tried to stand the cat up, but each time she let go the animal sank to the ground. An image of the snake on the front verandah flashed through her mind. *Oh no.* Had it chased the snake and been bitten when it escaped outside earlier?

Sophie scooped the cat into her arms and headed to the ambulance, locking the door of the house behind her. She placed the cat on the passenger side floor and ran around to climb into the driver's seat, praying under her breath that she could make it to town in time to find the vet clinic still open. 'It's okay, cat. Just hang in there,' she said, striving for a reassuring tone. The animal let out a feeble-sounding meow.

As she came around a sweeping bend she could just make out another vehicle up ahead, and within moments had caught up to it. The rusty old ute had a cage on the back and inside was the fattest pig she'd ever seen. The thing almost filled the entire back tray. This particular stretch of road was narrow and hard to overtake on. Sophie was counting on the driver to pull over and let her pass. The ute itself was barely doing more than forty kilometres—at this rate they wouldn't get into town for another half an hour. Sophie glanced down at the cat on the floor and made a decision. Switching on the sirens and lights would buy her a little extra time, and time was vital if they were dealing with snake venom. But the driver didn't pull over and just kept plodding along.

'Oh. My. God,' Sophie whispered beneath her breath. Finally, the driver looked up into his rear-view mirror and she saw his eyes widen into saucers. The ute jerked to the side of the road, leaving a cloud of dust in its wake. 'Thank you,' she muttered as she passed by and accelerated, leaving the enormous pig and its near-sighted driver behind.

Okay, so she probably shouldn't have used the sirens, but technically saving this cat's life would, in turn, save Bill's life, so really she was doing this for her patient.

There were no further holdups along the road and Sophie made it into town in record time, parking outside the small house at the end of the main street that housed the veterinary clinic. She gathered the cat into her arms and headed to the front door. 'Please, please, please be here,'

145

she whispered as she reached the door, breathing a sigh of relief when she found it open. The woman at the front counter looked up as Sophie came inside.

'Hi, I don't have an appointment, and I know it's almost closing time, but this cat needs to see a vet.'

'Cleo?' the receptionist stood up from behind her desk and eyed the feline and then Sophie suspiciously.

'I was feeding her for Mr Willoughby.'

'Bring her in here,' the woman said in a brisk tone. Sophie didn't know her, but she seemed like the kind of person you didn't want to get on the wrong side of.

Sophie placed the cat on the stainless-steel table as the woman bustled from the room, calling over her shoulder that she was getting Dr Conway.

'I'm sorry, cat. Please don't die.'

'No one's dying on my watch,' a deep voice said, making Sophie jump as she looked up at the man who walked into the room. 'I'm Zac Conway.'

He wore faded jeans and a checked shirt with the sleeves rolled to mid forearm, and Sophie found herself staring at the light tuff of chest hair exposed by the top button being left undone before snatching her gaze back up to his face. A bombardment of guilt interrupted the brief moment of whatever the hell that had just been. *Focus, Bryant. What's wrong with you?*

'Sophie Bryant,' she quickly introduced herself.

'I know. The new ambo,' he said matter-of-factly. 'Cleo, what have you done to yourself?'

'You know her?' Sophie asked, somewhat dumbfounded, then remembered where she was. *Of course he knew the cat.* Everyone knew everyone around here.

'Tell me what happened.'

Right, the cat. 'I was feeding her for Bill this afternoon,' she began.

'Why? Where's Bill?' he interrupted.

'He's spending the night in hospital. He had a fall this morning.'

'Is he okay?' Zac asked, looking concerned.

'They just want to run a few tests, but I think we've worked out what happened. Anyway, he was worried about leaving the cat alone so I offered to go out and feed it.'

'What are the symptoms?'

'He was a little confused and looks like he's sprained an ankle,' she said, then stopped when she saw the vet giving her an odd look.

'The *cat's* symptoms,' he slowly explained.

'Oh. Right.' *God, how embarrassing.* Sophie automatically kicked into professional mode and started rattling off the info the vet needed before mentioning her suspicions about the snake. This was just like any of a thousand handovers she'd done before—if you ignored the fact that the patient was a cat . . . and the doctor was a hot vet. *What the hell? Where was this coming from?*

'You saw her get bitten?'

'No,' Sophie said, eyeing the cat with a mixture of annoyance and regret, 'but I saw a snake on the front verandah when I got there, and she was outside for a few minutes alone.'

While Sophie spoke Zac had been running his hands along the cat's body with sure, confident strokes, peering into her eyes and checking her gums. 'I can't locate a bite mark site. Not surprising in a breed like this with so much hair.'

'Ah, there's also the *slight* possibility that she may have ingested some medication.'

He glanced across at her and lifted an eyebrow slightly. 'Snake bite *and* poisoning in the same day?'

'There was an incident and a container of medication was knocked off the table. I'm not sure if she ate any, but I can't be certain she didn't either.'

'When did you first notice any symptoms?'

'About ten minutes after that, I guess, when I went looking for her after I'd cleaned up the spill.'

'Well, to be honest, the symptoms she's displaying could be either snakebite *or* poisoning. I think we're going to have to run a snake detection kit to rule that out or confirm, as well as some blood tests to check for toxins. Before I do, I'll let you know the snake venom detection kit is going to cost $300 and the blood tests will be on top of that. Is it okay to go ahead?'

Sophie cringed. *Great.* 'Unless you happen to know of any pug-faced, fluffy white cats around the same age we can swap her for?'

For a minute the vet stared at her, seemingly taken aback by her comment. Sophie shook her head and let out a resigned sigh. 'Forget it, yes, I'll pay for whatever treatment is needed.' She couldn't very well tell Bill she'd killed his cat. Especially when it had been her suggestion that she go feed the damn thing for him in the first place.

'I'm going to need your help—my nurse has gone home for the day.'

'Sure. Tell me what to do.'

'I'll have to test her urine for the venom, since I can't locate an actual bite site under all this damn hair, and time is pretty crucial.'

'Will that work?'

'A swab from an unwashed site is preferable, but on occasions when the site's poor quality or it's been washed we have to use urine.'

Sophie had only seen the snakebite kit used once in all her time in the city.

Taking the sample, Zac placed drops of urine into a series of shallow vials and added drops of peroxide and the chromogen, waiting and watching for any colour change.

'Well, it's not looking like there's any snake venom being detected,' Zac said after checking his watch and holding up the small vials to study carefully.

'Are you sure?' Sophie asked, looking over his shoulder at the test vials uncertainly.

Zac sent her a brief glance and nodded. 'If the colour changes in any of these first five wells then that's an indication that there's snake venom present. And seeing as wells one to five have definitely not changed colour,' he said, looking back at the vials he was holding, 'I'm confident enough to rule the snake out as our culprit.'

'So we're looking at ingestion of medication,' Sophie said, feeling somewhat relieved that at least the cat hadn't been bitten by a snake when it escaped.

'You said a container of pills? Any idea what sort? Anything containing acetaminophen would be a huge concern for cats, and most pets, actually.'

Sophie frowned as she recalled the bottles she picked up. 'Yeah, there was some paracetamol,' she told him gravely, remembering that she saw the painkiller. 'There were also antidepressants, and a few naturopathic sleeping supplements.'

'Going by the symptoms, it's more likely she's ingested paracetamol. Any of the other things could potentially give similar symptoms but acetaminophen is deadly to cats, so that's what I'm more concerned about at the moment. We'll do some blood tests to see if we can trace any toxins, but we don't have the facilities here to get an answer immediately so, to be on the safe side, I'll give her some N-acetylcysteine, vitamin C and liver protectants to try to reduce the risk of liver damage as well as start her on intravenous fluids.'

Sophie stood by and watched for the most part, occasionally stepping up to hold something or simply pat the cat and offer some kind of emotional support while he deftly dealt with syringes and IV lines in a calm, professional manner that would put most doctors she'd seen to shame.

'That's about all we can do for now,' he finally said, looking up after he adjusted the drip on the IV. 'I'll monitor her tonight and we should know by morning if what we've done has worked or not.'

'Thank you,' Sophie said earnestly. 'This cat means a lot to Bill.'

'Yes, she does. I knew Mabel,' he said softly. 'I've treated this one since she was a kitten.'

'I'm really sorry,' Sophie felt terrible. 'I was trying to help Bill and instead I almost killed the damn cat.'

'Don't be too hard on yourself. Cleo is a bit of a princess at the best of times, and she has a mind of her own. You got here fast, which went a long way in helping to minimise any damage, and I'm confident she'll make a full recovery. We'll certainly do our best to give her every chance.'

'Thank you,' Sophie said as they reached the front door.

'You're welcome.'

She noticed up this close that his eyes were an olive shade, edged with hazel. They were kind eyes. She could see why animals would immediately trust him. She would—if she were an animal, that is. Blinking, Sophie realised she'd been staring and silently groaned her mortification. 'I better go and let you close up for the weekend. Thanks again,' she said, turning away and hurrying out the door.

'Wait up,' he called out and Sophie closed her eyes briefly before turning around with a wary expression.

'Here's my card,' Zac said, handing across a small rectangular business card. 'In case you want to call my mobile and check on Cleo over the weekend,' he added when she continued to watch him warily.

'Oh! Of course,' she said, feeling like a dope. *Why else would he be giving you his number, idiot?* Sophie felt her face

redden as she silently berated herself. 'Thanks. I will. Call
. . . to check on the cat.' *Shut up! Stop talking! Walk away!*

'Okay then,' he said, giving her a wave and a brief grin
before heading back inside and closing the door.

'Oh my God,' she whispered as she climbed inside the
ambulance and slammed the door shut. 'Could you have
been any more embarrassing?' Today had been one disaster
after another. She just hoped that it wasn't the start of some
kind of common theme for the remainder of her shift.

Sixteen

The next morning Sophie found Bill sitting up against a stack of pillows, doing a crossword puzzle. She really wasn't looking forward to telling him about Cleo, but seeing as he'd most likely be going home later today there was no way of putting it off.

'Sophie!' he smiled cheerfully.

'Morning, Bill. How are you feeling?'

'I feel great. Just like I told them yesterday. Although I'm pretty sure they're trying to kill me with their food.'

'Aw, come on, I'm sure it's not that bad. At least someone else cooked for you.'

'If you call it that,' he growled. 'I reckon I could show them a thing or two about baking.'

'Have you seen the doctor yet this morning?'

'Apparently he'll be around soon to do his rounds and then I can get out of here. Seems like I might have mixed up my medication or something.'

'About that, Bill,' she started, trying to think of the best way to broach the subject. 'Yesterday while I was feeding Cleo—'

'Oh, I know all about that. Don't worry yourself. Silly cat's always getting herself into trouble one way or another.'

'Wait, what? You've already heard about it?'

'Yeah, young Zac dropped by for a visit and wanted to fill me in on how she was doing.'

Sophie could only stare in disbelief. She'd been worrying all night about how to tell the man that she'd almost killed his dead wife's prized cat and Dr Doolittle had already been over to tell him?

'Seems like Cleo and me had the same problem—eating the wrong pills,' he chuckled.

'So about that—' Sophie started.

'I know, I know. The doc's already lectured me about mixin' up me medications.'

'Did he tell you that the chemist can make up pill packs so your medication is packaged in the correct dosages?'

'Yep. I'm going down to the chemist as soon as I get sprung from this joint and getting them to sort it out for me.'

'Great.'

'I want to thank you, Sophie. You didn't have to stay with me and then go out and make sure Cleo was alright.'

'All part of the service,' she grinned.

'That may well be, but it helped a great deal having you with me. It was a real kindness. So I want to thank you.'

The simple words brought a lump to Sophie's throat. What was wrong with her? 'I'm just glad you're okay. Do you have anyone coming to take you home?'

'Yes, thank you. But if it'd be lovely if you dropped by sometime. I've got plenty more stories to tell you about Archie and the Gilberts,' he said.

'I'd like that.'

Sophie didn't immediately head to the house when she got home but instead drove the now well-worn track towards what she called the back paddock, where the tree line thickened. She tried to come out every couple of days. Sometimes she caught a glimpse of the black horse, sometimes she didn't. The times she did put a smile on her face though, making her day complete. Each time she took a few slices of bread and left them; he never ventured out to take them from her hand, but every time she went back they were always gone. She'd taken to calling him Cobber. She was getting tired of thinking of him as 'horse' all the time and, after finishing Clarrie's diary, it just felt right. It was as good a name as any to call him, she supposed.

Today wasn't going to be one of the days Cobber decided to make himself known so after a while Sophie gave up, placing the bread on the smooth rock beside her and heading back to the house before it got dark. She wasn't sure why but gaining this animal's trust suddenly meant a lot. 'I'll be back,' she called out as she climbed into her car. 'See you tomorrow.'

෨

Sophie hadn't been for a run in far too long. She used to run every day, depending on her shift. After Garth died, she'd used it as a way to process her emotions, think things through. But then after the attack she lost her confidence. Where once she wouldn't have thought twice about running early in the morning or late in the afternoon, suddenly it terrified her. She seemed to find a lot of excuses why she couldn't run as far or as often, but the truth was she was too scared to run alone.

God she hated being afraid. All the time.

She didn't even know what she was afraid of, which was even more annoying. *Everything* scared her. Loud noises. Barking dogs. Motorbikes. She'd felt like she was losing her mind. While it had eventually become easier to handle these things in general, she'd never got back into running.

So today she decided she was going to try again. Out here there was nothing to scare her—no loud noises, no crowds, just open paddocks and nothingness. The rhythmic pounding of her feet on the ground gave her something to concentrate on and she soon fell into an easy pace.

After a while she headed for a huge old tree sitting smack bang in the middle of a paddock to stop for a rest. She'd seen it from a distance before and wondered then how it'd survived the clearing of most of the other timber in this part of the property. She was no botanist but she figured it was old, maybe even very old from the size of its trunk.

As she drew closer she noticed metal sticking out of the long grass that grew in a circle on the ground beneath the tree canopy. It was so dry out here that the grass had mostly died off, leaving patches here and there, but this looked like the weeds and grass were overgrown around *something*.

She picked her way across and pushed some of the grass and weeds aside, revealing a rusted metal fence. It was only thigh high, and when Sophie began pulling the weeds out, which came away surprisingly easily, she was astounded to discover what she'd revealed.

A grave.

'No way,' she breathed as she quickly continued clearing more of the long whisky-coloured grass, whispering a fervent prayer that no snakes were hiding in there. By the time she'd finished she was breathing heavily and sweating more than she'd done while running. Now she could see the modest headstone and just make out the inscription, which read *Edith Spicer*, and then *July 21st, 1865 – August 23rd, 1890, Loving wife and mother.*

Sophie stood back and considered the newly cleared gravesite thoughtfully. If this was Edith then there should be another grave too. From the conversation she'd had with Anne Harding she understood that her little girl had died a few months before Edith, who had taken her own life, so there should be a second grave somewhere nearby.

Sophie climbed over the rusty metal fence to continue exploring the area. There was long grass all along the fence line, but further away there was a promising area with more overgrown weeds, though it seemed an unlikely place to bury a child when the mother's grave was a good twenty or so metres away. Again she pulled aside the grass to get a look at what was hidden beneath and was rewarded by a crooked-looking headstone.

For a moment Sophie considered leaving it until she could bring back a whipper snipper or at least a shovel and a rake, anything to make the job a little easier, but curiosity got the better of her and she decided to make this her workout for the day. As she began clearing she noticed that unlike the other grave, this one was not alone. Beside it was a second headstone.

It took a lot of pulling and two falls onto her backside, but she eventually cleared the area and uncovered the two graves.

The name on the first stone was *Clarence Gilbert, June 1st, 1892 – December 26th, 1920. Age 28.* Sophie caught her breath as she read the name and felt her heart thud hard against her chest. Clarrie.

She swallowed past a sudden tightness in her throat and blinked back the unexpected sting of tears. There was no denying she felt a connection to Clarrie after reading his diaries and learning about everything he'd gone through in that horrible bloody war. The shock of finding his grave like this caught her off guard.

So this was where he'd ended up.

She remembered how much he'd missed this place when he'd been overseas, and how much the farm had meant to him. He would have been happy to know that he would be buried here, unlike so many of his fallen mates who were left behind in foreign lands, many without even a marker to identify where their remains would be. At least he was somewhere familiar and buried by people who had obviously cared enough to give him a headstone.

She shifted her gaze across to the other headstone and was surprised to see there were two names listed: *William Gilbert, March 5th, 1865 – December 29th, 1919,* and beneath that, *Maud Gilbert, September 3rd, 1868 – April 4th, 1936.*

Sophie took out her phone and took pictures of the headstones. When she got back home she intended to do a little research into her great discovery. Looking back over at the first grave she wiped an arm across her sweaty brow and frowned as she scanned the area. There were no more overgrown patches, nowhere else a grave could be hidden. So where was the little girl? And why would they bury the mother all the way out here by herself?

Seventeen

Sophie pulled up out the front as Bill opened the screen door and hobbled out onto the front porch to wait. One of the benefits of having a long driveway was that visitors usually couldn't sneak up on you.

'Good timing, I've just put the jug on,' he said, leaning onto the walking stick he'd been given to help him get around while his ankle healed.

'You're supposed to be resting that,' Sophie told him as she climbed the stairs, silently assessing his movement and feeling quite happy at his progress.

'I have been. I'm tired of sitting around and watching the clock. Hearing that car of yours was just what I needed. A visitor!'

Sophie was both touched and sympathetic to the old man's plight. He was obviously a man who liked to potter around in his garden and shed, and being limited by his injuries was taking its toll. 'Figured I'd come over and pick your brain some more about the Gilberts.'

'You mean you thought you'd come around and check up on me. Make sure I wasn't doing anything I shouldn't be.'

'Maybe I wanted to test out some of that home baking you were boasting about back in the hospital.'

'Ah, I see. Well, you're in luck. I've just made a date loaf this morning.'

As they sat out on the sunny verandah, Sophie gave a small groan of appreciation as she bit into the cake. 'Have you always baked?'

'No. I only started in the past year.'

'Are you serious?'

'Yep. Never really thought too much about cooking until Mabel passed away. She did all the cooking,' he smiled and shook his head slowly. 'You've never tasted a sponge like my Mabel used to make.'

Sophie smiled as she watched the old man's face fill with pride as talked about his wife.

'Then one day I was eating a packet of store-bought biscuits and I thought, *You know what? I'm gonna give this cooking thing a go.* I dug out Mabel's old recipes and I made myself a cake. Wasn't anything to write home about, but it was better than anything I bought at the shop. After that, I tried making one a week. But just between you and me, I reckon I might be giving her a run for her money with my sponge. Won myself first place in the show earlier this year,' he said with a grin.

'I think you need to enter this date loaf next year.'

'I might do that. But that's enough about me. You came here to talk about the Gilberts. What did you want to know?'

'Actually, I'm hoping you can tell me more about Clarrie. You said he died in an accident?'

'Ah, Clarrie. Now there's a sad story. He was a war hero. Was awarded the Distinguished Conduct Medal, which is only one step down from the Victoria Cross,' he explained, giving a nod of his head. 'He and his brother signed up and went off to war, and when he came back he was a changed man. My father knew him. Reckons he hardly ever left the property once he came home. They tried to throw him a welcome home dance to celebrate his medal and whatnot, but Clarrie wouldn't go. Refused to have anything to do with the war after that. He just worked the farm and kept to himself.'

'He was only home for about a year before he died?'

'Was probably something like that. Couldn't tell you the year, but not long after the war he was crushed by a tree he was felling down the back.' Bill shook his head and gave a sad snort. 'Survived the war, came back wounded— recovered from that—only to be flattened by a bloody tree!'

Sophie pictured the bushland at the rear of the property and wondered if maybe that's one of the reasons it hadn't been cleared like the rest of the property.

'I found his grave. He's buried on the property,' Sophie said, picking up her cup and taking a sip.

'Well, there you go. A lot of places around here have old graves. None on this place, but I have heard of a few elsewhere. I reckon that was a good way to be.'

It was kind of nice to think a family could remain on their property, but it was more out of necessity back then. It wouldn't probably sit well with people nowadays when you bought a house with freshly dug graves out in the backyard.

'I wouldn't mind coming out to take a look one of these days.'

'Sure, anytime. Just let me know and I'll show you where I found them—there were a couple of others too.'

Sophie had been back only the day before to continue clearing, intending to keep the place a little more under control than it had been previously. She thought she might plant some flowers and maybe even put a bench out there one day.

'So what do you think of young Conway?'

Sophie almost choked on her coffee at the surprising question. 'The vet?'

'Yeah. He seemed pretty interested in you,' Bill said, watching her keenly.

'I hardly think so. He probably thinks I'm some kind of moron.'

'That's not the impression I got.'

'Well, I'm not looking for anything like . . . that. I'm just out here to work.'

'Rubbish, young thing like you. There's got to be more to life than work.'

'I have the property to keep me busy.'

'You could do a lot worse than Zac. He's a hard worker. Needs a good woman in his life again.'

'Again?' Too late, Sophie realised she'd just opened a line of conversation she hadn't intended to.

'His wife, Christa, passed away about three years ago. Cancer, I think. Terrible thing. Such a nice young woman, she was.'

It *was* a terrible thing. Accidents, illness, death in general, really—no one was ever ready for it when it struck, and it was never fair. If only life was more like in the movies where the bad guys died and the goodies always triumphed. But life wasn't like that. It always took the good ones, the young ones, the children and the gentlest of souls too. It didn't discriminate. It sucked.

'I'm sorry for his loss, but I don't think I'm ready for a relationship yet.'

'Grief sets its own pace,' he nodded sympathetically, and they sat in a companionable kind of silence for a few moments, both lost in their own thoughts. 'You know, I miss Mabel every day. I still think she's just in the next room sometimes, and then I realise I can't hear her humming or singing. She was always singing when she did the housework,' he said with a faint smile. 'And then I realise everything's quiet. Just me and that bloody clock ticking,' he muttered. 'We were together sixty-four years,' he said wistfully. 'Still boggles my mind that all that time's just . . . gone.'

Sophie looked down into her cup, unable to bear the emotion on the old man's face.

'We were lucky,' he said, and waited until Sophie looked up. 'We had a lifetime together, but you're still so young.

I guess what I'm trying to say is not to push away the opportunity to find that kind of love with someone else if it comes along. There's an awful lot of living to be done—too much to spend it alone.'

'Maybe I'll get myself a cat,' Sophie said after a while.

'Nah,' Bill drawled, eyeing the cat, now miraculously recovered and curled up contentedly on a chair in the sun. 'They're overrated, and they can't bake. By the way, young Zac told me you fixed up the vet bill?'

'Well, yeah, I was responsible for her getting sick in the first place,' Sophie said.

'Rubbish. It was my fault for having the damn pills out like that. I'll get that money to you next time I'm in town.'

'Please don't worry about it. I'm just glad she's okay. I felt terrible.'

'She likes to act like a prissy damn thing, but that cat's pure street fighter underneath,' he said somewhat proudly.

'I better get going, Bill. Thanks for the cuppa and chat. As soon as that ankle gets better, give me a yell and I'll show you those graves.'

'Goodo. Look forward to it.'

'That means you better make sure you keep resting it.' Sophie gave him a stern look.

'You're a bossy one, aren't ya?'

'Someone has to keep you in line,' Sophie said with a grin as she collected their cups and carried them inside for him before saying farewell.

On the drive into town, Sophie thought over Bill's words about taking chances, but she couldn't actually imagine herself dating, especially the rugged-looking vet. Something told her he was one of those tough exterior, soft centre types. Yet she couldn't picture him, or anyone else for that matter, romantically in her life. It felt wrong.

Garth had been her best friend. They'd started off as partners, working side by side, and he'd made even her toughest day endurable. Gradually friendship had turned into more, and marriage had been an extension of their work life. It was comfortable, familiar and it just *worked*. He was everything she could ever want in a husband: loyal, kind, thoughtful. He always remembered their anniversary and her birthday; he made her laugh like no one else ever could. She loved him and he left behind a giant hole in her life. When he died, she'd lost not only a husband but her best friend as well. How did you replace something like that? No, she decided, looking out over the countryside as she drove, she didn't want to think about all that yet. She wasn't ready.

Eighteen

Waking up after a decent night's sleep for a change, Sophie decided to take her cup of coffee and toast out onto the verandah to eat. The sunny spot on the eastern side looked too good to resist. *A whole day off*, she thought, leaning back against the post and closing her eyes as she chewed, enjoying the warm morning sunshine on her face.

She could hear the happy chirping of birds, the maniacal laugh of a kookaburra somewhere high in a tree and . . . heavy breathing. Her eyes sprang open and Sophie jumped to her feet, almost spilling her coffee in the process. There was no one around, but the noise was still there. With her heart racing, Sophie carefully inched off the low verandah and moved to the bushes that grew in front of the fence and surrounded the house yard. Pulling back a few huge purple clusters of hydrangea flowers, she came face to face with a large brown eye and jumped again when a loud snort broke the sudden silence. A soft nicker followed and Sophie stepped away from the bushes, hurrying around to the gate to let herself out into the paddock beside the house.

Her initial surprise at finding a horse on her doorstep, particularly *this* horse, was shortlived the moment she saw the blood.

He was bleeding from a wound of some kind on his chest. Sophie had no idea what she was going to do: this was not a cat she could scoop up and throw into an ambulance, this was five hundred kilos of wild animal. Sophie pulled her phone from her back pocket and took out the business card she'd slipped inside, dialling the number quickly.

'Zac Conway.'

'Zac, it's Sophie,' she said, sighing with relief that he'd answered the phone.

'Hi there. Cleo's back home and on the mend,' he said.

'Who? Oh, the cat. Yes, I saw her yesterday . . . That's not why I'm calling. I've got an injured horse here and I don't know what to do.'

'A horse? How were you roped into feeding a horse?'

'This one lives here . . . I think. I'm actually not sure who owns it.'

'What kind of injury?'

Sophie glanced back at the horse where it was still standing near the fence and described the wound. 'It's like a puncture wound of some sort,' she added.

'Okay, I'm on my way out. Just keep him calm and confined. I'll be there soon.'

Confined? Sophie looked around and realised there was an awful lot of room for him to move out here. There was a set of old stockyards in the paddock behind the house, but she wasn't sure how she was supposed to get him into them.

'Hey, boy,' she said quietly, and saw his ears twitch at the sound of her voice. She was scared of moving closer in case he ran away. The last thing she wanted was for him to be running into the bush injured, but she wasn't sure how Zac was going to treat him if he wasn't contained in a smaller environment. 'What have you been up to, huh?' she continued to talk without moving, hoping to reassure him that she was a friend.

He shifted his weight from one front foot to the other and Sophie instantly noticed blood begin to ooze from the wound. Without being able to get close to him she couldn't even inspect it. She didn't want to try to chase him; if he got spooked and took off she was concerned about the effect that would have on the wound. Maybe he'd follow her, she thought, slowly turning away. 'Wait here, boy,' she said before running inside the house and reappearing with a slice of bread. 'Okay, let's try this. You want some bread?' She held it out and saw his nostrils flare slightly. 'Come with me and you can have the bread,' she said, slowly edging along the fence line. At first he didn't move and Sophie was wondering what else she could try to tempt him with, but then he took a step, and Sophie bit down on her lip to keep from startling him with a cheer of excitement. 'Good boy,' she said softly. 'Keep coming.' She waved the bread again and took a few more steps backwards. Slowly he followed her, each step making more blood gurgle from the wound, but at least it wasn't pumping like an artery wound. The fact that it was oozing made Sophie suspect that whatever had caused the wound in the first place was still in there, obstructing the blood from flowing out, but still deep enough for there to be substantial blood loss.

Gradually they made their way to the back of the house and were within a few metres of the yards. Sophie hurried ahead and opened the heavy timber gate, throwing the bread into the centre of the yard before moving to a safe enough distance not to feel like a threat to the animal.

For a few agonising moments, Sophie was sure the horse wasn't going to go in, but eventually he moved cautiously through the gate, sniffing at the ground until he found the bread and greedily gobbled it up. Sophie used the distraction to carefully move across to the gate and shut it behind him.

The sliding of the bar into the hole to secure it caused the animal to let out a high-pitched whinny, and Sophie tried her best to reassure him. 'It's alright, you've hurt your-self and we're going to take care of you. You'll be alright,' she soothed from where she leaned over the gate. 'Settle down or you're going to make that wound bleed more.'

He moved around the yard, his stride somewhat uneven and jerky. He was clearly agitated and Sophie was worried that he might do himself some kind of further injury.

The sound of an approaching car alerted her to Zac's arrival, and she breathed a sigh of relief as she circled the house and waved him over.

'So a horse, huh,' he said as he opened his door and looked across at the animal in the yards.

'It's a long story,' she said, distracted by the loud snorting the animal was doing. 'Is that normal?'

'He looks like he's in a bit of distress, I'll sedate him to calm him down and then we'll be able to get a better look at what's going on. Do you have a halter we can put on him?'

'No,' Sophie shook her head. 'I don't have anything.'

'How long has he been here?' he asked, reaching into the back of his car and withdrawing a long rope, a looped device that she assumed was the halter he'd been asking her for, and a medical kit.

'He was here when I bought the farm. He's never let me get close enough to touch him and he's never come this close to the house before.'

Zac wore a frown at that. 'I don't think he's been handled very often, probably not even broken in. I think for everyone's safety we should get him into the crush.'

She wasn't entirely sure where the crush was, but she hoped it wasn't as painful as it sounded.

Zac lightly swung over the rail of the yards and slowly approached the animal, forcing it gradually back towards the end of the yard where the rails narrowed into a long closed-off section that led up a small ramp. Zac slid a solid post in behind the horse once he'd manoeuvred it into position.

'Is he okay?' Sophie asked nervously, watching the horse protest loudly at finding himself trapped.

'He's not happy, but that wound needs attention. I'm pretty sure this horse hasn't had a great deal of human interaction.' He turned his glance on her, raising an eyebrow slightly. 'I don't even know how you managed to get him in the yards.'

'Bread.'

He gave an amused grunt before he turned back to the horse.

'The Spicers think he might have come from the national park.'

'Yeah, they could be right. I'm going to sedate him so I can do a thorough examination of the wound and give him a once-over,' he said, crouching down beside the medical kit on the ground.

The horse flinched a little and gave a low nicker as Zac gave the injection, rubbing his hand over the spot afterwards. 'Good fella,' Zac murmured.

'Will we need to lie him down?' she asked nervously as the horse seemed to become drowsy.

'Nah, it just makes them a bit groggy.' He took the halter and gently placed it over the horse's head, before clipping the other longer rope to it and handing her the other end.

She watched as Zac pulled on a pair of gloves and probed at the site of the wound. Again the blood oozed out.

'Do you think something's still in there?'

'Yeah, I do,' he said, glancing up at her with a concerned expression.

'What?'

'I'd like to do an ultrasound to find out what it is, and exactly how deep it's in. I don't want to go digging around in the wound if there's a chance it's lodged in something vital.'

He was back within minutes setting up a portable device. His frown grew deeper as he commenced the ultrasound.

'Is that what I think it is?' Sophie asked, disbelief colouring her voice as she leaned over to peer at the small screen.

'If you're thinking that there's a bullet lodged in your horse's chest, yep,' he said dryly.

'He's been shot?' A fleeting memory of pain pierced her, and for a moment she felt lightheaded before she forced the reaction aside.

'It would appear so. You okay?' he asked, giving her a second glance when he looked up from the screen.

Sophie brushed off his concern with a slight grimace and shake of her head. 'Who the hell would shoot at a horse?'

'Could be the work of some bored teenagers out joyriding. They spot a horse near a fence and decide to take pot shots at it, although I can't say I've heard of any incidents lately.'

'This is the first time I've even seen him up around the house, he usually keeps to the bush down the back . . .' She trailed off as she recalled her earlier conversation with Horrie Spicer. 'Son of a . . .'

'What?' Zac asked, glancing up.

'I don't think it's a carload of teenagers,' she bit off furiously. It was too much of a coincidence that Horrie would suggest shooting a feral horse as a solution only for the same horse to turn up with a bullet in him. She briefly filled Zac in on the conversation she'd had with Horrie at the butcher's a few days earlier.

'Let's worry about fixing him up before we think about how it happened. It doesn't look as though the bullet has penetrated anything major, and it's not all that deep. I can actually feel it. Sometimes with gunshot wounds in horses— and in humans, for that matter—it's safer to leave the bullet in because you can do more damage digging around to find it. But this one is fairly shallow and we've checked it hasn't nicked anything important, so I feel confident taking it out.'

'Okay. Do whatever you have to,' Sophie said, looking into the sleepy eyes of the horse she held. 'Poor old fella, why would anyone do that to you, huh?'

She watched as Zac preformed the minor surgery. His attention to detail and the efficient way in which he worked impressed her, and she found herself automatically handing him things as he worked.

'Is he going to be okay?'

'He's going to be fine. It wasn't deep. He's pretty lucky.'

'Do you get this happening a lot?'

'Now and again. Mostly it's kids mucking about.'

'I can't say that's exactly comforting. Kids running about the place with guns.'

'It's the country,' he shrugged. 'Shooting vermin is part of the job description.'

'Since when is a horse considered vermin?'

'Well, that depends. We get a lot of feral horses around these parts, and not everyone is a lover of them.'

Sophie frowned as she looked at the animal she held on to. How could anyone think this was a pest?

'Can you pick up that dish for me?' he asked, and Sophie looked down before passing him the small metal dish.

Zac looked at her and a grin broke out over his face. 'Listen to this,' he said, holding his hand over the dish, his grin widening at the distinctive ping of metal hitting metal. 'It never gets old,' he said as Sophie eyed him warily.

'It's like M*A*S*H and all those old war movies.' When she continued to look at him blankly he went on. 'You know, there's always that ping, as they drop it into a petri dish. You guys don't do that?'

Sophie shook her head slightly. 'Can't say I take out many bullets as a general rule.'

'Must be a vet thing then,' he said, in what she assumed was his odd way of trying to lighten the mood. 'You ever thought about trading in your ambulance to work as a vet nurse?'

'Not really. Your patients are a little bit bigger than I'm used to and they can't exactly tell you what's wrong—although come to think of it, some days that could be a good thing,' Sophie mused.

'They do tell you what's wrong, you just have to learn how to read the signs. But, yeah, I think you can keep your human patients. I prefer mine with more legs and less talking.'

Sophie switched her gaze back to the horse and marvelled again at how surreal this whole situation was. Suddenly she'd had this huge animal quite literally land on her front doorstep, injured and needing help, and he'd come to her for it. She gently stroked the horse's face and looked into the large brown eye, feeling something warm filtering in through the cracks of ice she'd carried around inside for too long. The sensation was so real that she felt the hand she rested against his neck shake slightly.

With the major part of the ordeal over, Zac turned to giving the animal a full examination of his mouth, eyes, legs and hooves. 'He's a fair age,' he said after inspecting his teeth.

'Really? How old?'

'My guess would be in his twenties.'

'Is that old for a horse?'

'It's no spring chicken, but I've got clients who have horses in their late thirties still going strong.'

Sophie looked at the horse, trying to digest some of this new information.

'Also, there's quite a lot of scarring on his hind legs and rump. My guess is he's had a pretty intensive injury at some point in his past. He's got a bit of lameness in his hind leg, maybe a tendon or ligament injury. I'm willing to bet he's been thrown out of his herd, maybe challenged by a younger rival and injured. Probably why he's this far from the national park—looking for his own territory.'

'I wouldn't have imagined wild horses to be in this decent condition.' For some reason, she pictured shaggy, skinny-looking animals when she thought of wild horses.

'I do a bit of work with the Heritage Horse Association up around Guy Fawkes River National Park. The horses they bring out of there are some of the best-looking animals I've seen anywhere. There's been wild horses surviving around this area for centuries—thriving, in fact,' he amended.

'I don't know much about horses but I know they cost a lot of money to keep, so how can these horses possibly survive without all the care they need?'

'Horses were wild a long time before humans decided to domesticate them,' Zac smiled. 'They cope just fine. Instinct is a pretty amazing thing. Horses kept in paddocks need their hooves trimmed regularly, teeth filed, feed supplemented, worming and shoeing if it's a competitive horse. These brumbies know how to take care of themselves without any help. They eat sticks and grind up small rocks to keep their teeth smooth, they graze in wide open spaces so their parasite load is much lower than a horse who grazes on a small holding, and they self-medicate by eating certain plants for things like tummy upsets.'

'Wow.' Sophie was amazed. She had no idea horses could be so self-sufficient.

'I can give the girls from the heritage association a call and get him taken over there if you like.'

'Oh.' Sophie sent a surprised look across at the horse and felt a wave of protectiveness wash over her.

'What were you planning on doing with him?' he asked, taking in her hesitant reply.

'I don't know. I hadn't really thought that far ahead.'

'Well, we can't release him back into the park. They're considered feral, despite the fact they've just been officially recognised as having heritage value. The national parks capture them and give them to places like the Heritage Horse Association to train and rehome. They're very experienced and they'd find him a good home.'

'Even with his injuries and his age?'

'I doubt he'll ever be able to be ridden, not without some kind of intensive surgery to try to correct that hind leg issue. But the association take anything that's pulled out of the park and do the best they can with them. They're good people.'

She was sure they were, but she had that weird feeling again—the same one that told her it was right to buy this place—telling her this horse should stay. Sophie chewed on her lip. 'I know it might sound crazy but I feel like he kind of belongs here. Maybe just while he recovers he could stay. I mean, we don't want to stress him out any more than he already is, especially if he's wounded.'

'He's going to take a bit of looking after.'

She nodded slowly; she had considered this. And with next to no experience in animal first aid maybe she should just ignore the feeling this time and let Zac take him to people who knew what they were doing.

'I've irrigated the wound to clean it out and now I'll just dress it,' Zac said, jolting her from the strange sensations. 'We'll leave these on until I come back and check on him, and in the meantime I'll start a course of antibiotics.

You want to do it?' he asked as he rummaged through his supplies for a large syringe.

Now he had her complete attention. 'No,' she said adamantly before softening her reply. 'I've never given an injection to an animal before.'

'Nothing to it,' he grinned, tearing open the packet to attach the needle and draw up the liquid antibiotic. 'You just make sure you don't hit a vein and Bob's your uncle,' he said, jabbing the huge syringe into the horse's rump.

'Right. No sweat,' Sophie said, not feeling as confident as she hoped she would.

'I'll come out and give you a hand for the first few until we see how he copes with handling,' he told her as he rubbed his hand over the spot where he'd injected.

Sophie looked back into the animal's big eye again. 'This is just so weird—I've been trying to make friends with him ever since I first saw him, but I've never been able to get close. I don't understand why he's suddenly turned up like this.'

'He obviously trusts you. He needed help and so he came and found you. My guess is that he's been keeping an eye on you for a while now. He obviously liked what he saw.'

Sophie shook her head as she stroked the dark head gently, the sedative allowing her to do what she'd only dreamed about doing before now. A fierce, protective streak surged through her as she remembered the bullet lodged in his chest.

'Well, that's about all I can do for now.' Zac pulled out the timber post from behind the horse's back legs and helped coax him backwards out into the main yards once more. 'Keep him confined in here for a few days so I can check on that wound and change the dressings. I don't want him running around until it heals.'

'Ah, do I need to feed him?'

'I'll bring something out tomorrow when I come and check on him. He'll be okay for the rest of the day while the sedative wears off. Just put some water in that trough for him.'

Sophie gave the horse one final glance before following Zac out the gate and walking him to his car.

'Glad you used that card I gave you,' he said as he packed his gear into the back of his vehicle.

'Glad you answered,' she said, dragging her eyes from his arms as he lifted the heavy case containing the ultrasound equipment high over the tailgate.

'You know, until you came to town it was pretty boring around here without cats being poisoned and mysterious horses turning up shot.'

'Accidentally poisoned,' she corrected gruffly.

'Well, it was a nice thing you did for Bill,' he said. 'Feeding his cat so he wouldn't worry.'

'Just doing my job.'

'I'm pretty sure offering to take care of a bloke's high-maintenance cat is going above and beyond your job description. Not to mention staying with him at the hospital to reassure him.'

Sophie looked up at that, somewhat surprised.

'Bill told me. It meant a lot to him. He gets lonely out there on his own, but he wouldn't have it any other way, I guess.'

'He's a nice man, and I understand what he's going through a little bit.'

'Yeah. I think that's what drew me to him as well.'

'I heard . . . that you lost your wife. I'm sorry,' she said genuinely. The pain was still there—she felt other people's losses a lot more keenly after Garth's death.

'Yeah, well,' Zac said, striving for a lighter mood, the sign to back off. Sophie could relate to that as well. 'I'll drop by tomorrow and see how he is.' He shut the tailgate at the rear of the four-wheel drive and stepped away, getting into the driver's seat.

'Okay. Thanks again,' she said as he gave her a wave out the window and drove off.

Sophie didn't know what to make of the local vet. There was something about him. He was good looking, but not in a polished, magazine kind of way. Each time she'd seen him he looked like he'd forgotten to shave that day, and his hair was in need of a good cut, but there was something she found a little too attractive about him. It was more than the fact he filled out a pair of jeans in a very not professional vet kind of way. In fact, he could easily be mistaken for a rodeo guy fresh off a damn bull, covered in dirt and God only knew what else, not at all like any vet she'd seen in the city. If it were only that she found him physically attractive she could dismiss it easily enough—she'd worked around plenty of well-built men and never had a problem with them. This was something different; it was more than his physical attributes. She'd noticed when she'd taken Cleo in to him, after the panic had ebbed, that he had a kindness that didn't automatically fit with his ruggedness. She'd watched it while he'd worked on Cleo and then again on the horse. He cared about them. His big, rough hands were gentle when he handled the animals, his deep voice calm and comforting. She always had been a sucker for a big softy.

Enough! she told herself, shaking off this line of thought. She was definitely not looking for anything more than veterinarian advice and care for a horse from Zac Conway. She had enough of her own problems to sort through without adding a vet with his own set of demons. No thank you. Next she needed to figure out what to do about the injured horse standing out the back in her stockyards.

Nineteen

The next morning, Sophie walked out of the house as she heard the vehicle approaching and met Zac over at the stockyards.

'How's the patient?' he asked, opening the back of his four-wheel drive to pull out a large bale of hay that he hefted up onto his shoulder.

Sophie found the action did lovely things to the man's already impressive-looking biceps. It clearly took a lot of strength to manhandle his patients, especially large farm animals, and it was probably offensive on some feminist level to be ogling the man's arms, but they certainly brightened up her afternoon.

'He's been a bit quieter today.' Although since the sedative had worn off, he'd gone back to that wary, standoffishness he'd displayed before.

'We might see how he goes without being put in the crush. It'd make it easier if we can treat him in the yards,' he said, coiling the long rope she'd held yesterday and slipping it over his shoulder. He pulled apart the bale of hay before carefully opening the gate enough to slide through, turning to close it behind him.

'Come on, old fella, let's get a look at you.' He approached the animal slowly, holding out the feed in his hand as a peace offering.

The horse gave Zac a sideways look and backed away, but Zac calmly continued walking towards him, keeping his tone low and gentle and his movements slow and steady until he was within touching distance. 'There's a good man,' he said softly as he held out the hay. 'Nice and easy now. Good boy, no one's going to hurt you. We're just going to get a look at you.' The horse reared and gave a high-pitched whinny that sounded like a scream, kicking out before dropping his feet back to the ground and tossing his head.

Zac didn't back off as Sophie had expected but continued to talk quietly in that low, soothing voice, gradually creeping closer to the agitated animal. After what seemed like an eternity he was finally close enough to gently place the end of the rope across the horse's neck, making soothing noises as it shuffled uneasily a bit but didn't pull away. He placed the hay on the ground and watched as the horse sniffed it warily before nibbling at it, while Zac continued to rub the rope along the animal's neck and head until eventually the horse didn't shy away or jerk in alarm.

After a while Zac gently guided the rope close enough until he could clip it onto the halter without too much fuss from the now somewhat subdued animal, who seemed happy so long as he could continue to eat.

'Good man,' he praised, still keeping his tone calm and low, and Sophie understood the soothing impact it had on the animal; she was fairly sure she would have done pretty much anything for him too if he asked her in that voice.

'Sophie, I need you to come over here,' he said, and suddenly she realised he *was* using that tone on her and she *was* about to do whatever he asked.

'I don't really know what to do,' she warned, even as she slowly made her way across to him.

'You'll be fine. I just need you to hold on to him while I get sorted.'

Oh, is that all? she felt like asking sarcastically. *Just hold on to the wild horse.*

He guided her in under his arm and slowly handed her the rope, all the while standing behind her. She wasn't sure which one of them he was reassuring the most, her or the horse. 'Stroke his head and speak gently to him, but don't wrap the rope around your hand.'

Sophie had a moment of blind panic when Zac moved away and she was left holding the horse all by herself, and she half-expected him to rear up and stomp her into the ground.

But then she realised that he was like any other patient, scared and in pain, and she needed to keep him calm. 'Well, look at us, huh?' she started a little nervously. 'We finally get to meet.' She gingerly lifted a shaking hand and lightly stroked his long face. Up close he was even more striking than from a distance. His hair was softer than she'd imagined it would be, although when she looked at her hand it came away dirty. 'You could use a good bath,' she said, keeping her voice low. He gave a soft blow of air through his nostrils and Sophie moved her hand to stroke along his neck.

'You're a natural,' Zac grinned as he came back across to them.

'I'm pretty sure he knows I'm not.'

'Horses are excellent judges of character,' Zac said. 'Clearly he's decided he can trust you.'

'He's never let me get this close before,' she said as Zac moved along to stand beside her at the horse's neck. 'I can't believe he's wild.'

'I've seen a lot of these horses and they're nothing like you'd expect a wild horse to be. They have this natural curiosity about them. I'm not sure if it's because they've had no contact with humans before and they have no expectations of what they need to fear, or if it's just their nature. I do know they build incredibly strong bonds with handlers once they're broken in. That was why they were so sought after by the military back in the day. They have incredible stamina, they're strong, sure-footed and intelligent.'

Zac decided to leave the dressings on the wound undisturbed, not wanting to risk opening it again, but he did manage to give the injection of antibiotics, and much to

Sophie's amazement the horse barely flinched as he munched at the hay on the ground.

'I'll come back out again in the morning. I don't want you doing anything too much in here with him alone just yet.'

'He seems so good.'

'He's still a wild animal and if anything startled him, he could hurt you unintentionally. Best to make sure there's someone around before you come in here with him by yourself for a while.'

'Okay.'

She waved him off and leaned against the rails of the yard, watching Cobber eat for a while before she had to go into work. There was something very soothing about just being near him. Who would have thought it?

⁓

'So what do you think of our hot vet?' Katie asked as they drove back from a patient transfer the next day.

Sophie was glad she had the added protection of sunglasses, which hopefully hid the fact her eyes had just shot wide open at Katie's unexpected question. 'You think he's hot?' she asked, trying to buy some time.

Katie's not too subtle snort was followed by a rather long list of Zac's attributes. 'So yeah, I think he's hot, and don't sit there and tell me you hadn't noticed. You've been spending quite a bit of time with Dr Hot Stuff lately.'

'Only because for some inexplicable reason I seem to be having a very bad streak of luck where animals are concerned.'

'Judge me all you like but I'd deliberately poison a cat too, if I owned one, to get a house call from the man ... Just sayin',' she said, giving Sophie a direct look over the top of her sunglasses.

'I did *not* deliberately poison the cat!' Sophie snapped. 'Why does everyone keep saying that?'

'All I'm saying is no woman would blame you,' she chuckled, seeming happy that she'd managed to get a rise out of her. 'Okay, I'm sorry, I know you wouldn't. But, come on, he's pretty easy on the eyes, right?'

'I guess. If you like the rough around the edges look.'

'Give me rough around the edges and a nice butt in a pair of jeans over a suit any day.'

Okay, so she had a point there. He *did* know how to wear a pair of jeans.

'So I hear he even paid a house call?'

'What? How on earth would you know that?' It'd only happened the day before.

'Tammy Bowbridge.'

'Who's Tammy Bowbridge?'

'She's my husband's cousin,' Katie said, as though she should have realised. 'Anyway,' she continued, 'she was waiting for her dog's appointment and cranky Gail, the receptionist,' she explained as Sophie was about to open her mouth to ask, 'told her that Dr Conway was on a house call to your place and would be late.'

Shouldn't vets have a confidentiality clause somewhere to protect their patients' owners from becoming gossip fodder?

'So what happened? Does he seem interested?'

'He was looking at a horse.'

'But did he seem interested in *you*,' she persisted, undeterred by Sophie's lack of co-operation.

'Nope.'

'I bet he is. I mean, seriously, look at you. You're a catch!'

'Thanks . . . I think,' Sophie said, eyeing her friend sideways.

'You're the first fresh meat to move to town in ages. He'd be stupid not to make a move on you before someone else does.'

'I'm going to ignore the fact that you just referred to me as meat and do my best not to be offended while I point out the fact if I'd wanted to find a man, I probably would have stayed in a city where there were a lot more to choose from.'

'You've got plenty of choice here. There's an entire football team—most of them are single, not to mention the local farmers. Wait till the weekends when everyone comes into town. If I were single and a few years younger . . .' She shook her head.

'Yeah, no. I'm perfectly happy with the way things are, thanks.'

'If you say so,' Katie said, seemingly unconvinced, but thankfully letting the subject go for now.

Sophie mentally shook her head. She didn't have to worry about her status, not when she seemed to have the entire town more than happy to do the worrying for her.

Twenty

It had been a quiet day in the station, and Sophie was on with Jackie for the day doing some training. As a reward, they decided that a counter lunch at the pub would be suitable compensation for a long day of office work.

They placed their orders at the bar and were heading across to find a table when Sophie noticed a familiar face. 'I just need to speak to someone,' she told Jackie, stopping to change direction. 'I won't be long.'

Sophie walked up to the two men sitting at the other end of the bar laughing at a shared story, and waited for a break in the hilarity before she butted in.

'Uh oh, who ordered the ambulance?' Horrie asked, leaning his arm back on the bar, holding his near empty beer glass, a small measure of amber liquid in the bottom.

'Did you shoot that horse?'

'What?'

'The horse. The one that's on my place. Did you shoot it?'

Horrie put his glass of beer down on the bar and looked away from her. 'I shot at it. Missed the crafty bastard though,' he muttered.

'No. You didn't. You managed to hit it.'

He turned his sidewards glance onto her narrowly. 'Yeah? Well, I'll be. Not as rusty as I thought I was.'

'Who gave you permission to shoot it?'

'Permission?' he said with a slight laugh, lifting a brow in her direction. 'Why would I need permission to shoot at feral pests?'

'It was on *my* property. You can't just go shooting whatever you like on someone else's land.'

'I can if I want to protect my property from damage.'

'It's a horse,' she reminded him pointedly.

'It's a *wild* horse. You didn't even know who it belonged to.'

'It belongs to *me* now. My lawyer assured me that I owned everything on that property as of the day of settlement. That includes any livestock. You do not have the right to harm any animal on my property.'

'Now you listen here, girly—' he started, losing his previous cockiness.

'No, *you* listen,' Sophie said, calling on her most authoritative tone reserved for difficult patients. 'If this animal needs any further treatment I'm sending you the vet bill and, I swear, if you *ever* shoot another living thing on my property,

I don't care if it's a fox, a rabbit or a bloody rhinoceros, for that matter, I will take you to court, so help me God.'

Horrie did a lot of spluttering at that before he managed to get out, 'Court?'

'Stay away from my horse.' Sophie turned away, leaving behind her a murmur of angry male voices.

'That probably wasn't wise,' Jackie said, following Sophie as they went in search of a table in the next room. 'The Spicers, especially Horrie, aren't really a family you want to get on the bad side of around here.'

'No. Probably wasn't,' Sophie conceded, but it was too late now to do anything about it. She was furious that Horrie had taken it upon himself to come onto her land and shoot an animal that wasn't hurting anyone. Well, if he expected her to be some kind of pushover, he better start thinking again. 'But he doesn't want to get on the bad side of an angry paramedic either,' Sophie said, taking her seat.

Julie Spicer smiled a welcome, opening the door wider for Sophie to come inside. 'I heard about your run-in with Horrie,' she said, shaking her head. 'He's a loose cannon that one. How's the horse?'

'He'll be alright. Luckily Horrie didn't get a clear shot.'

'Silly old fool. We don't have a great deal to do with him. It's sad, really. The rest of the family are so close, but that lot just seem to have distanced themselves over some ridiculous dispute spanning two generations. Can you believe that?'

'That is sad. Horrie and his family don't talk to the rest of you, at all?'

'Oh, I see Lois, that's Horrie's wife, in town occasionally and we've always said hello. But they're getting on now, so I don't see her as much anymore. I just think it's silly for the men to continue ignoring each other.'

'It must be nearly impossible not to run into each other in this town.'

'Yes. It's never been easy. So, what brings you over here today, dear?' Julie asked, bustling about her kitchen to gather cups and prepare the coffee.

'I was hoping to pick your brain a bit and get some information about the history of my place.'

'Oh, I love history. I've just finished doing my side of the family tree not long ago—took me years. I don't know how much help I'll be to you, but I'm happy to if I can.'

This news brightened Sophie's day. 'I found some old graves on my place while I was out looking around a few days ago. There was one belonging to a Spicer.'

'That would be Edith, I presume.'

'Yes. I understand she was married to Danny Spicer, who used to own my place, and that they lost a daughter shortly before Edith's death, but I can't seem to find the little girl's grave.'

'No, you wouldn't. She's buried in the Spicer family cemetery over the back of our place. When they divided the original property, Hill Song ended up with the Spicer family cemetery. Some of the graves go right back to the eighteen hundreds.'

'So if the daughter is buried in the Spicer family cemetery, why would her mother be buried on my place?'

'I vaguely remember Lennard's mother making some kind of comment years ago about the whole thing. It was because of the suicide.' Julie shook her head sadly. 'Apparently the little girl wandered off and fell into a dam and drowned. Poor little pet. Edith blamed herself and became inconsolable. They found her face down in the same waterhole a few months later. Went off to be with her baby, they say.'

Sophie thought over Julie's words in silence, saddened by the tragedy of it all.

'You have to remember that back when this all happened it was very much a taboo subject. Anyone who killed themselves wasn't allowed to be buried in consecrated ground.'

'But surely on a private property that wouldn't have made any difference?'

'The original Spicers were very stout Catholics. They used to hold regular church services on the property—in fact, there was an old church built on their land but it burnt down years ago. The Spicers took religion very seriously, so when Danny wanted to bury Edith next to their daughter, you can imagine the kerfuffle that would have caused.'

'So they refused to let him bury her in the family plot?'

Julie nodded sadly. 'Danny would have had no choice but to bury her on his property. It was after that he packed up and sold the place to the Gilberts. He'd just lost his wife and daughter, and the family doing this was the last straw. Selling his land was his final act of vengeance, knowing full well that the rest of the Spicers would have hated it going to anyone outside the family.'

How hypocritical that a family so obsessed with religion—a religion based on love and forgiveness—could refuse to allow a mother to be buried alongside her own child. Where was the humanity in that decision? Sophie felt inexplicably saddened by the story.

'But that all happened such a long, long time ago.' Julie patted Sophie's arm.

Sophie managed a polite half-smile but time seemed irrelevant. Julie placed a cup and plate of homemade biscuits in front of her and conversation moved to more general topics, which filled in the rest of the visit. She left with an invitation for Julie to drop by and take a look at the renovations she'd made to the old house and a container of mouth-watering shortbread biscuits.

On the drive home Sophie once again thought about that lonely grave. She supposed it wasn't really lonely with the Gilbert family nearby, but it would have been out there for a long time before any of the Gilberts died. It seemed that even the Gilberts felt a need to keep their distance from a woman who, in the eyes of society at the time, had to be ostracised. Anne had said Edith was 'a bit nervy'—what did that mean? It could have related to a lot of things. It was quite possible that Edith's issue was something that today could have been treated. What a sad ending this woman must have had, to have lost a child and felt so much guilt and grief that she thought her only way out was to commit suicide.

Twenty-one

Sophie had just finished cleaning out the ambulance a few days later when an urgent call came in. Police were attending a domestic dispute and they needed ambulance assistance for an injured female.

As she reached for the radio, a horrible sensation of déjà vu washed over Sophie and her hand began to tremble. She closed her eyes tightly and took a deep, calming breath as she waited for it to pass. *Pull yourself together, Bryant.*

John glanced across at Sophie and she realised too late that she may not have said it inside her head after all. She sent him a distracted smile and waved away the question she saw in his gaze as they climbed into the ambulance.

As they pulled up out the front of the house, Sophie ran around the back to open the doors of the ambulance and grab her bag before heading inside. As she neared the front door a sudden dizziness came over her, making her stop in her tracks. A cold sweat broke out across her forehead and her breathing sounded loud inside her head.

No. Not again. She hadn't had an anxiety attack like this in months. Sophie blinked hard and took two slow, deep breaths until the lightheaded feeling passed and she continued walking.

'You okay?' the police officer standing inside the front door asked as she approached, watching her carefully.

'Yeah, I'm fine. Not used to this heat yet. Where is she?'

'In the bedroom—Lisa's in with her,' he told her, referring to the female officer Sophie had met briefly before.

'What's the patient's name?'

'Kadie Parker.'

Sophie manoeuvred her way along the hallway, stepping over scattered toys and clothing. As she entered the bedroom she saw the huddled figure of a woman curled on the bed, holding her face and sobbing quietly.

Sophie nodded a silent greeting to the female officer sitting on the side of the bed and took her place, speaking gently but firmly to the woman. 'Hi, Kadie, I'm Sophie. I'm here to help. Can I take a bit of a look at you?'

Kadie slowly lifted her head and took her hand away from the side of her face where she'd been holding a scrunched up t-shirt against a laceration.

Sophie pulled on her gloves and gently lifted the shirt away from the wound, inwardly cringing at the deep, jagged cut that ran along her cheekbone. This was going to be a plastic surgery job, she thought, realising the location and size of the wound would leave a disfiguring scar if it wasn't treated properly.

Sophie cleaned and dressed it as best she could and moved on to assess the rest of her injuries—and there were multiple. At least one suspected fractured rib, a possible fractured wrist and extensive bruising to the head, torso and legs. 'Okay, we're going to get you to hospital so they can have a better look at you.' She turned to John and nodded that they would need the stretcher and followed him outside, leaving Lisa with her to continue taking her statement, while she went back to the ambulance to call in what she'd found.

'You okay, Soph?' John asked quietly once they were out of earshot of the police.

'Yeah, sorry,' she said, tucking a stray strand of hair behind her ear and lowering her gaze. She swore silently as she noticed her hand had a slight shake.

'The thing about trauma,' John continued in a conversational way without looking directly at her, 'is that it's a bastard of a thing to try to shake. It comes back the minute you let your guard down. I remember not long after I came back home from Rwanda I went out with a few mates shootin' roos. I'd been doing it ever since my old man gave me my first rifle, but this time we were out there and one of the blokes took a shot and only nicked this roo. I couldn't stand to see it thrashin' around on the ground like it was so I went over to put it out of its misery,' he explained, while Sophie tried her best not to feel horrified.

'But as I got closer to it I suddenly wasn't seeing a roo on the ground, it was a kid.'

Sophie's heart lurched slightly, as dread welled up inside.

'He was layin' there lookin' up at me with these big brown eyes.'

Sophie saw his Adam's apple moving in his throat as he forced back emotion before lifting his gaze back to hers. 'I tried my damnedest to never think about the messed-up shit I'd seen over there during my time in the army, but it just kept reappearing unexpectedly.' He shook his head a little as though to leave his ghosts back in the past again and settled a level look on her once more. 'It'll get better,' he told her gently. 'Until then you just gotta ride it out. If you ever need someone to listen, or talk to, I'm told I'm a regular Dr Phil,' he said, giving her a brief lopsided grin.

'I thought that the moment I met you,' Sophie agreed with mock sincerity. Despite the fact she hadn't told any of the others about the shooting, she knew that it would probably only be a matter of time before they found out. Then again, maybe John didn't know the details, just the signs that she was a fellow sufferer of post-traumatic stress. 'Thanks, John,' she added in a more genuine tone, and managed a smile as he went back to getting the stretcher from the rear of the ambulance.

It was decided that they'd take the patient straight to Grafton in order to get a transfer to a specialist who would deal with the facial lacerations elsewhere, so Sophie had a long drive to think over what had happened.

Following her attack, in the first few days back on the job, Sophie had tried to cover up the nausea and shaking that followed any of the more violent calls she received. It was impossible to hide them from her eagle-eyed mentor Darrell though, and he'd eventually had to call her out on it.

Sophie had denied having any problems; she'd just wanted to get back to normal. She'd wanted to forget all about that day and move on with life, but her body and state of mind had other plans. She'd packed away all the emotions relating to losing her husband and the attack, squashing them firmly into a tiny compartment and storing them as far back in her mind as she could. Each time something came up that threatened to open that compartment, she'd shove it in there too, until eventually there was no more room to cram any more emotions inside it. Her fear was that at any moment all those feelings she'd stuffed away would burst free. Darrell had been waiting for it to happen, and seemed quite unsurprised when eventually things had begun to unravel.

'You need to deal with everything, Soph,' he'd said, sitting her down in his office after she'd flown off the handle at a trainee unnecessarily.

'I shouldn't have yelled at him,' Sophie acknowledged, 'but he let the siren off in the station. It scared me and I just reacted. I'll apologise to him.'

'It's not the first time you've lost your temper. It's not like you, Soph. I'm worried about you. *Everyone's* worried about you. You shouldn't be back at work yet.'

'I *need* to be back at work!' Sophie yelled, then squeezed her eyes shut when she saw Darrell send a pointed glare at her raised voice. 'I can't sit at home. I'll be fine,' she sighed at Darrell's unhappy frown. 'I need to get back to work now, or . . .'

'You're worried you won't be able to,' Darrell finished quietly.

It had been eating at her ever since she'd woken up in hospital. The fear. This sudden anxiety about returning to the job she loved more than anything. 'When you fall off a horse, they make you get back on straight away,' she told him. 'Or is it if you fall off a bike?'

'Getting shot and almost dying isn't like falling off a bloody horse, Sophie! Look,' he said softening his tone slightly, 'I get it. I know it shook you up. Hell, it shook everyone up, but no one expects you to rush back on the job. It's normal to feel what you're feeling.'

'It's normal to feel scared? Jumping at my own shadow?' she snapped.

'I want you to go and see the counsellor the doctor referred you to.'

'I don't need to see a counsellor. I can get through this if I'm kept busy. I just need to get back out there and get used to it again, that's all.'

'I can't send you out, Soph,' he said gravely.

'What do you mean?'

'You're not ready to be out there. I can't put your work-mates or patients at risk.'

'Darrell, please don't do this. You can't fire me.'

'I'm not firing you. Jesus, Sophie. What do you think I am?'

'Then what the hell am I supposed to do if you won't put me out in the field?'

'I have a few suggestions. Don't look at me like that, just hear me out.'

Sophie couldn't hear anything except that she was effectively being suspended.

'You could do something else. Dispatch, maybe? Or you could train. You'd be an excellent trainer,' he said, and sighed as he saw her expression hardening. 'Or you could take a temporary transfer.'

'A transfer? What the hell, Darrell?'

'Look, I was talking to an old mate the other day. He's looking for someone. It's a small town, actually, *really* small, but it's quiet and they're in desperate need of a paramedic. I think it would be perfect for you. Just take it for a few months and see how you feel. I think this is your only real option at the moment,' he said, holding her hurt look before his voice softened slightly, 'Soph, I want you to see that counsellor.'

Darrell had been right—there was no way she could stay in an office all day, watching her workmates go out on calls without her. She had to take this transfer. For months after the attack she'd been adamant she hadn't needed to talk about things, but even she couldn't lie to herself any longer about how *fine* she was.

In the end, it hadn't been as bad as she'd feared. There was no couch to lie on, no delving back into any deep, dark family secrets, but they had touched on a lot of things that still hurt.

The eventual diagnosis had been that Sophie was suffering from a mild form of post-traumatic stress disorder. At first she'd denied it—she didn't think she'd been under the kind of long-term emotional stress that she'd seen police offers and military personnel suffer—but her ordeal with the gunman and the domestic dispute had triggered some similar symptoms. For Sophie, who'd never liked sharing her emotions with an audience at the best of times, talking about her husband's death and the following attack to a complete stranger had been extremely difficult, but she'd done it, and although it was no miraculous cure for her anxiety or grief, she did feel more in control and positive, now that she had a plan of attack and people there to help.

As they headed back to Hilsons Ridge following handover, the afternoon shadows began to sweep across the wild mountains in the distance and she realised just how right Darrell was to have suggested the transfer. Of course she'd never actually tell him that, but Sophie had to admit she would never have imagined herself being in a place like this . . . owning a farm, for goodness sake! She shook her head slightly and chuckled as she glanced out the side window. She was starting to wonder who she'd become. No wonder her sister kept calling and sending regular messages. They were all worried she was having some kind of mental breakdown. Maybe she was. Although it couldn't be a bad thing if she was actually feeling happier . . . could it? Today's relapse hadn't been terribly major, and she'd managed to pull through it, but it had shaken her recent belief that she'd recovered from her anxiety and it was finally in the past. Maybe the damn counsellor had known what she was talking about after all.

⁓

Pulling up outside her house that afternoon, Sophie sat in her car for a few moments, listening to the soft ticking of the engine as it cooled down. Inside she felt like a tightly pulled rubber band, stretched to its limits. At any moment she feared the strain of holding herself together would snap it. She knew she could use her medication tucked away in the back of the bathroom cabinet, but she hadn't touched it since coming here and she didn't want to now.

She pushed open the car door. She'd felt ill walking inside that house, finding Kadie battered and bruised. Another time and another place had tried to force its way in, but, once again, she had pushed it away, slamming the door shut behind her.

She didn't want to feel this way: anxious, sick and full of remorse. She didn't want to see Mandy's beaten and bloodied body on the floor. She didn't want to hear the gun or smell the blood.

Sophie grabbed hold of the fence rail and rested her head on top of her folded arms. She just wanted to forget it. She wanted to feel normal again. She wanted to feel . . .

The soft nicker made Sophie lift her head in surprise. She hadn't consciously made a decision to come here, she'd just been walking blindly, distracted by the painful memories.

Cobber took another step closer and nudged her arm.

Sophie barely dared to breathe. This was the first time he'd approached her of his own accord, without food being used as an incentive. The hot sting of tears burned behind her eyes. This unexpected moment, the gentleness she saw in the animal's eyes, touched a place inside her that she'd buried deep beneath the professionalism she tried very hard to hide behind.

Sophie slowly opened the gate and slipped inside the yard. Cobber didn't shy away, he just stood there as she raised her hand and placed it on his neck. She leaned forward and buried her face in the horse's soft hair, breathing in the earthy, musk smell that clung to his coat. *God, why didn't anyone bottle this stuff?* It smelled so good. She ran her hand along his neck in long, rhythmic strokes and after a few minutes her inner turmoil had settled down, replaced by the wonder and privilege of being able to stand here next to this animal that had lived its entire life wild and free.

Sophie lost track of time as she stood there, but when she noticed the sun had begun to sink and evening had started to roll in, she realised she was calm once again. She felt better.

It was hard to pull herself away from the fragile bond she'd forged with the big animal, but she found him some lucerne and checked his water before dragging herself inside to fill a tub for a bath. She'd survived her meltdown and was able to put things back into perspective. She was okay. Tomorrow was a new day.

Twenty-two

'Look at you.'

Sophie glanced over her shoulder and was surprised to see Zac leaning on the rail of the stockyards. She hadn't even heard him arrive.

'Hi,' she said, feeding Cobber the last treat. 'We've been getting to know each other a bit.'

'Looks like it. He's really taken to you.'

Sophie had really taken to him too, but she still wasn't sure why he'd chosen her of all people. She'd never even owned a goldfish before.

'So how's our patient?' Zac asked as he opened the gate and crossed to her side.

'Wound's looking good. Antibiotics must be working.'

'Excellent. He's a tough old bugger, this one. Aren't you, boy?'

Sophie followed Zac's big hands as they ran down the animal's neck smoothly. He looked so comfortable and confident; Sophie still wasn't sure that she was doing anything right. Handling people was one thing, administering medical care to a horse was something different altogether.

'I heard you had an encounter with Horrie the other day.' He looked across at her.

'Of sorts,' she hedged, uncertain where the conversation was headed.

'Word has it that Horrie was given a serve. You may be little but apparently you've got a mean streak,' he grinned.

'He's a coward who thinks shooting defenceless animals somehow makes him a big man.'

'I don't condone what he did, but you should know that graziers are within their rights to get rid of feral animals.'

'He shot it on my land.'

'He won't be making that mistake again.'

The way he said it gave Sophie pause.

'I also had a quiet word with him. But do me a favour and steer clear of Horrie for a while. He's not the type who'll forget being publicly castrated by a woman anytime soon.'

Sophie scoffed at his phrasing but did heed the warning. Something told her Horrie would indeed be the type of person who held onto a grudge.

'How's he been eating?' Zac asked, changing the subject.

'Like a horse.'

He threw her a lopsided grin and Sophie felt a zing hit her square in the chest. *Knock it off, already!*

'Well, that's a good sign. Have you thought anymore about what you want to do with him? I can still take him to the Heritage Horse Association.'

A mixture of panic and irritation vied for position at his question. 'I'd like him to stay.'

'You're sure?'

'He can't go back to the national park, and it seems a shame to move him when he seems happy enough here,' she shrugged.

'He can't be ridden,' he reminded her.

'I wasn't really planning to ride him.'

'He's getting older. Those previous injuries are going to continue to worsen over time. Are you sure you want to take on that responsibility? He'll need ongoing treatment at some point.'

'He was kicked out of his mob.' She stroked the horse's face gently. 'He's all alone; he doesn't have anyone else.'

'Alright,' he said, running his hand down the horse's neck again. 'Just wanted to make sure you knew what you were getting yourself into.'

It seemed like she'd had very little say in most choices she'd made since coming out here. Things just kept happening and they all somehow felt right.

'He's a lucky guy,' Zac said after he'd checked the wound and finished up.

'That bullet could have done a lot of damage,' she agreed.

'Well, that too. I meant he was lucky having you to look out for him.'

She glanced up quickly and found Zac staring at her from the other side. 'Oh.' She had no idea why his comment flustered her the way it did. 'I guess you think he and I make a bit of an odd pair,' she eventually said, filling in the silence that followed.

'Not at all. I think certain people and animals end up together for a reason. Maybe you need him just as much as he needs you,' Zac commented, giving Cobber one last pat before throwing her a wave as he headed off.

Sophie followed his departure with a thoughtful frown then looked back at the horse. 'You think he's right?' she asked softly. 'Am I here to fix you, or are you here to fix me?'

The horse gave her hand a nudge when she'd stopped scratching his rump and Sophie grinned as she obediently continued. 'Oh, I see. I'm just here to serve you, huh?'

She supposed there were worse things in life.

The phone rang as Sophie heaved herself up off her knees. Weeding the garden at the side of the house was one of a long list of outside chores she'd been trying to find time to get to on her days off.

'Sophie, it's Bill. Listen, I was wondering if you'd like to come over for dinner tonight. I wouldn't normally impose, it's just that today is a kind of hard one . . . it's Mabel's and my anniversary. We always made a special dinner and used the good china. It's going to waste with just me.'

Sophie instantly had an image of Bill seated at the table with candles and fancy dinner plates set out, all alone. 'I'd love to,' she said. 'What time?'

'Seven o'clock? Does that suit you?'

'I'll see you then,' she promised. She hung up and checked the time, seeing it was already four. She'd been out gardening longer than she'd expected to. Oh well, at least she didn't have to worry about what to make for dinner.

At seven, she pulled up in front of Bill's and grabbed the bottle of wine she'd packed. She didn't know if Bill was a wine drinker or not, but if things got emotional she knew she'd certainly need a glass or two.

Inside the table was set with a beautiful red rose china dinner set. Her mother had inherited a similar patterned set from Sophie's grandmother and it was her mum's pride and joy, only used for special occasions and Christmas dinner. It brought on an unexpected wave of homesickness.

Sophie didn't comment on the three settings; clearly Bill was having trouble letting go of Mabel's memory, and on such a personal occasion like their anniversary it was kind of fitting that she was represented.

'I brought wine.' She held up the bottle and placed it onto the counter.

'Lovely. I'll get you a glass,' he said, moving his walking stick to the other hand.

'No, stay there, I'll get it. Which cupboard?'

'Oh no, tonight we use the good stuff. Mabel would skin me alive if I let you use anything less than crystal. It's out in the cabinet in the lounge room.'

Sophie passed Cleo on the way to the cabinet, who lifted her head and swished her tail at her. The cat sure could hold a grudge. 'You're welcome,' she muttered.

Taking out a glass and closing the cabinet door, Sophie heard voices coming from outside and returned to the kitchen cautiously, just as Bill hobbled through the door followed by Zac Conway.

'Ah, there you are, Sophie. Look who's joining us tonight,' Bill said with a grin, avoiding her surprised glance by pulling out a chair and sitting down.

'Hello, Zac. I didn't know you were going to be here,' she said, sending Bill a narrowed glance. Somehow she didn't think this was an innocent slip of the mind on his behalf.

'Apparently it's the night for surprises. Nice to see you, Sophie,' Zac said.

'Would you like a glass of wine?' she asked, self-consciously looking down at the solitary glass in her hand and now needing it more than ever if she was going to share a meal with Zac Conway.

'Sure,' he said.

'I'll get you a glass.' Bill started to get up.

'Sit!' Zac and Sophie both said in unison.

'Jeez, a man only offered,' Bill muttered, easing back in his chair.

'I'll get it,' Sophie said, already leaving the room. *What the hell was Bill thinking?* She mentally kicked herself—it was *obvious* what he was up to. Matchmaking. She grabbed another glass and gave Cleo a glare before heading back into the kitchen.

'Well, isn't this nice.' Bill beamed at the two of them as they sat and sipped their wine. 'Makes tonight so much easier, having company over,' he added. Sophie wasn't sure if the anniversary thing was part of this whole ruse or not but found that some of her irritation at being duped had begun to subside.

☙

The oven timer went off and Sophie stood before Bill could get up. 'Let me serve—you sit and talk to Zac.'

'You're supposed to be the guest,' Bill protested.

'Yes, but I'm also supposed to be making sure you don't put too much weight on that foot, so you sit and I'll dish out.'

Sophie worked quickly, her mouth watering at the tempting aroma of roast beef and baked vegetables. 'This looks delicious, Bill. You did a great job,' she said after following all his instructions on where to find everything and bringing the plates across to the table.

'Love a baked dinner, but I don't bother cooking them for just myself much.'

'Beats a tin of baked beans and toast,' Zac agreed, picking up his cutlery and eyeing the meal eagerly.

'So Zac tells me you've found yourself a fella,' Bill announced.

The fork she held froze halfway to her mouth as she swung a startled gaze across at Zac. 'Pardon?'

'The horse,' Zac supplied helpfully as he continued to eat.

'Oh. Right. Well, he kind of found me.'

'Archie mentioned something about a brumby once. Said he found him out the back one day, his leg was in a bad way.'

Sophie stared at Bill, her meal forgotten as she gaped at him. 'You knew about the horse?' All this time she hadn't been able to find *anyone* who knew about a damn horse on her property.

'I'd pretty much forgotten until Zac mentioned it. This was a good few years back now. I figured he'd managed to patch the horse up, or it died. He never spoke about it again.'

'Patched it up? Archie knew how to take care of a horse?'

'Archie probably knew more about healing horses than anyone around here. If he couldn't fix it then no one could.'

'He was a horseman?'

'Whole family was. The Gilberts made a living out of catching and breaking brumbies, well before the First World War. Archie may have given up on farming towards the end but he was still an active old bugger.'

Sophie threw a dumbfounded look to Zac across the table, before turning back to Bill. 'You never told me any of this before when we were talking about the Gilberts.'

'Well, you never asked,' he pointed out calmly.

'I knew Clarrie owned a horse and he took him from here when he signed up for the war, but I didn't know about the brumby breaking business.'

'Back then there weren't many fences, and the national park wasn't national park. The early settlers often let their stockhorses and cattle free range and, as a result, the livestock become more muscular and sure-footed from living in the rough terrain. Over the years, they continued to turn out well-bred stallions and mares, introducing a mixture of bloodlines to strengthen their qualities. The British Army were looking for strong horses like this and the colony began a trade exporting horses to the British Army. The horses bred from here were used to supply the military way back even before the Boer War. Farmers could make a year's worth of wages out of catching and selling war horses. It was big business around these parts back then.'

'But everyone around here is so anti horses.'

'Well, all this was a long time ago. Horses kind of lost their value once the motor industry came along, and then tractors. They pretty much became obsolete. And once they were no longer being controlled, the wild population grew unchecked and became a competitor with cattle for grazing. Anything that competes with livestock is considered a pest. Back in about 2000 they had a cull to try to get numbers back under control. Caused a bit of an uproar.'

'That's when the Heritage Horse Association was formed,' Zac added. 'They managed to get a genetic study commissioned into the heritage value of the horses in the national park and it proved that they are direct descendants of the Walers used by the military,' Zac told her.

'Walers?' Sophie was only vaguely familiar with the term.

'That's what they called the brumbies, due to the fact they originated in New South Wales from the first horses brought over to stock the colonies,' he explained. 'Now they remove and rehome the horses in order to manage the numbers.'

'That's a pretty amazing outcome,' Sophie said, listening intently.

'They're a great organisation,' he agreed.

'So do you own any horses? You seem to be a pretty strong advocate for them.' She saw Zac slow the carving of his next bite.

'No.'

There was a subtle change in the mood, and Sophie wasn't sure exactly what had caused it, but Zac was displaying all the classic signs of 'end of discussion'. *Maybe I've been reading too many articles on horse behaviour,* she thought.

In an effort to change the subject she looked back at Bill. 'So do you think this horse is the same one Archie mentioned?'

'Sounds like it, although as I said it was a while back now. He said he'd heard it out his window at night.'

'Do you think Archie tried to train him?'

'I don't know about that. But he wouldn't have turned his back on an animal that was suffering.'

'I wonder why the horse stayed on the property for so long.'

'Wouldn't have any reason to leave—the bush was undisturbed and Archie kept to himself. You ask me, old Archie probably saw a lot of himself in the animal—both outcasts and alone.'

Sophie thought over Bill's remark for the remainder of the meal. It was easy to understand that Archie had felt a connection to the horse—after all, hadn't she felt the same thing?

Twenty-three

Sophie thanked Bill, leaning up to kiss his cheek and say goodnight.

'Well, if I knew this was all it took to get a pretty young thing to give me a kiss I'd have invited you over for dinner sooner,' he chuckled.

'Tomorrow I turn back into the nazi who nags you about taking care of yourself,' she warned before looking across at Zac and giving him a quick nod and saying goodnight.

She heard the men saying farewell as she slid into her seat and turned the ignition . . . only to have nothing happen. She tried again and still nothing. No click-click of a flat battery. Just nothing. *Great.* She pulled the bonnet latch and climbed back out. Zac was already at the front waiting for her by the time she walked around.

'Doesn't sound like a flat battery.' He peered into the depths of the engine bay and wiggled a few things before asking her to try starting it again.

Sophie tried multiple times at his request, and each time the engine refused to start.

'I think it's your starter motor,' he said, coming back from his four-wheel drive with a rag to wipe his greasy fingers on.

'That sounds expensive,' Sophie sighed.

'Yeah, maybe. Might not be, but you'd better get Terry from the garage to take a look at it. He'll come out and tow it back into town for you. Just give him a call in the morning.'

'I'll take care of that,' Bill said, catching the last bit of the conversation as he came over to see what was going on. 'Zac can take you home tonight and I'll call Terry first thing tomorrow.'

Sophie frowned, sending a suspicious glance at Bill as it suddenly occurred to her that he was being very positive about this whole situation. But surely he wouldn't stoop to tampering with her vehicle in his matchmaking pursuits?

'Sure, I'll drop you home. There's nothing much else you can do about it tonight.'

'Okay. Thank you,' Sophie finally conceded, heading back to get her handbag and handing the keys to Bill. Somehow his cheerful smile did nothing to reassure her that this was all some very unfortunate coincidence.

She glanced around as she climbed in to the passenger seat next to Zac and did up her seatbelt. In the back of the car there were two big bales of hay.

'Yeah, sorry about the smell. Wasn't expecting company. I occasionally pick up feed for clients when I go on visits. Got an early farm appointment in the morning.'

'I've come to like the smell of lucerne. I'm sorry to do this to you—driving all the way out to my place is probably the last thing you feel like after being ambushed by a dinner party.'

'It's not a problem, although I *was* kind of surprised at finding you there tonight.'

'Oh, it was a surprise alright. But somehow I think Bill intended it to be.' Sophie glanced sideways at him. 'I think he's trying to play Cupid.'

'You think?' he said dryly.

'Sorry about that,' she apologised.

'Why are you sorry? You didn't ask him to—did you?'

'Of course not,' Sophie scoffed. He lifted an eyebrow at her and she realised it sounded more insulting than she'd intended. 'I mean, I'm not looking for anything like that.'

'I see,' he said noncommittally, keeping his gaze forward.

An awkward silence filled the dark cabin between them as they both stared off through the beam of headlights that lit up the long stretch of narrow bitumen ahead. After a few more minutes Zac turned off the road and headed up the long dirt drive.

'What made you decide to buy a place all the way out here?'

Sophie let out a small sigh as thought how to answer the now familiar question. She'd tried to find an answer that didn't sound as though she were some kind of weirdo—telling people that she was inexplicably drawn to it sounded a bit odd. 'I just like the peace and quiet.'

In the darkness of the car interior she felt less self-conscious around him than she usually did. Sitting this close she was acutely aware of the warm scent of male deodorant and hay that swirled around them, sending her senses into overdrive. Her eyes drifted across his torso, the fabric of his buttoned shirt stretched across his shoulders, emphasising the size of the man. He filled the other side of the cabin.

'I felt that too when I came out here the other day after you called about the horse,' he said.

'You did?'

'Yeah,' he said, sounding just as surprised as she did. 'It was weird, actually.'

Oh, she knew all about that weird feeling. 'I saw it from the road not long after I got here and couldn't stop thinking about the place. Then one day I came out for a drive, and I don't know, I called the agent . . . and bought it.'

'You usually do impulsive things like that?' he asked quietly, turning in his seat to look at her as he pulled the vehicle to a stop outside her house.

'Never.' She shook her head as she looked at him, feeling her gaze trapped in his. The pull happened slowly, and she wasn't sure if it was her moving or him, but somehow the space between them disappeared and she felt the gentle warmth of his lips moving slowly on hers, coaxing a response and yet not demanding any more than she wanted to give. A wave of heat instantly rushed through her body, faster than any drug entering a bloodstream, and a moan of something long forgotten escaped, igniting a powder keg of emotion. Her moan sparked one from him, and what started out as a gentle, probing kiss spontaneously combusted into something urgent and volatile.

Sophie pulled back, her breathing heavy as she fought to gather her scrambled wits. *What the actual hell? What was she doing?* 'Thank you for the lift home,' she managed, turning away as she searched blindly for the handle. 'Goodnight.'

'Sophie,' Zac said, but she ignored him, pushing open the door and feeling the cold slap of fresh air hitting her face as she headed for the house.

'Sophie, would you wait up?'

Oh God, he's out of the car. She tried not to panic, but she wasn't sure that she was ready for the kind of discussion he had in mind about what had just happened.

She stopped at the front door. Her house key was on the key ring she'd left with Bill. The spare one was in one of those fake rocks that had a hidden compartment for keys. Damn it, she hadn't realised how dark it would be if she needed to find it at night. Maybe she could pull a window out?

'Sophie!' Zac said, snapping her out of her break-and-entering thoughts.

'What?'

He stared at her, exasperated. 'What?' he asked. 'What do you mean, what? You practically ran from my car. I want to make sure you're okay.'

'I'm fine. It's just getting late,' she said, biting her lip and then realising that was a bad move when it only brought back memories of how fast her heart had raced only a few moments earlier when he'd nibbled on her lip just like that.

He ran a hand through his hair and blew out a long breath. 'Look, I wasn't planning on doing that, but I'm not saying I regret it. I've wanted to do it ever since I first saw you.'

Sophie almost gave herself whiplash at that. 'You did?'

'Yeah. But that wouldn't have been very professional.'

'Professional?'

'Considering the first time I saw you was when you brought in the cat you'd just poisoned.'

'Accidentally!' she automatically corrected, then rolled her eyes when he grinned.

He stepped closer and Sophie watched him warily, but couldn't deny the jump in her heart rate was a direct response to the effect this man had on her. He approached her calmly, gently, like she was one of his damn flight-risk animals, which wasn't an altogether unrealistic comparison.

'Are you okay?' he asked again, his face mere inches from her own.

'I don't know,' she whispered.

'Do you want me to go?' he asked, leaning in to touch his lips against hers in a feather-light kiss.

Did she? Her body screamed *No!* but her head was desperately trying to act like a responsible adult. She couldn't deny she hadn't had her own moments where she'd thought about Zac in a situation very much like this one, but was she ready for this? 'No,' she finally breathed, barely getting the word out before he lowered his head and kissed her again.

Sophie felt the wall of the house behind her, solid and strong, and in front of her was Zac, equally hard and strong, pressing so tightly against her that it was impossible to tell where he stopped and she began. It was madness. She hardly even knew him, but right at this very minute she couldn't get enough of him.

'We should probably take this inside, I think I just got a splinter,' Zac said as he pulled his hand away from the wall beside her head. 'Where are you going?' he asked, sounding alarmed when she ducked under his arm and started down the steps on unsteady legs.

'To look for the key.'

'In the garden?'

She took out her phone and switched on the torch, shining it around the garden edge.

'Why are we looking for a key in the garden? he asked, joining the search.

'Because that's where I put it. Inside a rock.'

'What kind of rock?'

'A fake rock. It looks just like a real one.' An impromptu treasure hunt was not conducive to sating a raging libido.

'They all look real.'

'Found it!' Sophie held up the rock triumphantly before opening it and grabbing the key.

As she unlocked the front door, Zac slid his arms around her waist and turned her back to face him, picking up where they left off moments before. Sophie wound her arms around his neck, stretching up to anchor his lips to hers, and felt a shiver of desire run through the length of her. He cupped her jean-clad backside in his palms and lifted her up, her legs wrapping around him securely.

'Which way?' he asked against her lips, barely breaking their kiss to ask for directions.

'First on the left,' she murmured, leaning back slightly to undo the buttons on the front of his shirt as he carried her down the hallway.

When they reached the edge of the bed, he slowly lowered her down the length of him and Sophie closed her eyes as a million different sensations ran through her. When her feet touched the floor she opened her eyes and looked up, her breath catching at the hunger she saw in Zac's eyes as he slowly moved his hands along her waist and down to her hips.

His shirt fell open as she reached for the last button and she was allowed only a moment to feast her gaze upon him before he let go of her to remove his jeans. Sophie reached for the hem of her top and pulled it up over her head before tackling the button of her own jeans and slithering out of them quickly. He pulled her back into his arms and reclaimed her mouth, gently lying them down on the bed and covering her body with his own.

The cool evening air touched her skin and sent a shiver through her body as he lowered his face to her neck. The stubble on his jaw scratched in a satisfying way as his mouth burnt hot kisses down and across to her collarbone.

There was no room for rational thought, no possible way of forming the most basic of sentences. All she wanted was to lose herself in the sensation Zac was creating and forget everything else around them.

∽

As they lay side by side, Sophie replayed the mind-blowing sex they'd just shared.

Sex had always been great with Garth but it had never been like *that*.

The moment the thought entered her head, she felt like a traitor. What was wrong with her? She'd just acted like a complete nymphomaniac. Sophie squeezed her eyes shut tightly, feeling mortified by her behaviour. She'd never been one to sleep around much in her youth. Until she'd met Garth she'd had very little experience with sex, just a few unimpressive encounters in her late teens that had made her wonder what all the fuss was about. After that she went on dates during university, but she rarely went out with the same man more than a few times, and none of them had sparked enough enthusiasm within her to sleep with them on a first date. She didn't really have time for a social life between uni and the part-time work she had to do.

Zac sat up on the other side of the bed, and Sophie braced herself for what was to come. What *was* to come? What did she say to the man after this? She'd just had sex with practically a stranger . . . Well, maybe he wasn't exactly a stranger, but still, she barely knew him. How did she explain that this was not who she usually was?

'I better go. I've got an early start in the morning,' he said, already reaching for his clothing on the floor without turning to look at her.

Sophie chewed the inside of her lip as she watched him dress. They still hadn't turned the lights on and Sophie was grateful for that small mercy. Although the moonlight was bright enough to make out most of his outline, his facial features were hidden from her. He didn't bother doing up the buttons on his shirt, leaving it to gape open as he sat back down on the bed to pull on his socks and boots without a word. The silence between them hung heavily and Sophie wanted to say something but she didn't know what. Her emotions were all over the place and she could see the tension in Zac, his back straight, and in his side profile she caught the tightness of his jawline. For a moment she was distracted by the discovery. He seemed angry. Had he realised this had been a mistake as well?

She was still pondering this when he stood abruptly and headed for the door. He moved so fast she'd barely had time to register her surprise, until he paused in the doorway and half turned towards her, his gaze on the floor between them.

'I'm sorry,' he said. His voice had a raw huskiness to it that sounded as though it was being torn from his throat. Then he was gone. Before she could even ask what the hell *he* was sorry for. Had he sensed her self-reproach somehow? Had she been too easy, and he had realised afterwards how unattractive that actually was?

As she lay there listening to his engine start and then fade into the distance, her emotions were going haywire, shifting between self-loathing, and anger at Zac. Why the hell was he *sorry*?

She had no hope of sleeping so she got up and made herself a cup of tea, sitting at the small kitchen table long into the early hours of the morning.

Twenty-four

Sophie avoided town as much as possible on her next two days off, keeping a low profile and praying she wouldn't need a vet in that time. She had been tempted to text Zac and ask what was going on, but the fact of the matter was that she was too scared of his answer. She had enough confused feelings of her own to sort through without discovering what his problem with their encounter was.

She'd congratulated herself on managing to avoid Zac for four whole days when her luck inevitably ran out, as it had to in a town of this size. There was just no avoiding anyone for any length of time around here. She was coming out of the grocery store, juggling plastic bags to get the weight ratio right for balance, when she ran into something warm and solid. With an apology on her lips, her shock seemed reflected on Zac's face as she stared up at him, frozen to the spot.

Sophie could feel the warmth of his hands where they wrapped around her upper arms through the shirt of her uniform as he held her steady.

'Sorry, are you okay?' he asked.

'I'm fine. I should have been looking where I was going,' she finally managed, taking a step back to break their contact. She couldn't think straight when he was this close. *Wow, he smells good.*

Focus, Bryant.

'How's Cobber?'

'Fine.'

'That's good,' he nodded, shoving his hands into the small pockets at the front of his jeans, his shoulders hunched forward slightly.

'I need to get back to work,' she said, hitching the bags in her fingers, which were in jeopardy of having their circulation cut off at any moment.

'Oh. Yeah, right. Do you need a hand with those?' he asked, seemingly just noticing the bags she was holding.

'No, thanks. I've got it. See you later.' She edged around him to get outside.

'Yeah. Okay.' He waved a hand briefly as she brushed past.

That went well. She gave a small cringe at the thought. This was why she didn't understand one-night stands—how the hell were you supposed to treat the person when you happened to bump into them again? What was the protocol in this situation? How were you supposed to face a guy who had been in such a damn hurry to leave that he barely stopped to finish getting dressed before he practically ran from the room? What the hell had she been thinking?

'Sophie!'

She froze, barely withholding the groan of despair that threatened to escape at her name being called, and looked up as a big pair of boots planted themselves in front of her.

'I just wanted to say . . .'

She waited silently for him to continue and saw him move his weight from one side to the other as he seemed to search for the words.

'About the other night,' he started again. 'I wanted to apologise—'

Oh no. No, she could not stand here and listen to him say out loud how much he regretted sleeping with her. What little amount of self-esteem she had left couldn't take that kind of brutality. 'It's fine!' she said hastily, cutting him off. 'It was just one of those things,' she shrugged, having absolutely no idea what she was saying as the words came tumbling out her mouth. 'It didn't mean anything. We're both grown-ups and all that.' She edged away from him once more. She needed to distance herself from him right now.

'Okay,' he said, and she wasn't sure if he sounded relieved or resigned by her response. Either way, she didn't care. She just wanted to move on and forget about it.

'See you around,' she said over her shoulder, heading for her vehicle and praying he wouldn't follow. On the upside, now that the first awkward meeting was done and dusted, hopefully things would be slightly less so when they eventually crossed paths again. Well, she could only hope. She was fairly certain he'd be just as relieved as she was not to have to speak of it ever again after this.

She just needed to remember why she came out here—to concentrate on a new beginning and rekindle the love of her job. That was it. Now that all that sexual frustration was out of her system, she could focus on what was important. Starting from . . . now.

⁓

'Okay, spill,' Katie said after a morning where Sophie had been full of distractions.

Sophie gave her friend a confused look.

'What's going on with you? You've been acting weird for the last few days.'

'Nothing. I've just got a lot on my mind.'

'Like?'

Sophie bit back an exasperated sigh. She'd never met anyone as persistent as Katie before. The woman seriously knew no boundaries, but it was almost impossible to be annoyed with her when you knew the depth of her compassion and caring on the job. Everyone loved her; she was a bouncy, happy, cheeky ray of sunshine who could reassure and put at ease the most anxious of patients with just a smile.

'Like a lot of things—work, the farm, this horse who seems to have adopted me, bills . . . stuff.'

'It's more than that,' Katie said, tilting her head sideways slightly as she studied Sophie. 'If I didn't know better I'd say it was more like . . . man trouble,' she declared as her eyes lit up. 'That's it, isn't it?' she said triumphantly as Sophie rolled her eyes and turned away. 'What happened?'

'Nothing. Nothing happened.'

'You fibber! You know, you're a terrible liar.'

'Oh, for goodness sake,' Sophie muttered.

'You've been on edge all week. Just tell me what the problem is and I might be able to help.'

Sophie slammed the boxes of twenty-one-gauge needles she'd been unpacking onto the shelf a tad harder than may have been required. 'Unless you can turn back time so I can undo a terrible decision then there's nothing you can help me with.'

'Was it Zac?'

This woman just doesn't quit. This was new territory for her. She didn't have a large number of women friends, none that she'd hang out with for coffee and chats about her private life, anyway. Even during high school she'd never really had that one best friend you'd share all your secrets with. She'd been part of a larger social crowd who would just hang out and have fun. It wasn't until she'd met Garth that she'd felt comfortable telling someone her deepest, most private thoughts. Maybe she was odd that way.

But for whatever reason, Katie didn't seem deterred by her unwillingness to divulge any information, and maybe it was due to lack of sleep lately or, quite possibly, Katie's unrelenting questioning, but Sophie felt her resolve weaken. 'Fine! If it'll stop you going on about it—yes. It was Zac. We slept together, okay? Now will you please get off my back.'

'You *slept together*?' Katie's eyes widened almost as much as her mouth.

'Would you keep your voice down, please,' Sophie hissed, looking over her shoulder.

'There's only us here,' Katie protested, but like a cat with a mouse in its sights, her attention was unwavering. 'So what's the problem?'

'The problem is that it was clearly a mistake.'

'Why? How could jumping that fine man's bones be wrong?'

Sophie stared at Katie, silently dumbfounded by her unapologetic enthusiasm. 'Okay, firstly, I did *not* jump his bones,' she said prudishly. 'Secondly, he obviously thought it was a bad idea as well if his hasty retreat afterwards was any indication.'

Katie frowned a little as she digested this new information. 'Were you smiling?'

'What?'

'Afterwards, because I bet you were wearing your "keep your distance" face. He probably felt intimidated.'

'Intimidated?'

'You *are* a bit intimidating, you know.'

'I am not.' Sophie's denial wasn't sounding as assertive as she'd hoped it would.

'You are, a little bit.'

'You don't seem intimidated,' Sophie said with a slight huff. *Otherwise you'd have stopped trying to get me to spill my guts ever since we met.*

'To men,' she amended. 'You kinda give off a bit of an ice queen feel.'

'What!'

'Hey,' Katie held up her hands. 'Don't shoot the messenger.'

Sophie suppressed a groan and massaged the centre of her forehead with her fingertips before calming her tone. 'Maybe if everyone were a little more interested in my job instead of my love life I wouldn't come across that way.'

'Your job ain't gonna keep you warm at night, just sayin',' Katie grinned. 'So anyway, back to Zac. What happened then?'

'Nothing happened, there's no more to tell. We both agreed it was a mistake and that's it.'

'How was it a mistake? You're single, he's single—what's the issue?'

'The issue is that he was clearly freaked about something and I'm not about to revisit that particular experience again.'

'What could have freaked him out? Did you two do something kinky?' she asked, wriggling her eyebrows.

'No, we did not,' Sophie snapped, turning away from the open amusement on Katie's face.

'Oh come on, Soph. I'm married to a farmer who I barely get to see and I have two kids under seven. I have no sex life of my own—I need to live vicariously through you.'

'Well, sorry to say, you're out of luck. Here, live vicariously by finishing unpacking the stores.' Sophie handed her the inventory list as she passed by. 'I have a meeting to go to.'

'I say give him another chance,' Katie called out after her. 'And this time, smile!'

'I'll give you smile,' Sophie mumbled under her breath as she walked into her office to prepare for a phone conference with the regional area manager. She caught a brief reflection of herself on the blank computer monitor and frowned, tucking a loose strand of hair behind her ear and trying a quick smile. 'Ice queen my arse,' she muttered, turning away from the monitor and reaching for a nearby folder. But if it wasn't her that freaked him out then what had happened? Why had he seemed so eager to leave? This is why she didn't need a man in her life right now, she thought irritably. Who needed this kind of drama? She already had more than her fair share at the moment.

Twenty-five

Sophie knew they wouldn't have any trouble finding the location of the car accident. Grafton were also sending out a crew, but Sophie and John were closer and would have to handle the situation as best they could if there were multiple injuries.

God, she hated car accidents. She hadn't been at the scene of Garth's accident, she'd been at home asleep having been on night shift, but she'd attended enough of them to have instantly been able to bring up a mental image of just how gruesome it would have been. Every time she'd closed her eyes afterwards she pictured Garth's poor mangled body, waking herself up from the nightmares with hoarse screams.

Up ahead she could see a flash of light, and as she drew closer it became a bright blur of red and blue saturating the darkness. Sophie had been to more of these than she cared to remember and each time she felt the same pit of dread in the bottom of her stomach. As she pulled the ambulance up, the scene before her was nothing short of horrific. The remains of a car, broken in two and wrapped around a tree, shocked even her, a veteran of road accidents; and it was clear from the faces of the police and firemen already on the scene that she wasn't the only one affected by the severity of the impact. She could tell that these people were all professionals; there was a common, poker-faced look that emergency personnel seemed to adapt. It had more to do with personal coping mechanisms than any form of indifference. In order to do what needed to be done in the aftermath of an accident like this, a person had to find a way to somehow detach themselves from the confronting trauma of the things they would see.

She grabbed her bag and hurried towards an older policeman who was heading across to intercept her. The initial report that came through was one fatality and one critical; she didn't have any further details. 'Where's the survivor?' she asked as she reached the sergeant.

The police officer shook his head. 'Two fatalities,' he corrected. 'The critical one was gone by the time we got here.'

Sophie let out a long, defeated sigh and felt her shoulders slump at the news. 'Who was first on the scene?' she asked, following the sergeant. She still had to confirm that the bodies were both actually deceased.

'That guy over there. He came down the road only a few minutes after it happened.'

Sophie knew that any civilians who may have witnessed the accident would need to be examined for shock if nothing else, but her eyes widened as she followed the policeman's gaze. *Zac.*

Her instinct was to rush to his side, but she knew that she needed to follow protocol and the victims were her first priority. There was no need to double-check the driver who looked no older than eighteen; his condition made it perfectly clear that he would have died on impact.

Sophie circled instead to the passenger side of the vehicle and found a young girl, maybe fifteen or sixteen years old, trapped in her seat by the front of the car and part of the tree trunk. She leaned inside the vehicle and searched for a pulse, even though she could observe that there were no signs of life. She closed her eyes to regather her composure before straightening. Anger, sorrow and regret surged through her at the utter waste of precious life that had happened such a short time ago.

There would still need to be the official identifying of the two bodies, but from the look on John and a few of the other emergency personnel's faces, they already knew who these two kids were. It was hard to remain professionally detached when you knew a victim by name.

Two lives had ended and a hundred more would soon be affected once the police made that horrible knock on two families' doors tonight. Family, friends, teachers and the community in general would be left to grieve and pick up the pieces of their lives. Lives that would never be the same after tonight.

Zac lifted his head as she walked towards him and Sophie momentarily faltered, seeing the torment and grief etched on his strong face. As she reached his side, she willed herself to remain strong. She needed to be the calm and professional paramedic right now, offering empathy and comfort even though all her instincts were screaming at her to hold him and cry.

He was seated in the back of the police car, his long legs on the ground, elbows resting heavily against his thighs, and as she approached he stood up.

'You should sit,' she said, reaching a hand out to direct him back into the car.

'I can't,' he said softly. 'I need to do something, anything except sit.'

'I need to check you out, Zac.'

'I'm fine,' he said irritably.

'You're not fine. You couldn't possibly be after what just happened. You're in shock.'

She ran her gaze over him quickly, trying to assess and stopping when she saw his hands, covered in blood.

He followed her glance and she saw his face still, but he didn't protest as she gently picked up his hand in hers. 'It's not mine. It's . . . hers,' he said, his eyes darting briefly to the car before coming back to stare at the ground between his booted feet.

'Actually, some of it *is* yours,' Sophie said with a frown as she examined his hand, a deep gash running between his wrist and the centre of his palm. She could see glass protruding from the cut and crouched down in front of him, opening her medical bag. 'You've picked up a bit of glass in your hand, possibly from the window as you leaned in.' The location of the cut was a bit of a concern for nerve damage, but she needed to clean the cut of debris before she could assess it and get a clearer idea. As she irrigated the wound with saline she could better see the fragment wedged in the centre of the cut. 'Do you have any tingling sensation in your fingers?'

'No,' he said, and she glanced up at his hollow-sounding tone.

'Can you feel this?' she asked, touching his fingertips, and was relieved when he gave a brief nod of his head. Satisfied that there wasn't any major nerve damage, she carefully removed the cube-like safety glass that had lodged into Zac's palm, then deftly dressed and wrapped it securely.

'Thanks,' he said, looking down at his hand after she'd finished.

'Were you out on a call tonight?'

Zac looked up, a little startled. 'Yeah,' he frowned, as though trying to remember. 'I was on my way back into town.' He glanced over at the car briefly and she saw him swallow painfully before he continued. 'They came from nowhere and overtook me about half a k back . . . then I found them like this,' he said, swallowing hard without looking at the nearby wreckage. 'She was alive, Soph,' he said, looking up at her. 'When I got here, I heard her calling out, and I tried to get the door open, but it was stuck . . . her legs were trapped. I called the police and stayed with her till they got here, but she just . . .' His words faded and he dropped his head, his shoulders shaking with silent sobs.

'You couldn't have done anything more than you did.' She took his large hands in hers carefully. 'They're going to have to cut them out of that wreck . . . No one could have got her out of that in time.'

'I just felt so bloody helpless,' he said, shaking his head.

She could understand his frustration and heartache; he was a man who was used to handling emergencies. He calmed frightened animals, often in great pain, for a living; he knew how to work in potentially dangerous situations, but he couldn't help a young girl trapped in a car.

The sergeant came across to them and exchanged a brief look with Sophie before addressing Zac. 'Mate, if you're feeling up to it, we'd like to get a statement, but it can wait till tomorrow if you don't think you can do it right now.'

'Let's get it over and done with.'

Sophie hated the gutted sound of his voice but knew it all too well. It was going to be a long road ahead as he learned how to deal with tonight. She left him with the police and headed back to her ambulance to get on with the formalities that needed to be handled before she left the scene. It was never a good day when they arrived too late to do anything. At least if they managed to stabilise and get victims to hospital, giving them the best possible chance at survival, you felt as though you'd done something worthwhile. Situations like this just left everyone feeling sad and angry at such a senseless waste of life.

✍

Sophie walked up the wonky pathway leading to the rather ugly fibro apartment at the rear of the veterinarian hospital and knocked on the door, feeling a little nervous.

She'd just come off shift after a miserable evening filling out reports relating to the accident earlier on and wanted to check on Zac. She wasn't sure if her visit would be welcome or not, but she had a fair idea what he was going through and knew he'd be in a pretty horrible place right now. Maybe he'd need a friendly face. Unless, of course, he was the type to need space in which to deal with his emotions, but she felt as though she needed to check on him anyway.

She heard the sound of approaching footsteps and braced herself for whatever reaction she was about to encounter.

The door opened and Sophie felt her heart clench in sympathy at the tired, bloodshot eyes that greeted her. 'Hey,' she said quietly, watching him.

'Hey.'

'I was on my way home, but I just wanted to see how you were doing . . . if you needed anything.'

His gaze locked onto hers fiercely and Sophie felt her breath lodge in her chest at the intensity of his look. 'Yeah, I need something,' he said hoarsely, taking a step closer and sliding his arms around her waist. 'I need you, Sophie.' His lips slid over hers in a hard, urgent kiss that took the remainder of her breath away. 'Please?' he asked, lifting his mouth from hers to speak roughly. 'Stay with me?'

She didn't need to think about it; there was no way she could turn her back on him in this condition, even if she'd wanted to. She reached up and wove her fingers into his thick hair and pulled him back down to her in silent agreement.

She heard Zac kick the door shut without breaking the kiss, and shuffled her backwards towards a room somewhere behind her. They removed clothes between fervent kisses, both of them needing that physical contact, a connection to another warm body to chase away the chill of death and grief and helplessness that continued to haunt them.

There were no practised niceties, no frivolous foreplay, there was only need. The need to bury themselves in each other and feel something other than the horror that they'd both witnessed tonight.

Sophie ran her fingers lightly through Zac's chest hair and savoured the warmth of his body next to hers as they lay in the quiet of his bedroom in the early hours of the morning. She wasn't going to push him to talk, even though he probably needed to at some point. She'd never been a big believer in compulsory counselling immediately after a traumatic event, and she should know; she'd been through more than her fair share. Everyone reacted differently in these situations. Some people needed time to come to terms with their emotions before they tried talking to anyone about them. She'd always been that way. It didn't mean she was shutting herself off from people, she just didn't need to talk about her feelings when she didn't understand them herself. But eventually, once the inner turmoil settled, she found it easier to voice what she needed to say. Others needed to talk to someone straight away. Grief and stress were responses everyone handled differently.

'How do you do it?' he asked, his low voice breaking the silence.

'It's part of the job, I guess.'

'I couldn't imagine going through that more than once in a lifetime. How does that not affect you?'

'You'd have to be a robot for it not to affect you.'

'So how do you deal with it?'

'I guess in one sense I'm lucky because I have a great support group. The people I work with become more like family than workmates, and then there was Garth, my husband,' she said, faltering only slightly over his name. 'He was on the job as well, so we were able to help each other through it a lot of the time.'

'He was a paramedic too?'

'Yeah. That's how we met. He was my first partner.'

'That must have been pretty special.'

Sophie swallowed past the slight tightening of her throat but was surprised when she realised it wasn't as bad as it usually was whenever she spoke about Garth. 'Yeah. It was.'

'He died on the job?'

'Yeah.'

'You don't have to talk about it if you'd rather not. I guess I'm just trying to distract myself.'

'No, that's okay.' And oddly enough, it was. She didn't feel any of the usual walls going up whenever someone mentioned the accident. 'He was killed in a collision with another vehicle on his way to a call.'

'Were you there? Were you in it too?'

'No. Once we were engaged, we decided to get other partners. It's one thing to work in the same industry, but working together all shift and then bringing everything home as well . . . We were worried it might put too much pressure on our relationship.'

'I get that. Is that why you took a transfer out here?'

'No. Well, I guess, in a way. Everything started feeling different without him being there,' she admitted, thinking back. 'But I still loved my job, so I probably wouldn't have transferred just because of that.'

'So then why did you?'

'I was injured on a job . . . I was shot,' she said, hearing the words tumble out and bracing herself for whatever was to come next. She wasn't sure what to expect, considering she'd rarely spoken about it to anyone other than the people who knew her when it had happened.

His hand on her hip tightened involuntarily and she felt his sharp intake of breath beneath her ear. 'What happened?' he finally asked.

In the dark room, held securely by his side, Sophie didn't feel any of the usual trepidation that talking about the incident usually brought with it. 'My partner and I were called to a woman who'd been beaten and shot by her partner. We got there before the police, and I could see her through the front door, lying there, bleeding to death. We convinced the husband to let me in to help her. Then the police turned up and he started shooting. I caught one of the bullets.'

Sophie remembered working frantically on the woman, trying to stop the bleeding, while all around her people were yelling. For a brief moment the cold metal of the gun pressed against her temple before the sound of a gunshot rang out as he opened fire on the police, catching Sophie in the crossfire as she threw herself across the injured woman on the floor.

'Is that the scar you have here?' he asked quietly, lightly touching the pink-skinned shallow groove near her right hip. She'd been lucky it hadn't hit anything vital—missing the bone too, which would have done far greater damage with shards of bone causing internal trauma.

She nodded against his chest and his arms tightened around her in response. His arms felt good around her. Sophie felt safe and for a moment she forgot about everything else going on in her life.

'I'm sorry about your husband,' he said softly after a while.

'I'm sorry about your wife,' she told him back. She knew he had to be thinking about her as much as she'd been thinking about Garth.

The first light of morning began peeking around the edges of the blinds on his bedroom window, intruding on their dark, cosy cocoon of intimacy that had allowed them the freedom to discuss things neither of them would normally speak about in the harsh light of day that was rapidly approaching.

Sophie reluctantly pulled out of his embrace. 'I better go so you can get to work, and I have a hungry horse at home waiting for his morning feed.'

He opened his mouth to protest, or maybe he was about to suggest the same thing; she didn't really want to find out either way. The vulnerability of everything they'd shared suddenly made her feel nervous. Zac Conway confused her. He made her do and say things she never did or said with anyone else. A combination of last night's tragedy and reliving painful memories of Garth and the shooting were suddenly taking its toll on her. She needed some time alone to process everything.

Sophie finished buttoning up her shirt and pulled on her shoes before turning back to look at Zac in bed, who was currently staring up at the ceiling. 'Okay. Well . . .' Her voice trailed off as he turned his steady gaze onto her face, studying her silently for a few moments before swinging his legs to the floor and bracing his arms either side of him on the mattress as he held her eyes.

'Thank you,' he said quietly.

Sophie swallowed hard before managing a jerky nod of her head. 'No worries.' She wanted to say something professional about looking out for things like insomnia, fatigue and mood swings over the next few days, but she was struggling to keep her own jumpy emotions at bay. She did manage to tell him to make sure he made an appointment with Dr Tomovic about his hand before giving him a brief smile as she left the room.

'Sophie, wait,' she heard him call just before she reached the front door.

He appeared only a few seconds later. He'd pulled on a pair of jeans and she found herself more than a little distracted by his bare chest and bed-tousled hair.

'Look, I don't want this to end the way it did last time,' he said, rubbing at the stubble on his chin as he looked at the floor and shifted his weight slightly. 'I acted like a real dick. I panicked,' he said, finally looking up.

Sophie felt bad that he was so uncomfortable and a little of her own awkwardness eased. 'No, it wasn't just you. It kind of freaked me out too. I thought you'd think I was a . . . that I had casual sex all the time. I wouldn't have blamed you for thinking that after the way I—' *practically jumped your bones*—'acted,' she finished lamely.

'I didn't think that. I wasn't thinking anything. I was too busy calling myself all kinds of names for cheating on my wife.'

'What?' Sophie was momentarily alarmed.

'I mean, *feeling* like I was cheating on her.' He shook his head irritably. 'It caught me off guard. *You* caught me off guard,' he said, holding her surprised gaze steadily. 'You're the first woman I've . . . been with since she died.'

'Same,' Sophie admitted. 'I'm not sure what happened that night. That wasn't the usual me,' she assured him. Although seeing as he barely had to ask twice only a few hours before didn't really back up that theory. 'Last night—'

'Was my fault,' he cut in before she could finish. 'I'm sorry. I know you only came over to make sure I was okay . . . I wasn't. Not until I saw you standing there on my doorstep. I had no right to put you in that situation.'

'You didn't put me anywhere I didn't want to be,' she said. 'Sometimes sex is just an adrenaline release. It's a natural reaction.'

'So that's all it was? Two people reacting to a traumatic situation?' he asked, watching her carefully.

All of a sudden, Sophie wasn't sure how to answer. She couldn't read him at all. Was he giving them an escape clause here? A free pass to avoid any complicated emotional drama? Or was he waiting for her to disagree and say that it meant a lot more than a biological reaction? And if it did, what would that mean? Was she ready for a relationship? She wasn't sure. What she did know though was that friends with benefits wasn't something she particularly wanted either. She hadn't had anywhere near enough sleep, or coffee for that matter, for this kind of discussion. 'I'm not sure what it was. *Yet*,' she said with a tired sigh. 'Both of us come with a lot of baggage and I don't think it's anything that can be rushed into.'

'Fair enough,' he conceded, stepping back to allow her to open the door. 'Thanks again for being here.'

She smiled and squeezed his hand. Regardless of what was going on between them, she was glad she'd decided to drop by. She'd needed the contact of another person more than she'd been willing to admit. The coming days were going to be rough enough to face.

Twenty-six

The next day was full of talk about the accident and Sophie, although expecting it, was not quite prepared for just how fast the news had spread. The driver was a seventeen-year-old boy who'd just got his licence that day and was taking his sixteen-year-old girlfriend out for a drive. So much freedom to enjoy and it had been cut short in the space of a heartbeat.

Sophie soon realised there was no way of closing herself off professionally from anything that happened in this place. It didn't matter if she'd been on a call-out for a farming incident or a tragic car accident, here in this small community she was always going to cross paths with either a patient or the patient's family after the event. It wasn't an issue in the city; rarely had she encountered her patients while grocery shopping or refuelling her car. There were of course those lonely, sad few who were frequent call-outs and would phone the ambulance regularly in order to have some kind of human contact, but she had never had to deal with this kind of ex-patient contact before.

It was confronting to witness the devastation the accident had on the whole town. Everywhere she looked, people shook heads and dabbed at eyes with well-used tissues as they huddled in small groups and tried their best to deal with the shock of losing two young lives from their community.

Sophie didn't know either of the families involved, but it was clear to her that they were both very much loved and respected if the level of grief she saw was any indication. She did her best to stay away from the gossip as much as possible, declining to comment by changing the subject whenever she was asked about the accident. She knew no one was asking questions out of malice or disrespect, rather they were just trying to make sense of a completely senseless act, but Sophie couldn't help them with that. She'd had more than her fair share of raw deals, losing Garth and then almost her own life. She had no answers to offer. Life sometimes dealt out shitty hands, and it sucked.

Around the station it was equally as depressing because, unlike her, most of the others *did* know the families and both of the deceased kids. As the senior member of staff, it was up to her to make sure her volunteers were okay and had access to any kind of counselling they needed. This kind of accident was always going to hit a team like theirs especially hard. It was a tight-knit community and all of them were acutely aware that every day they ran the risk of turning up at an incident and discovering that the victims were someone they knew or were even related to. There was no way to prepare for something like that. But these volunteers were the backbone of this community—they gave those injured in a serious accident a fighting chance before the victims could make it to hospital. Sophie's admiration for her team grew with every passing day she spent working with them. Their level of dedication was second to none and she couldn't be more proud of them.

At home, her daily routine had become a soothing habit. Morning and evening she fed Cobber and spent time talking to him, but she needed to make some decisions soon. His wound had all but healed and she'd soon need to release him from the yards. The thought saddened her more than she liked to admit. Although she could approach him and pat him, she knew that mostly he only allowed it because he was in a somewhat confined area. Once she opened those gates and let him go, she was pretty sure his instinct would kick in and he'd run without looking back.

The sound of an approaching car drew Sophie's head up and she let herself out of the yard, wiping her hands on her jeans as she tried to figure out who her visitor was.

A woman in jeans and a bright green t-shirt waved, her boots crunching in the gravel. 'Hi there. I hope you don't mind me dropping in unannounced like this but I was headed past this way and I've been meaning to stop in for a while. My name's Alison Sherman. I'm with the Heritage Horse Association.'

'Oh, hi. Sophie.' She shook the woman's outstretched hand.

'Zac told me about your stallion. I hope you don't mind but I'd love to take a look at him.'

'Ah, sure,' Sophie said, caught a little off guard by the visit.

Her alarm must have shown on her face because immediately Alison smiled. 'Don't worry, I'm not here to steal him away from you. Zac told me you've been taking care of him. I'm just here for a stickybeak.'

'Oh. Sure, he's in the yards.'

'Wow, look at this guy,' Alison said, folding her arms across the top rail. 'He's gorgeous.'

Sophie felt absurdly proud. *This must be what it's like when people gush over your baby.*

'When Zac told me about him, I had to come and see if I was right.'

'About what?'

Alison dragged her gaze off the horse and Sophie saw her eyes alight with excitement. 'Years ago there was a black stallion that led one of the biggest mobs in the park. They named him Devil. No matter how many times they tried, they could never catch him. Then one day, he just disappeared. There were no sightings of him, and a younger male had taken over his mob. It happens that way; they get hurt or sick and they die. But when Zac told me about this injured old stallion you'd found, I immediately thought of Devil and wondered if it could be him.'

'So you think it is?'

'The age is right, and those scars look very much like something he could have suffered in a fight, not to mention his markings . . . I'd say it couldn't be anyone else but him.' She turned back to look at Cobber, who had begun pacing back and forth, tossing his head. 'Zac mentioned you'd been doing some basic handling of him. How's that going?'

'Oh, I wouldn't call it handling, exactly. I actually have no idea what I'm doing. I've just been feeding him and talking to him . . .' She felt stupid saying it out loud, when everything about this woman beside her screamed professional horsewoman.

'Well, that's handling,' she grinned. 'The first step is always gaining the animal's trust. Sounds like that's exactly what you've done. If you like, I can give you a hand with the rest.'

'Really? But he can't be ridden, so he can't really be broken in,' she said hesitantly.

'There's still lots of ground work we can do with him. Training is all about forming a bond with your horse. It just takes patience and time. He's getting too old to live on his own out there, even though that's what he's done his entire life. If he were still in the wild, he'd eventually get too old to continue fending for himself. If you want to keep him here, it's probably in his best interests to be trained so you can better handle and take care of him.'

Alison's words filled her with a surge of optimism. Maybe she wouldn't lose him after all. If she could train him, then maybe he wouldn't leave her. 'I'd really appreciate your help.'

'My daughter's started training horses, so I reckon between the three of us we should be able to do the job.'

'Thank you,' Sophie said as they walked back towards the car.

'No worries. Zac mentioned you might need a hand.'

'He did?'

'He was worried about you being alone so much with an unhandled horse, I think.'

'Oh. I guess he has a point.'

'I'm happy for the chance to pay him back with a favour after all the time he's donated to the association.'

'For someone who spends so much time looking after them, it's surprising he doesn't actually own a horse himself.'

'That was Christa's department,' Alison said with a smile.

When Sophie sent her a curious glance, a melancholy smile touched Alison's lips. 'Christa was a founding member of the association; the horses were her life. Even when she was sick, she still made time for the place. After she died, Zac took over as far as the veterinary side of things went, but he's never been a horse lover the way Christa was.'

That explained his abruptness at dinner with Bill that night. 'Well, anyway, I'm grateful for your help. I'm a bit of a newcomer to this horse thing.'

'Once you get it, it's usually terminal. There's no cure. You've got it for life,' she grinned.

'I think you might be right.'

Sophie walked back to the yards feeling a lot happier. 'What do you think, boy? You want to be a kept man?' She tried to imagine what life would be like for him if she allowed him to return to the bush, but the thought of him disappearing back in there, never to know what had become of him, was too horrible to consider. It would be for the best. She tried to ignore the way he stared out over the rail at the bushland beyond, longingly.

Twenty-seven

Sophie had been kept busy with a training weekend and follow-up meeting with her supervisor in Grafton the next week and the days had flown by. She hadn't seen Zac since the accident and she'd been thinking about him, but every time she went to call she ended up hanging up before he could answer.

'Have you seen Zac lately?' she asked Katie as they sat in the lunch room having morning tea.

'No. Why?'

'No reason. Just wondering how he was since the accident.'

'You haven't seen him since then?' Katie asked, leaning forward.

'I've been busy.'

'Not *that* busy,' she pointed out. 'You two aren't still pussyfooting around that sleeping together thing, are you?' Katie asked, her eyes narrowing.

'It's complicated,' Sophie muttered.

'What's complicated about it?'

'I don't know, it just is,' she said irritably. It didn't *sound* complicated if you didn't factor in the bit about them both having hang-ups about moving on. She'd wanted to check on him, but what if he thought checking on him was just a cover for her wanting an encore of the last time they'd seen each other? After all, the last two times they'd seen each other had both ended with them in bed. Yes, she knew it sounded irrational, but late at night as she tossed and turned trying to fall asleep, her mind found a sick kind of amusement in torturing her with all kinds of terrible things—it particularly enjoyed playing her a newsreel of Zac's thoughts on how he would see any kind of drop-by visit as a thinly veiled excuse for a booty call.

It didn't help that on some level she knew that if that *did* happen it wouldn't be the worst thing in the world.

It shouldn't be this hard. She liked the man, she just wasn't sure if she wanted to move things further along. All this accidental sex they'd been having during moments of weakness wasn't exactly a solid foundation to build anything very secure on. She was getting too old and jaded to waste her time on casual affairs—especially in a small town like this. The last thing she needed was to discover she had a reputation for casual sex. There were certain professional standards she needed to maintain, especially out here where she was in a senior position and needed credibility in the community.

'For goodness sake,' she muttered, disgusted with this senseless debating. She needed to make sure he was okay after the accident. The other stuff wasn't important right now. Decision finally made, Sophie got to her feet and grabbed her phone. 'I'm going out for a minute,' she told Katie. 'I've got my phone if you need me.'

Katie sat back in her chair wearing a smug I-told-you-so smile. 'Say hi to Zac for me.'

❦

The vet surgery was reasonably quiet when she opened the front door. Zac's dusty four-wheel drive was parked outside so she figured he was in, taking the chance she would be able to pop her head in between patients.

'Hi.' Sophie smiled brightly at the receptionist who eventually dragged herself away from the computer monitor to acknowledge her. 'I'm just wondering if I'd be able to see Zac for a moment.'

'Do you have an appointment?' the woman asked in a bored tone.

'No, I don't. I just wanted a word with him.'

'He's with a patient.'

'Is it okay if I just wait?'

'Up to you,' she said, turning back to the computer screen.

Alrighty then, Sophie thought, taking a seat in the small waiting room. The strong smell of antiseptic and bleach took a few minutes to get used to, and the various posters depicting different types of intestinal worms were an absolute delight as she filled in her waiting time. Finally, there was movement at the far end of the room and a door opened, an enormous dog dragging its flustered female owner from the room on the end of a lead.

'Cedrick, heel!' the middle-aged woman yelled, while Cedrick completely ignored his owner's request, straining and choking as it barked excitedly and scrambled forward.

'I just need to weigh him before you leave,' Zac said to the woman, whose knitted beanie had slipped down over one eye as she struggled to hold onto the overexcited animal with both hands. After more yelling, the dog was manoeuvred onto the scales.

'Cedrick, sit!'

Zac took out a small treat from behind the desk to try to pacify the animal into staying still long enough to get a reading, but the woman narrowed her eyes and glared at him. 'No treats,' she said in a haughty tone. 'We do not give treats to reward behaviour. We're training *without* food rewards.'

Sophie lifted an eyebrow at that. *And how's that working out for you, lady?* Although she had to give the woman points for tenaciousness; she never once let go of the lead no matter how hard the dog lunged and dragged her about the place.

'Cedrick!' she hollered again over the ear-splitting barks of the excited dog. 'Sit!'

Zac, clearly having reached his tolerance level, took the lead from the woman and firmly got the canine under control long enough to get the weight recorded. Then there was more barking as the woman opened the door and the dog bounded through, dragging his owner like a kite on a string behind him as it took off at a run out into the carpark.

The room seemed to let out a sigh of relief once the barking and yelling faded into the distance, and Zac finally noticed her sitting there. 'Sophie! Hi.' He gave her an exasperated glance, shaking his head in silent apology for the bedlam she'd just witnessed. 'What brings you here?'

'I just wanted to see you . . . I mean, check on you . . .' She closed her eyes briefly before trying again. 'I was thinking about you—but not in a weird way,' she hurriedly corrected. *Good lord!* What was happening to her? The words were pouring out uncontrollably.

Zac slid a glance across at the receptionist, who was watching with a bored kind of tolerance, then waved Sophie into his examination room.

'Okay, so maybe you could start again?' he said as he leaned back against the high stainless steel table and folded his arms across his chest.

Sophie raked a hand through her ponytail nervously as she looked at him. 'I've just been wondering how you've been . . . since the accident. Did you go and see Ado?'

'Nah, I was fine after I got a bit of sleep.'

Sophie frowned at the casual brush-off of concern. She'd dealt with stress and emotional trauma after witnessing horrific events long enough to know that you *weren't* always fine. Men in particular tended to dismiss concern and chose to play the tough-guy card. Although, in all fairness, she knew she had been guilty of doing the same thing on occasion, but it was only ever a quick fix—don't think, just move on. Eventually these things had a habit of sneaking up on you and making you acknowledge them one way or the other. Hers resulted in a near nervous breakdown on the job. It wasn't fun.

'If you want to talk about it, I'm always here to listen. It helps.'

'What's to talk about? It won't bring back those kids, will it?' he said cynically, dropping her gaze.

'No, but it can help digest everything you went through.'

'I'm good.' He flashed a smile at her and pushed away from the table.

Sophie wasn't convinced he was as good as he was letting on, but she let it go. She'd been there too. There was nothing worse than someone badgering you to talk about it when you weren't ready.

'I'm glad you came by.' He took a step closer to her and Sophie was distracted by the strange reaction her body was having at his close proximity.

'I was worried about you.'

'There was no need. I'm fine. But there has been something playing on my mind,' he said, probing her gaze intently.

Sophie swallowed nervously. His lowering tone was igniting all kinds of weird emotions. 'What's that?'

'I've been thinking about your theory.'

'My theory?' she repeated weakly as he came within touching distance and she breathed in a warm scent of man, soap and something uniquely Zac that always reminded her of the outdoors.

'The last time I saw you, you were under the impression that we'd only ended up in bed due to some kind of delayed adrenaline rush.'

'We'd both been under a lot of strain,' she managed to point out, distracted by the stubble on his lower jaw.

'I'd like to test that theory,' he said, moving closer.

What? Test? How? She didn't have time to voice her fears. He was only a breath away when she realised it was too late and he pulled her towards him, his lips covering hers.

Why did kissing this man feel as natural to her as breathing? It felt like an eternity since she'd last been this alive. She opened her eyes as he pulled back slightly, but left his hands linked around her waist.

'Nope,' he said quietly. 'It's still there.'

Sophie let out a long breath and bowed her head. 'Yeah. It is.'

'I'm trying not to take your decided lack of enthusiasm personally.'

'It's just—' Sophie started then gave a frustrated sigh. 'I'm not sure we're ready for this. I mean . . . you freaked out the first time because you felt guilty about your wife, and I get it—I was the same. I'm still a little freaked out, to tell you the truth.'

'I can't tell,' he added dryly as she moved away from him.

'People are going to talk about us,' she said, eyeing him sternly.

'People are always going to talk. They talk about everyone.'

'Yeah, but . . . I haven't been in town long and if we . . .' she faltered trying to find the right words to describe their situation. 'If it doesn't work out, people are going to think I'm . . .'

'Human?' he supplied helpfully.

'That I'm not serious about my job.'

Zac slowly crossed his arms again and eyed her doubtfully. 'I think you're blowing this all out of proportion.'

'Oh really? Easy for you say when it won't be your career on the line.'

'Soph, I don't think you're giving people the credit they deserve. Sure they like to gossip and speculate on things, but it's not done maliciously. They're not going to run you out of town with pitchforks just because you decide to date someone.'

'I'm just not used to this kind of scrutiny,' she sighed. She couldn't go anywhere, talk to anyone or do anything without someone later mentioning that they'd seen her or spoken to someone who saw her. It was more than a little disconcerting. In the city she never had to think about anyone recognising her down the street, or taking notice of where she ate dinner.

'I won't lie—it took me some time to get used to it when I first moved here as well, but you do eventually adjust. If it helps, I'm nervous too.'

She saw the truth of the statement in his serious expression and felt some of the tension in her shoulders ease a little.

'We don't have to rush into anything—I'm not suggesting we jump into moving in together,' he shrugged. 'All I'm saying is that I don't really want to do casual sex any more than I think you do. Why don't we just go slow and see what happens?'

In theory it sounded good. But could they go slow? Would it be that easy?

'Let's do dinner. What do you say?'

Sophie instantly thought of the prying eyes that would watch their every move at the pub or RSL club but, before she could say no, he was already one step ahead of her.

'Somewhere else. We could go to Grafton, or Glen Innes. We could even make a weekend of it if you aren't rostered on.'

Well, that sounded doable, and a hell of a lot better than what she'd first imagined. 'I can't do a weekend away, but I could do dinner on Saturday,' she said slowly.

'This Saturday? Sounds good,' he smiled.

'Okay then.'

'Right. I'll talk to you beforehand and sort out a time.'

Sophie nodded and they looked at one another awkwardly for a moment before she took a step towards the door. 'Right. I should get back.'

'Yes, my next appointment is probably waiting.'

They exchanged a self-conscious wave and smile before Sophie left the room and headed for the front door.

She'd come here to check on the man and she was leaving with a date for Saturday night. She was still trying to understand how it all happened long after she returned to work.

Twenty-eight

It had been one of those shifts where it was quiet patient-wise, but hectic in the office. Every time Sophie thought she was getting on top of the paperwork she'd find more. If it wasn't getting that side of things sorted it was the phone constantly ringing. When it rang as soon as she'd finished her last call Sophie almost decided not to answer it, but on hearing the familiar gruffness on the other end of the line she felt an unexpected rush of affection wash over her.

'That was more than three rings, Bryant. What kind of circus you running out there?'

Darrell was a stickler for his rules. No phone was ever allowed to ring more than three times or there'd be hell to pay. 'I don't exactly have the staff numbers here that you have, so give me a break.'

She heard his grunt on the other end of the line and smiled at the familiar sound. She missed the grumpy old bugger. 'Is that all you were calling for? To give me grief about how many rings it took to answer?'

'Well, that, and I have something that will brighten up your day.'

'Oh? And what would that be?'

'I just heard that there's an opening in SOT.'

Sophie had been flicking through the folder on her desk while she was talking but stopped as Darrell's words sunk in. The Special Operations Team was a branch of the service that had always fascinated her, and joining it had long been a dream of hers. Just completing the course was an astronomical challenge. It involved training to treat patients in the worst of environments, including in water, bushland and hot-zone areas that may contain hazardous chemical spills. They worked alongside police and fire and rescue units as well as federal organisations. She'd been waiting for this opportunity for years.

'Oh my God.'

'You don't have to call me God, Darrell will do.'

'But . . . what about . . .'

'There was nothing terrible in that psych report,' he said, guessing about her concern over the hostile domestic situation she'd been caught up in. 'Do you think you're okay?'

'Yeah,' she said slowly as it dawned on her that she was. She felt better than she had when she'd first came out here. Back then she'd been unsure what her future had held, and she'd been fragile and a little nervous. Now she felt stronger and more like herself than she had in a long time. 'I think I'm okay now.'

'Well, there you go then. There's nothing stopping you from applying is there?' he said in his practical, no-nonsense way that managed to pull a smile from the corner of her lips.

As she said goodbye her smile petered out and died, to be replaced by a dipping of her eyebrows. There was nothing stopping her from applying . . . except this strange emptiness that had suddenly appeared at the thought. If she was selected for the course she'd have to move back to Sydney. She'd have to give up this place, leave her property. That moment of excitement the news brought her was now a distant memory. To chase one dream, she'd have to give up on another. But which one was more important?

∽

Sophie had just finished cleaning out the ambulance when she heard her name being called from the doorway. 'Someone here to see you,' Katie called.

Putting the rubbish in the bin, Sophie crossed the garage bay and stopped short as she came through the door. 'Mon?'

'Surprise,' her sister volunteered, eyeing Sophie a little warily.

'What are you doing here?' Sophie winced at the words and quickly shook her head. 'I mean,' she gaped at Monique, 'I wasn't expecting you.'

'I know, I'm sorry.'

Sophie stepped forward to hug her sister, now that some of the initial shock at finding her in the station had worn off. 'Don't be silly, it's great. I just didn't expect to see you. Here.'

'It was kind of spur of the moment.'

Sophie finally noticed Katie sitting at the desk and introduced the two women before turning back to her sister and eyeing her slim-fitting skirt, low, strappy heels and tailored blouse. 'Is everything alright? Mum and Dad—'

'Oh no, don't worry,' Monique quickly reassured her, 'they're fine, I just wanted to come out and see how you were going.'

'Ahh,' Sophie said, eyeing her sister with a hint of amusement. 'You're checking to make sure I haven't lost my mind.'

'No,' she said, folding her arms and sticking one hip out slightly. 'It's not like that at all.'

Sophie didn't believe her for a moment. Her sister couldn't help herself: ever since they'd been kids she had always felt a need to mother her. After the initial conversation they'd had when Sophie told her about buying her property, the two women had only had brief chats and Sophie had a feeling her older sister still worried that she'd made some huge mistake.

'How'd you get here?' She couldn't imagine Mon driving the whole way, but she wasn't sure how else she'd have managed.

'I flew to Grafton and then hired a car to drive the rest of the way.'

Sophie was impressed. Mon must really be convinced her little sister was in need of an intervention of some sort to go to all that trouble. 'Well, I'm here for another few hours, but I can give you directions to my place if you like, or you could go and have something to eat at the pub until I finish?'

'I can stay back, Soph,' Katie said from her desk. 'I have my in-laws staying with us at the moment, so I don't need to rush home for the kids.'

'I don't want to cut into your family time,' Sophie protested.

'Trust me, a little distance is probably a good thing at the moment. I don't mind *at all*,' she said pointedly.

'Well, in that case, call me if you need me,' Sophie smiled before leading the way out of the office to take her sister home.

'Shall do,' Katie said, waving goodbye as she swivelled her computer chair back and forth in front of the computer monitor. Hopefully it remained quiet, Sophie thought and prayed that now she'd thought it she hadn't just jinxed them.

❧

'This is it,' Sophie said as she held open the front door for her sister to walk inside.

'The photos didn't do it justice, Soph,' Monique said as she looked about, dropping her sunglasses into her handbag. 'What a quaint little place.'

Quaint? Only her sister could describe something as *quaint*. 'Thanks. I like it.'

She led the way down the hallway to the guest room that, so far, hadn't been used. Thankfully she'd finished unpacking all the boxes that had been stored in here since she'd moved in the weekend before. 'The bed's not made up, but I'll get some sheets and blankets.'

Monique waved off Sophie's fuss with one elegant hand. She'd inherited their mother's artist-like hands, long and slim with perfect nails. Sophie had got her work hands from her father's side of the family—short and somewhat stumpy compared to her sister's. Everything about Mon was elegant. Sophie had often felt like an ugly duckling beside a graceful swan, but it stood out in far greater detail now with Sophie in her blue trousers, boots and work shirt next to Mon in her heels.

Sophie left her to get sorted while she headed to the kitchen and rummaged through the fridge and pantry to throw together a plate of soft cheese and biscuits. She opened a container of dip, giving it a cautious sniff before deeming it safe enough to eat, and added that to the platter as well. Two glasses and a bottle of wine completed their feast and she carried it all out to the verandah, placing it on the table and taking a seat.

'This all looks rather refined,' Mon said, coming out and eyeing the platter.

'It's remote up here—it's not uncivilised,' Sophie said, reaching for a biscuit.

'You're looking good, Soph. I wasn't sure what I was expecting, but you look healthier and . . . more relaxed?'

'It's a little more laid-back here. Guess I must be acclimatising,' she smiled.

'That's good,' her sister said, picking up her wineglass. 'I still think you're crazy for buying a farm though,' she added and looked out over the paddocks before them. 'You're planning on staying here long-term then?'

Sophie let her gaze fall on the mountains in the distance. She found it difficult to think about moving back to the city and living that fast-paced life again. The old Sophie was beginning to feel more and more like a stranger every day. 'I guess I am,' Sophie said softly. She wasn't even sure when she'd made the decision—it seemed to be happening without her becoming aware of it.

'What happened to your career goals?' Mon pressed. 'I seem to remember you had very specific targets you wanted to reach not so very long ago. Are you just going to throw all that away?'

Sophie's eyes narrowed as she eyed her sister. 'You've been talking to Darrell? Is this why you've come out here? To talk me into moving back?'

'I'm just worried you're making decisions without thinking about the long-term consequences.' She stopped as she saw Sophie's expression close. 'Look, I think it's great that you've been able to come up here and slow down. You needed to get away for a while. I'm just worried that you're shutting yourself off from everyone and hiding.'

'Hiding? What would I be hiding from?'

'I don't know. You've been through a lot. Maybe you're avoiding dealing with it all by staying up here instead of coming home.'

'I've dealt with what happened to me. It was a hazard of the job and it was terrifying, but I'm okay. And yes, the stress of work was getting to me, but since coming here,

I feel like I've found my passion for the job again. People out here need us.'

'It's just so . . . I don't know. It's not the kind of place I'd have ever imagined my baby sister ending up.'

Sophie gave a small smile at that. 'You and me both, but I guess that's what happens when you take a chance and try something new. Look around, Mon,' Sophie said after a moment. 'Just stop and listen for a minute.'

Monique rolled her eyes but stopped talking. After a few moments Sophie saw her tilt her head slightly and close her eyes before opening them to glance over at her. 'It's so . . . quiet.'

'Peaceful,' Sophie agreed.

'Yeah, it is,' she said with a small sigh, looking at her sister thoughtfully. 'I don't think I could live here, but I can see the attraction. Just don't close the door on returning to the city one day. If you're happy for now then I guess that's all we can ask for, but you're still so young—all that work over the years to become an intensive care paramedic and you're stuck here wasting all those skills. I'm just worried you're going to wake up one day and realise you've missed an opportunity to do more with your career.'

Sophie could understand her sister's concern. Monique was happily single and proudly independent. She'd always said that she was never going to be the kind of woman who depended on a husband to support her, and that her career was the single most important thing in her life. She'd put in the hard yards and the long hours to work her way up the corporate ladder and she was beginning to reap the rewards. Sophie admired her—she couldn't imagine a more tedious job, being a credit analyst, but she was proud of her. Once upon a time, Sophie was just as determined to go as far as her career would allow her but, unlike Mon, Sophie wasn't doing it for financial security—she was just passionate about her job. Out here she had that same job satisfaction, albeit on a smaller scale.

'My skills have saved lives, Mon. If anything, *because* of my training I'm more important to have out here. This place is remote and the community deserve to have an ICP stationed nearby.'

She saw her sister nod reluctantly at her logic. 'I just hope you don't decide you've made a terrible mistake a few years from now.'

The voice of doom and gloom put a slight damper on the rest of the conversation but, for the most part, Sophie brushed it off. Her sister was just being her usual over-cautious self. She'd made the right decision buying this place, and she didn't have to defend it to anyone else.

Twenty-nine

Sophie stood on her verandah and watched the dust leave a trail behind her sister's hire car the next day. Sophie was a little sad to see her go. As sisters they'd fought for most of their teenage years but had grown closer after high school. They were so opposite in nature that it wasn't exactly easy to find anything in common, and although they were now close, she always got the feeling that she was a bit of a disappointment to her older sibling. Maybe it was just Mon being a big sister. She wouldn't have come all this way if she hadn't been worried about her, but she wished she hadn't. Their conversation about her job had left a niggling feeling in the base of her stomach that remained, despite her best attempts to ignore it.

Is that really what it looked like to people who knew her? That she'd given up? Taking this position had started

274

out as a temporary thing, a way to take a breather of sorts, and she'd had her doubts about handling the quieter pace initially, but as she'd learned, there were quiet days and then there were the days when they could be run off their feet with emergencies. She hadn't counted on settling into the job or the community as quickly as she had, but she was beginning to enjoy it. Wasn't that what taking chances and trying something new was all about? Opening your mind to new experiences?

She wasn't settling or giving up anything . . . was she?

❧

Sophie slid her sunglasses on top of her head as she pulled the ambulance up beside the bowser and climbed out. Zac's four-wheel drive was parked across from her and she reminded herself that she was a professional, grown-up woman and not the blushing, giggling teenager that threatened to explode out of her as he walked from the service-station shop back towards his vehicle.

'I heard you've had a visitor.'

'My sister,' she confirmed, sending him a droll glance as she unhooked the nozzle and inserted it in the tank. Of course he'd heard. Everyone had heard.

'She didn't stay long?'

'Nope.'

'Is everything alright?'

'She just dropped by to reassure herself that I hadn't completely lost my mind.'

'Fair enough. So was she reassured?'

'Who knows, but she wouldn't have left if she had any major concerns, I guess.'

'So, are we still on for Saturday?'

Sophie busied herself with the nozzle of the bowser as an attack of nerves swarmed her. 'Sure.'

'Good,' he said and she felt him watching her keenly. 'I'm looking forward to it. There's a new little place in Glen Innes I thought we could try.'

'Sounds good. Yeah, I'm looking forward to it too,' she added, hoping he couldn't read the panic in her eyes.

'Soph,' he said, making her glance up hesitantly. 'We're taking it slowly, remember? There's no pressure. It's just dinner.'

'I know,' she said and managed a small smile. She wasn't sure why she was so nervous all of a sudden. Except maybe because she knew that spending an evening with this man would almost certainly turn into the night, and then what?

'It's a big step for me too,' he said quietly.

Sophie looked at him again, this time her gaze softening as she saw a shadow of uncertainty there and knew that he was battling some of the same demons she was. 'I know it is, and I'm looking forward to it,' she told him, and meant it. Despite the nerves, she was excited about going out for dinner on a real date. How long had it been since she'd done that? She pushed away the question, knowing that it would only bring up more anxious butterflies.

'Okay. I'll pick you up about five? Factoring in travel time.'

'Great.' She knew there was nothing to fear with Zac—except maybe him breaking her heart, but she didn't want to go with that train of thought yet. The bowser clicked off and Sophie quickly finished up and wiped her hands along the legs of her work trousers.

'See you then,' he said, turning to his vehicle and climbing inside with a lopsided grin.

∽

Sophie muttered under her breath as she threw the third change of outfit on the bed in disgust. This was beyond stupid. When had she last cared what she looked like? When had it mattered? A swift glance at her bedside clock sent a fresh wave of frustration through her. She had ten minutes before Zac pulled up outside. With a low growl, she snatched up the long skirt and peasant blouse she'd first tried on and grabbed her tan boots with the low heel. She twisted her hair into a messy bun at the back of her neck and secured it with enough bobby pins to sink a ship, but she wasn't sure if it looked as though she'd purposely gone for a messy look or just hadn't actually done her hair. As she stared at her reflection critically, she bit her lip and began to stress. Taking a quick selfie, something she rarely did, she sent the photo to Katie and typed in: *Tell me honestly, does this look okay?* She waited anxiously for a reply.

It came back disturbingly fast. *Bow chicka wow wow.*

Sophie still wasn't sure how Katie had managed to get their date tonight out of her, but in her usual annoyingly persistent yet somehow loveable way she'd extracted the details and had been sending completely unnecessary snippets of advice all day, like pack a clean pair of underwear

. . . just in case. Wear something that's easy to take off. Don't order anything with garlic. The texts went on, and Sophie had just about given herself a headache with the amount of eye rolling she'd been doing. She *did* pack spare clothes, but that was a completely valid precaution. They could break down between here and there and it was always good to be prepared for any emergency. Okay, so it was unlikely, but why take chances?

Not too much? she typed in.

He's going to have to be superhuman not to drag you into the nearest motel. I'll be surprised if you make it to dinner.

Sophie's hands clutched the phone tightly. *Oh dear God.* Her fingers flew across the keypad. *Does it look like I'm expecting sex?!!*

Relax, you look like you're expecting a date, possibly a make-out session, but definitely doesn't suggest that you're hanging out to get laid.

Sophie went to roll her eyes once again but stopped, giving a long-suffering sigh instead. There was nothing she could do about her decision now though, because outside she heard Zac pulling up.

Tossing her phone in her bag, she grabbed a coat and headed out to meet Zac at the front door, and gaped.

Dressed in taupe trousers and a dark blue button-up dress shirt, he'd not long been out of the shower if his newly cut, wet hair was any indication. The neatly trimmed sides and slightly longer top gave him a tougher, edgier look that did strange things to her insides.

'Wow!' He stared at her through the open door.

'It's too much, isn't it,' she said, feeling self-conscious as she went to turn away. 'I'll go get changed.'

'No!' he said, almost shouting and startling them both. 'No,' he said, lowering his voice. 'You look beautiful. I've never seen you in a skirt before.'

'Well, they're a bit of a pain in the back of an ambulance,' she told him drolly.

'Yeah.' He gave a half-hearted chuckle and rubbed the back of his neck with one palm. 'I guess it would be.'

'Should we get going?' she prompted when an awkward silence fell between them.

'Yes,' he said, dropping his hand and standing back to wait for her to lead the way. 'We have reservations.'

Sophie locked the door behind her and walked towards his four-wheel drive, which she noticed he'd recently washed. Oddly she felt a little bit better about her own nerves. His small attention to detail may not have been a big deal for most people, but considering she'd never seen it *not* covered in mud and dust it meant that he'd taken the time to wash his car especially for the occasion.

The car ride was initially a little awkward until he pressed the CD button on the dash and the soothing music of Ministry of Sound and their chilled-out sessions filtered through the cabin and gave them both breathing space from trying to come up with conversation to fill the void. 'This is rather ... surprising,' she said, searching for a word.

'Let me guess, you were expecting country music?' he said drily.

She gave a half-hearted smirk before looking out the window. 'It *is* pretty prevalent out here.'

'Yeah. It is. Which is why I occasionally like to take a break from it. This relaxes me.'

The silence fell once more as the music swirled around them, but Sophie found herself anything but relaxed, sitting so close to him and wondering what the hell they were going to talk about for an entire meal when they could barely make conversation for the ten minutes they'd been in the car.

Why was it so awkward? She was beginning to think she'd made a terrible mistake agreeing to this when Zac suddenly pulled the vehicle off to the side of the road.

'What's wrong?' Sophie asked, turning in her seat to glance over her shoulder and search for something amiss.

'Nothing,' he said, before undoing his seatbelt and leaning across to kiss her. Sophie was too surprised at first to respond, but within moments surrendered to the warm, coaxing mouth that was slowly teasing a response from her. When Zac pulled away slightly, she opened her eyes and blinked.

'That needed to be done.'

'It did?' she murmured.

'I don't know about you, but I was feeling like a fifteen-year-old on a first date.'

Sophie's lips twitched slightly at that. 'There was a slight degree of weirdness happening.'

'It *was* pretty weird,' he agreed.

'So you figured kissing me senseless would fix that?'

'Did it work?'

'Kinda,' she said. 'But maybe you should do it once more just to make sure.'

It seemed Zac didn't need to be asked twice, and it was some time before he reluctantly pulled away. 'I didn't plan a sophisticated evening only to end up making out on the side of the road,' he told her before he started driving once more, his gaze fixed firmly on the road ahead.

'You don't have to impress me.'

Zac sent her a brief look and grinned. 'Yes, I do. I want you to know there's more to me than dusty jeans and cow poo.'

'There is?' she asked innocently.

His grin turned into a narrow-eyed glare. '*This* is why we're not turning around.'

'Fine,' she said, giving a pout and looking back out the window. She glanced down as his warm hand covered hers on the edge of the seat, and felt herself relax as they continued the drive in a much more comfortable silence.

The restaurant was a pleasant surprise—a small house that had been lovingly restored and converted into a cosy, intimate dining experience. Soft candlelight filled the room with a warm glow and a fire crackled invitingly in the far corner.

Zac spoke to the hostess, an older woman who smiled warmly as she led them from the foyer into the main dining room and their table.

There were three other couples seated at tables scattered about the room and Sophie was relieved to discover she didn't recognise a single face.

'Wow, this is a bit fancy,' Sophie whispered as she reached for a glass of water from the table.

'A little swankier than the pub.'

'Just a tad.'

They spent a few minutes perusing the menu before placing their order and ordering their wine.

'Have you been here before?' Sophie asked.

'No, believe it or not, I'm more a counter lunch at the pub kinda guy, but I've heard good things about it.'

'Well, it's very nice. Thank you for bringing me.'

Zac held her gaze and the candlelight cocooned itself around them. The moment was broken only when their hostess appeared with a bottle of wine and poured them each a glass before leaving them alone once more.

'So, how was your sister's visit? You didn't really say much about it.'

Sophie gave a small offhand shrug. 'Mon was being Mon.'

'How so?'

'She's my big sister. She likes to have input into important decisions. She's a bit of a worrier.'

'What did she want input into?'

'It's been a run of things really,' Sophie said, taking a sip of wine. 'First it was coming out here, and then buying the property, and I guess the job offer thing was the last straw and she couldn't bite her tongue anymore.'

'What job offer thing?' he asked, going still as his eyebrows dipped slightly towards his nose.

Bugger. Sophie suddenly remembered she hadn't got around to telling him about that. 'My old boss called the other day to tell me there was an SOT position available if I wanted to apply.'

'What is that?'

'A special operations team. It's kind of the elite of paramedics.'

'Is that something you were thinking about?'

'It used to be. Once.' She dropped her gaze to the glass and traced the rim with her finger. 'I always wanted to prove something. I'm not sure why or even who to, really. Just always wanted the opportunity to try.'

'So it's a big deal?'

She looked up at that and saw the carefully neutral expression on his face. 'Kind of. It doesn't come up very often.'

'Are you going to apply?'

'I don't know . . . I'm not as sure about it as I used to be.'

'Why?'

'Things have changed, I guess,' she hedged, but seeing that he wasn't about to let the topic drop, she let her gaze wander around the room as she answered. Something about his steady, searching gaze made her feel as though he were trying to peel back the layers and reach inside. 'I didn't expect to love it out here so much. I didn't expect to feel needed again or accepted into a community. I wasn't planning on staying here too long, but then I bought my place and, I don't know, everything just seems right. I don't feel like the same person who needed to prove herself by beating a bunch of alpha males to be in the team.'

'But you could have?'

'Who knows? Maybe,' she smiled a little. 'I don't know, it all seemed so important before. The things I thought I wanted just didn't seem to be the same after Garth died.' She absently toyed with the cutlery in front of her. 'He always wanted kids but I kept putting it off. I didn't want to put my career on hold, or rearrange things. I know that sounds selfish,' she said, lowering her eyes to the tabletop, 'but I just wasn't ready for that and then later, after his accident, all I could think of was how disappointed he must have been.'

'I don't think that's true. I didn't know your husband, Sophie, but I know you. And there's no way any man could be disappointed in a woman who cares so deeply for other people.'

Sophie felt her throat tighten as emotion swelled inside her. 'I don't know why I suddenly want to settle down, here and now. I don't know why I didn't feel that way while I was married. Garth would have loved it out here, living this kind of life . . . Monique thinks that maybe I'm trying to compensate for everything I didn't want back then. That I'm living here out of guilt or something.'

'Are you?' he asked, reaching for his glass and taking a sip.

'I don't think so,' she said after a while. 'But I can't explain it either. I think that's what frustrates my sister the most: she doesn't believe in gut instinct. She believes in facts and figures and smart decisions based on research and graphs. Me telling her that it just *feels* right drives her nuts. And I can't really blame her. It *is* out of character for me. Even I can't explain it.'

'Maybe you don't need to,' he suggested. 'Maybe you just trust in that feeling. It's been right so far, hasn't it?'

Sophie raised her shoulders and nodded. It *had* been right. Maybe she needed to stop over-thinking everything and just enjoy life while it was good. God knows she'd been through enough of the bad side of life lately, so why not just accept that everything was great and go with it? She was out for dinner in a nice restaurant with a man she was attracted to. She needed to stop analysing everything and just . . . be.

Thirty

Over their meal, Sophie had managed to unwind. The nerves of earlier had finally gone as they'd laughed and chatted through dinner. Zac told her stories about his early uni days and outrageous encounters he'd had over the years with pets and their owners. Apparently an accidental poisoning of a cat and a shot horse were the least of his weird dealings.

As the evening drew to a close, Sophie realised she was disappointed that it was coming to an end. She'd offered to split the bill but was given a firm, 'I got it,' as a reply. She wouldn't have minded paying for half of the meal, but it was nice to see he was a traditional kind of guy. Sophie waited while Zac paid for the meal and they walked back to his car, the town now quieter than it had been earlier. There was a decided chill in the air with winter fast approaching.

Zac unlocked the car and started the engine to get the heater working. Sophie noticed that he seemed a little less relaxed than he had been back in the restaurant as he made himself overly busy turning the knobs and adjusting the temperature of the heater.

'Thank you for tonight,' she said, relieved that the warm air was finally beginning to defrost her hands.

'You're welcome.'

The lights of the town flashed past as Zac drove through the streets and headed back onto the main road back to Hilsons Ridge. After a huge meal and a glass of wine, Sophie was feeling contented. She gazed out at the darkness and listened to the gentle hum of the engine. It was a pity they couldn't have stayed the night as it seemed such a long way to travel just for dinner, but Zac didn't seem to mind. 'It's a small price to pay for living where we do,' he told her when she broke the quiet mood to ask him about it.

They filled the trip home with more stories from their pasts, and chatted about their families. All too soon they were turning into her driveway.

Zac pulled up outside the house and turned slightly to face her. 'Well, I guess—'

'Would you like to—'

They both gave an awkward chuckle as they spoke over each other.

'Would you like to come in for a coffee?'

'Yeah, I would,' he said, turning off the engine and opening the door.

Sophie smiled to herself; she hadn't needed to twist his arm very hard. Unlocking the front door, she dropped her bag on the foyer table and turned on a light before making her way to the kitchen.

Zac pulled out a chair at her small kitchen table and picked up the diary that lay on top. 'What's this?'

'That's Clarrie's diary.'

'Who's Clarrie?'

'Clarrie Gilbert. He used to live here before Archie. I found some old stuff out in the shed and I've been reading it.'

'Oh, right. The guy you were talking about with Bill. Wow, this is old,' he said, gingerly turning the pages.

As she prepared the coffee, Sophie filled him in on everything she knew about the Gilberts and Clarrie's war, and was surprised when they'd finished their coffee. 'Sorry, I didn't mean to go on about it that long. You must be bored out of your brain.'

'Hardly. It's amazing to think you've got all this history right here on your kitchen table.'

'The fact it lasted in a box out in the shed and who knows where else for almost a hundred years doesn't make me worry any less about taking care of it. I usually keep it in a sealed container. I need to talk to a professional about how to store it properly.'

She took the diary and placed it back in its container, moving towards the kitchen bench when she finished. 'Do you want another cuppa? Or a tea or something? I think I have wine in the fridge.'

Zac had got up from his seat and was standing behind her when she turned around to wait for his reply. 'Actually, there *is* something I've kinda felt like all night,' he said, and lowered his head.

Oh yeah, she thought dreamily, this was so much better than wine—if not just as inebriating. His warm lips coaxed and toyed with her own, and a growing frustration gnawed at her insides as they moved against each other, the friction and heat building between them and making her impatient to feel more.

With only a low growl from his throat as warning, Sophie found herself lifted and deposited on top of the kitchen table. She had a brief moment to thank her lucky stars that she'd moved the hundred-year-old irreplaceable artefact beforehand, and then she had no time to think of anything else.

She briefly wondered if it was acceptable to have a sex bucket list and, if so, she was pretty sure this was going to be one she could cross off rather smugly. On the kitchen table—check.

Later that night she could also tick off in the bathtub as well. At the rate things were going, she was a little worried her bucket list would be complete within a few weeks.

༄

The mornings were very crisp, and Sophie was wondering why she hadn't just stayed in bed a bit longer, particularly since there was a very large, very sexy male still in there keeping it warm.

Cobber snorted and gave a low whinny as he saw her approach, and she sent him a rueful smile. 'You are so lucky that I love you.' She mixed his feed and put out his bucket, deciding to give him a quick brush while he ate since she was up and out of bed anyway.

He'd come a long way since that morning when he'd showed up, scared and bleeding on her doorstep.

Alison and her daughter Tiah had been coming out three times a week to work with him, leaving Sophie to continue in their absence, and the difference in the big stallion was remarkable. Alison's initial observation that he wasn't as inexperienced around humans as she'd suspected, despite the recent treatment and care he'd received here, made her wonder if Archie had maybe had more contact with him than anyone had suspected. This made sense as he'd grown up with horses in his blood and wouldn't abandon a wounded animal. Maybe he'd found where Cobber had entered the property and fixed it, keeping the horse on the property for its own good? With no other horses around to chase him out of the area, he'd have his own territory to live in, uncontested by younger horses and yet still free to roam the vast acres of bushland without danger.

The first week of training had been spent gaining the horse's trust, gently patting him and then rubbing him over with rope, getting him used to having a halter on and to eventually being led around. It was a far cry from images she had of what horse breaking was going to entail. There was no rearing or kicking and squealing; everything was amazingly peaceful and calm.

'It's not necessary to train a horse by breaking its spirit,' Alison told her. 'That used to be how it was done, but a horse will respond so much better with a calm approach, and by gaining trust. It's a little slower but, in the long run, it makes for a better, safer horse if its trust issues are handled early on in training. We have to address its fears and show it that there's no reason to worry. There's nothing more satisfying then that moment a horse allows you to touch it without flinching for the very first time.'

The past few weeks they'd been able to get him to accept putting a halter on and off. Seeing as they'd only got the halter on the first time when he'd been sedated, it was important they start from scratch, as they worked on desensitising him to noise and movement. The next stage would be leading in order to venture out of the yards. Already he was like a new horse. He came to greet her now, and there was no more flinching and pulling away. There was a calmness to him now and Sophie was in awe of the whole process.

'Hard to believe this is the same horse.'

Sophie turned to discover Zac watching her, one dusty booted foot resting on the bottom rail, hands in his pockets. Sophie needed a moment to get the heavy thudding of her heart under control as flashes of the night before raced through her mind. 'Morning,' she said, briefly holding his gaze before hers skittered away.

'You're doing a great job with him,' he said, taking his hands from his pockets and draping them over the top rail.

'Thanks. Alison and Tiah have done most of the work; I just keep him practising.' She unclasped the lead rope from his halter and walked across to the gate, hanging it on the rail. 'You could have stayed in bed. I had to feed Cobber.'

'It was no fun in there alone.' His deep voice dropped a notch, sending a giddy flutter through her and bringing a shy smile to her lips. She busied herself with closing the gate behind her before risking a look at him.

God, he was gorgeous.

He snaked his arms around her waist and pulled her close to nuzzle her ear. 'You smell like horse,' he murmured, and immediately all awkward shyness vanished.

'And that's a problem how?' she asked, tilting her head to give him better access, despite the chill in the air. Horse was one of the best smells in the entire world.

'No problem. I think you smell great no matter what.'

'Good answer. I'm starving. What are you cooking me for breakfast?'

'Me? But I'm the guest.'

'No freeloaders around this place,' she told him briskly.

'What about him?' Zac nodded towards Cobber with his head buried in a bucket of food.

Sophie gasped. 'He's my horse. He doesn't *have* to do anything.'

'Typical,' Zac muttered. 'Alright, fine, lead the way to the kitchen and I'll see what I can do. Freeloader,' he muttered under his breath at Cobber as they left.

'I heard that,' she said in a singsong voice as they walked up the steps of the house.

'I know,' Zac replied in the same tone. 'Upstaged by a horse.'

'Don't be jealous. I'll keep you around for your other talents.'

'Oh yeah? Like what?' his mood lifted slightly.

'Like how well you cook breakfast,' she grinned, slapping him on the backside as he ambled past inside.

Thirty-one

Sophie re-read the same paragraph for the third time in ten minutes and gave up with an impatient huff. All morning she'd been distracted. The weekend had been nothing short of amazing. She knew this thing with Zac had the potential to develop into something serious—he was funny and thoughtful, and they were great together in every way. He was different to Garth, not just in looks and personality, and yet she felt that same kind of connection, which was both confusing and comforting. After shutting herself off from human contact for so long, it was nice to be held again, and wanted. She felt herself warming from the inside out once more.

And yet, that damn offer to apply for the SOT position still niggled at her. There was an email from Darrell waiting for her when she got into the office. She remembered how badly she'd wanted it—how she'd waited so damn patiently for the opportunity to apply in the past and now here it was being offered to her. It was hard to say a flat out no, even though the thought of leaving here in order to do it wasn't something she really wanted.

The phone on her desk rang and Sophie groaned silently when she saw the name come up on the screen. The guy must have ESP or something.

'Hi, Darrell.' She put the call on loudspeaker so she could continue typing up the reports that needed finishing.

'So have you given it any more thought?'

'The SOT job?'

'Of course the SOT job!'

'I haven't really been able to think of anything else,' she admitted. 'It's a big decision.'

'I honestly didn't think it would take you this long to decide. This is what you've wanted for the whole time I've known you.'

'Yeah, I know,' Sophie sighed, closing her eyes as she tipped her head back against the headrest of the chair. 'But that was before . . . everything.'

'I know I don't have to tell you that it won't be an offer left on the table for too long.'

'I know.' She did know. And she knew that if she turned it down, she wouldn't be getting another shot at it any time soon.

'What's the problem?'

'I'm just not sure I'd be able to jump straight back into the craziness again.'

'Maybe you need to try it and see. I didn't suggest sending you up there with the intention that you stayed there for the rest of your career. I figured it would be until you got back on your feet again, or Hilsons Ridge found themselves another candidate.'

'I wasn't planning on staying here either—it just happened.'

'I think you're always going to regret it if you don't take this opportunity, Soph,' he said quietly.

'I don't know, Darrell. What if I fall apart again? What if I'm just not cut out to work in that kind of environment?' Flashbacks of her reaction to the domestic situation a few months earlier crossed her mind. She knew in this line of work there was always going to be a high probability that she'd be called out again but, in the city, the frequency of them would be considerably higher with a bigger population. What if she froze up and couldn't do her job?

'Maybe that's something you need to face in order to move on.'

'Can I think it over tonight and let you know tomorrow?'

The silence on the other end of the line spoke clearer than words. She knew what Darrell was thinking—the old Sophie wouldn't need to think about it. But she hadn't been the old Sophie for a long time now. She wasn't exactly sure who this new Sophie was either, but they were two very different people.

'Sure, Soph. Give me a call tomorrow,' he said before saying goodbye.

Sophie disconnected the call and bit her lip, deep in thought. She jumped a little when Zac moved from his position in the doorway, where he'd been standing unnoticed until now.

'You're still considering the job offer?'

Sophie couldn't read his expression, but his tone may have held a slight edge that wasn't normally there. 'I don't know. I didn't think I was, but now . . . I don't *know*.' She picked up a pen on the table before tossing it back down again and glancing up at him. 'I just . . . It's a big deal, Zac. If I let this go, I'm worried I might always wonder what if . . . you know?' She searched his eyes hopefully, but she couldn't read what he was thinking from the carefully guarded look he was holding hers with.

'So you're going to take it?'

'I didn't say that,' she shook her head.

'But you haven't told them no, either?' he prodded.

'I haven't told them anything, yet. I'm just trying to sort it out in my head first.'

'I was under the impression you were happy here.'

'I am.' His pushing on the topic was starting to irritate her. 'But I don't think you appreciate what a huge thing this is. I've wanted this since the very first day on the job. This has been my goal—the thing I'd been waiting for . . . the thing I put off having kids for.'

'Sounds to me like you've made up your mind.'

'Well, I haven't,' she snapped, and regretted it. She didn't know why she was so defensive about it.

'I guess, after the weekend, I was under the impression you were thinking about something serious.'

A flood of emotions washed over her at that. She had been thinking long-term thoughts—she could easily picture her and Zac sitting on the verandah watching the sun go down together. When he was near her, it all made perfect sense—it all seemed so doable. It was only when she was alone that her doubts would try to resurface and the under-mining would start. What if she *was* hiding here? What if she *was* using this place as a crutch? What if she *had* given up? She hated thinking that somehow the whole hostage ordeal had stolen away her drive and ambition.

How could she explain it all to him when she could barely explain it to herself?

'I only said I was thinking about it. I haven't given them my answer yet,' she sighed.

He tilted his head slightly and gave a brief nod before turning away. 'Fair enough. When you know, let *me* know, okay?'

'Zac!' She gave an irritated huff when he didn't turn back and disappeared out of the office. She supposed he had a right to be peeved, but she hadn't told him she'd said no to the job on their date. He'd just assumed that since things had gone so well she'd changed her mind. Maybe, to some degree, that's what had happened . . . maybe she *had* made up her mind at some point over the weekend, but it still didn't guarantee that she'd never look back one day and regret turning the offer down.

His attitude suddenly highlighted one of those fundamental differences she'd noted earlier. Garth had always stood by her decisions, never trying to influence her one way or the other, just as she'd always stood by him. Their career was important to both of them. They were equal when it came to making their own job decisions. Zac, on the other hand, seemed to think that she could turn down something like this and be content with what she had. Was it a sign of things to come if they went into a serious relationship? Would he assume that she'd just back down and be the one to make the sacrifice because she was the woman? Would he be willing to do the same if she needed him to? Not many men would. She'd seen it happen before; the man considered himself the breadwinner and the woman was simply the extra income, until she could be spared to give up work to have children, and then try to pick up her career after years out of the workforce.

Sophie stood up and crossed to the window of the station. Maybe she should think about taking a trip back to Sydney, just to see if that helped put things back into perspective. A sick, hollow feeling settled back inside her at the thought.

Resting her head against the windowpane she smothered a groan. Why did everything always have to be so complicated?

⨏

Sophie pulled on the handbrake of her car and let out a long, weary sigh. When had the traffic become so bad? She opened her door and the high-pitched squeal of tyres on smooth concrete somewhere in a higher level of the car park grated on her nerves.

Outside she could hear horns beeping and buses roaring between stops as people rushed from one place to another, heads down, eyes glued to their phones or fixed on a destination somewhere in the distance.

Had it always been this noisy? she wondered as she locked her car and headed for the exit. Sophie passed a few people she recognised and waved, knowing that the gossip mill in the station would work just as fast as the one back in Hilsons Ridge, and in no time everyone would know she was back.

Sophie paused as she heard her name and turned, a smile coming to her lips as she recognised the blond-headed beanpole who was loping over.

'Hey, stranger!' Mac said, coming to a stop before her.

Sophie waited for a flash of memory or the horrible, empty feeling she'd carried around with her after the siege to reappear, but there was nothing. Her smile broadened and relief filled her. 'Hi, Mac. It's good to see you.' And it was. After the incident, Mac had taken it hard. He'd blamed himself for not preventing her going inside the house that day, despite the fact Sophie had told him there was no way he'd have been able to stop her. She took full responsibility for her actions, but looking back she knew that she'd put him in a horrible situation and she felt bad about that. If she'd died that day, he would have been left to carry around the guilt.

'Are you back now? For good?'

'Just for the day. I came down to talk over something with Darrell.'

'It's different around here without you. They gave me a rookie to train,' he said with an exaggerated groan.

'I hope you're teaching them everything by the book?' She raised an eyebrow doubtfully.

'Of course,' he said, placing a hand across his heart as though her words had wounded him. 'Well, mostly,' he amended.

'They couldn't have a better teacher.' She reached out and put her hand on his arm. She did miss this old camaraderie. These people shared a history with her. They'd known Garth, most had been at their wedding, many had been regular visitors to their home.

An alarm sounded and Mac gave her hand a squeeze. 'I gotta go. Take care of yourself, Soph.'

She watched him race back down the hallway, off on a call-out, ready to save a life somewhere. And that was that. Life continued. Everyone moved on.

She knocked on Darrell's door after saying a brief hello to the receptionist and waited for the gruff 'Enter' before she opened the door.

She didn't speak as Darrell continued to scribble down notes without looking up to acknowledge his visitor, finally muttering a bored 'Yes?' and glancing up. She grinned at the irritated frown he wore.

'Jeez, you're still a grumpy old bastard, aren't you?'

'What are you doin' back here?' His expression barely changed but she knew she'd managed to surprise him.

'Just thought I needed to check up on you lot.'

Darrell leaned back and the chair creaked in protest as he studied her thoughtfully. 'So you made up your mind yet?'

'You know, I think I have,' she said, sounding a little surprised herself at the ease with which the answer came to her.

Thirty-two

Sophie sat curled up on her lounge looking out the window at the rain falling in a constant drizzle outside. A cold front had blown in over the past few days and she'd had to dig out extra layers of clothing. The mountains were a lot cooler than Sydney. Further up the range it had even snowed. Today she was on call, but so far it had been quiet. She'd been expecting it to be busy, but was glad she'd been wrong, at least so far, because she only had John as backup. Everyone else was either out of town or stuck at home with sick children.

Ever since her return from Sydney, she'd felt at peace with her decision. As soon as she pulled into her driveway a sensation had filled her, warming her from the inside out, and she knew she'd made the right choice. This was her home now. This is where she belonged. Surprisingly, Darrell hadn't tried to talk her out of it. Maybe he could see that she'd changed. The uncertainty—the what-ifs—had all but vanished after her visit back to the city.

Her life goals had changed. She still loved her job, but now she knew that she loved it in a different context. She didn't need to prove herself to anyone anymore, and that included Zac. She wanted to tell him that she'd made up her mind, but part of her was still a little bit annoyed with his attitude. But she got why he was upset: he'd assumed she'd been just as happy as he was about the weekend they'd just spent together, only to walk in on a conversation about the possibility of her taking a job somewhere else. She knew he deserved to hear that she'd turned down the offer, but she wasn't quite sure how to broach it. She figured she'd have to sooner or later, but right now, later sounded good.

The rain dripped off the edges of the gutter out over the verandah and the steady, gentle patter on the tin roof above made her wish that she could be snuggled up in her PJs in front of a fire with a good book. Instead of dressed and waiting around for the first of the standard calls that rainy weather always brought with it. Slippery roads and dingles were the usual. A few minutes later when a call came in, she knew she should have stopped thinking how lucky she was that it was so quiet.

Sophie pulled the ambulance up in the car park of the national park where she'd arranged to meet John to save time, and waited until he got in.

'What have we got?' John asked, shaking the rain off his sleeve after he shut the door.

'Hiker called it in. Came across a man in his early twenties who looks like he's taken a fall, down near the camping ground. Unresponsive, but breathing. I've already called the chopper and the police will meet us out there to help sort out a landing zone.' They couldn't take any chances with a fall and possible spinal injuries. 'We should be able to drive down to the campsite, I take it?'

'Yeah, it's gravel road all the way down there,' he confirmed as Sophie headed down the track that was signed as leading to the camping area. 'Who the hell goes out hiking in this weather?' he muttered, ducking his head to look up at the sky through the windscreen. 'Forecast said storms are predicted this afternoon and it's starting to look pretty nasty.'

'The sooner we get this guy out of there the better then,' Sophie agreed. They parked near a small, soggy-looking camping area a few kilometres down the road. Sophie pulled on her heavy jacket before closing the door behind her and helping John grab the gear from the back of the ambulance.

Down close to the river, a woman standing next to a crude structure of a tarpaulin draped across two branches waved them over.

They carefully negotiated the rocky shoreline that led to the now rushing river. Usually these rivers were pretty tranquil, making a happy gurgle as the water meandered its way downstream, but after all the rain they'd been having, the quaint trout steam had grown into an angry whitewater rapid.

'Hi. You called it in?' Sophie asked, raising her voice above the rain.

'Yeah. I came out to get some photos and I spotted him down here. He's only just started to come to. I've tried not to move him. He was complaining about a sore neck.'

'You did a great job.'

The woman shook her head. 'I don't know how long he was lying out here for. There's no one else around; I was getting a bit creeped out actually.'

John reached the man and immediately began to reassure him. 'It's okay, mate. We're going to help you. Just stay nice and still. Can you tell us your name?' John asked as Sophie quickly pulled the neck collar from the kit.

'Ian,' the young man said as he looked up at them with frightened eyes. 'My neck really hurts.'

'Ian, my name's Sophie. I know you're scared, but you need to stay calm right now and lay still. We're going to get a brace on you, just as a precaution, okay?' Although not completely reassured by her words, he did seem a little less agitated.

John and Sophie carefully manoeuvred the brace into position, immobilising the neck to avoid any further injury, while reassuring Ian he was doing great as they worked.

'Do you remember what happened?' John asked.

'I was walking and I slipped, I think. I'm not sure,' he said uncertainly. 'Do you think I've broken my neck? Am I going to be paralysed?' There was a growing note of panic in the man's voice.

'Ian, you need to calm down. We're going to get you to hospital, and they'll be able to see what's going on.'

The rain began to get heavier and all three of them ducked their heads instinctively, huddling further into their jackets. A rumble of foreboding thunder shook the air around them.

'Look, you can get out of this rain if you want, we can take it from here,' Sophie called to the woman over the growing noise of the river and rain.

'Okay, thanks,' she yelled back, clearly not needing to be told twice.

'I don't like the look of that river,' John said, casting a wary glance over his shoulder. 'It's rising really quickly. Flash flooding is a real issue with rain like this and these creeks have a nasty habit of catching people unawares.'

A loud crack of lightning split the sky followed by a loud explosion and boom as it hit a tree nearby. Sophie's heart felt as though it had just been pulled from her chest. She hadn't even had time to scream before another loud crack sounded and she looked up in time to see an enormous tree falling towards her.

There was a moment of shocked horror before she was thrown backwards, John's voice yelling over the top of the blood rushing through her ears, then she felt the water—icy fingers pricking her skin and her face as she went under. The muted sounds of water pushing through the narrow stream surrounded her. It was too murky to see anything, but a few moments later she was thrust upwards and the roar of the river almost deafened her as her head broke the surface and she gasped, air piercing her lungs like sharp needles as she struggled in her thick jacket to keep her head above water.

In the distance she thought she heard her name being called, but she couldn't be sure as the river tried to drag her under once more and she had to use all her strength to fight it. The sides of the bank were flashing past at an alarming rate, and she gasped as her body came into contact with rocks and branches as she was carried relentlessly forward. She needed to grab hold of something—anything. Sophie felt the strength seeping from her body as her fingers went numb. She had to get rid of her jacket, but the water tossed her about violently as she tried to make her freezing fingers work. As she went under again, she managed to get one arm free of the jacket before bursting back to the surface and gulping a breath of air. She twisted and turned, fighting with the sodden fabric that clung to her body and refused to let go, until using her last ounce of energy she finally managed to untangle herself from its clutches, floating backwards as the current swirled her about ruthlessly. She couldn't feel her legs and could barely even lift her arms. Cold crept into her body, and she struggled to keep her head out of the water, then her leg caught on something sharp and she was being pulled down below the water once more and this time she didn't have the strength to fight it.

It was quieter down here. Almost soothing. Sophie could see sticks and rocks on the bottom of the riverbed, the brown water so different to its usual crystal clearness. Moss-covered trees, fallen and buried in their watery graves from previous floods, lined the edges of the river and she wondered if they'd find her body one day wedged underneath one of them. She'd never see Zac again. The thought cut through the fog-like sensation in her brain. She didn't want to die. A movement caught her eye, something white, and she turned her head slightly. A white gown floated like a sail billowing in the water around the shape of a woman with long blonde hair. She held her hands out and Sophie instinctively reached for them, feeling herself floating towards the woman with the saddest blue eyes she'd ever seen.

She wasn't frightened; there was something about this woman that comforted her. The woman gave a small smile, but it didn't quite reach her eyes, there was a despair too deep to hide there, but her smile was gentle and Sophie knew she meant no harm. As her fingers touched the fabric, Sophie felt a wash of pain and longing so strong go through her that she gasped and everything around her suddenly faded and she fell into lonely, gaping darkness.

Sophie went to moan but it hurt too much and she was confused for a moment as to why. Slowly she opened her eyes, lifting a hand to cover them protectively when even that movement hurt. Her surroundings began to filter through and the sounds of rushing water soon brought everything flooding back. She was cold, colder than she could ever recall being in her entire life.

Where was she? It was dark and wet—everything was wet. Beneath her she felt the squishy sensation of mud and earth and was momentarily relieved she was at least somehow on solid ground and not at the bottom of the river. She tried to move her toes and then her legs, and gradually worked her way up her body until she was satisfied she hadn't broken anything, but she ached all over—a bone-numbing, cold ache that made her want to go to sleep and escape the pain, but she couldn't do that. She needed to stay awake and find help.

Sophie carefully pushed with her hands and eased herself up into a sitting position. A stabbing, throbbing pain made her glance down at her leg to find a nasty gash, and she clenched her teeth together tightly as she tried to pull herself upright, using the trunk of a nearby tree to support her without placing any weight on her injured leg. It was still raining and fat drops splashed her as they fell from the branches of the tree above. Just below her the river still raced downwards and onwards to its ultimate destination, taking everything in its path. She had no idea how she got washed up on the bank where she now stood, and she didn't really care at this point. All she knew was that she needed help before hyperthermia set in, and seeing as it was now dark, it was looking pretty doubtful that she was going to find it standing here.

She took a tentative step and gasped as pain shot through her leg, making her stop and lean back against the tree trunk. Her teeth chattered uncontrollably and it took a considerable amount of energy to lift her hand and wipe the rain from her face as she searched her surroundings. How far downstream had she been washed? She couldn't work it out from memory—it could be only a few hundred metres or a few kilometres. The river was certainly flowing fast enough for it to be a considerable distance. If she followed it upstream, surely she'd eventually run into someone out looking for her. She had no idea how much time had passed, but as she took in the harsh terrain around her she knew that access and nightfall were going to make it difficult for a search party to move very quickly. As she reassessed her options, Sophie soon realised that with her leg out of action and the steep inclines along the river edge where she'd been washed up, there was no way she was going to be able to walk out by herself. She was going to have to wait for a rescue party to find her. Not far from the edge of the water she noticed a cluster of rocks with one that slightly protruded, offering a fraction of protection from the rain. She searched for a long stick to use as a crutch and then tore the bottom of her shirt, which was relatively easy considering it already looked as though Jack the Ripper had gone through it, securing the long piece of fabric to a branch that overhung the river in case someone came along and didn't see her near the rocks. Sophie hobbled across to her flimsy shelter and saw that although the ground was wet, it was somewhat protected. She collapsed in an exhausted heap, doing her best to huddle out of the rain.

Sophie groaned as she moved, unsure what had woken her. She didn't remember falling asleep and on some level she knew that was really bad, but she was too tired to think why. Then she heard something: a noise above the ever-persistent roar of water nearby.

'Sophie!'

Her eyes opened and she rolled her head to look out through the darkness. Maybe it was her mind playing tricks on her. A tiny glimmer of hope began to flare to life inside her. *Please let it be real,* she thought, her eyes searching the shadows. Then something moved and she focused in on it, as gradually little beams of light began bobbing about on the opposite side of the river.

'Help,' she tried calling, but it barely came out as a whisper and panic surged through her—if they didn't see her, she wasn't going to make it through to morning. 'Help!' she tried again and the sound almost slit her aching head in two. Her gaze clung to the light that started growing larger. 'Help!' she called again.

For a moment the lights seemed to be moving away, but then she realised they were negotiating the steep banks and she heard a loud shout and more people talking in excited babble. There was a long wait before she saw someone approaching, and guessed they must have found a safer place to cross further upstream. They reached for the strip of shirt on the branch but hadn't seen her yet. 'Help!' she called, praying they'd hear her over the sound of a crackling two-way radio and the river. 'I'm here!'

'Sophie!'

Her heart jumped at the familiar voice and she knew if she could have summoned the energy she would have bawled like a baby in relief as Zac's face appeared before her.

'Are you alright?' he asked, his eyes, frowning and full of concern, searching her face and then what he could see of her body in torchlight.

'My leg,' she murmured.

Zac pulled out his radio and spoke into it before cupping her face in his large hands. 'Thank God, Sophie. I thought we'd lost you.'

'I'm okay.'

'You will be. We're going to get you to hospital.'

Sophie felt her eyes fluttering closed—she was safe. She didn't even feel the cold so much now and her fingers and toes had stopped hurting a long time ago. She just wanted to go to sleep.

'Sophie!'

Her eyes sprang open at Zac yelling at her and she tried to remember what was happening.

'Stay awake, okay? Help's coming.'

She tried to talk but she couldn't, everything hurt, but Zac refused to let her sleep. She heard him yelling to other people, and she felt him gather her close to him, the warmth of his body seeping into hers. It felt so nice to be a little bit warm again but it wasn't enough, she was still so cold.

Something warm covered her and then she was being lifted, and beneath her the ground moved as though she were floating along above it. The warmth and rocking movement soon lulled her to sleep and she knew it was okay. Zac was here and he would take care of her.

Thirty-three

'For the last time, Sophie, we've got it under control!'

Sophie rolled her eyes and crossed her arms as she glared at Katie. She'd been in hospital twenty-four hours now and was more than ready to go home.

'We managed to run the station without you for three months, I'm fairly sure we can do it for another few days.'

'I'm not worried about that. I just want to get out of here. I'm perfectly able to go back to work.'

'Have you *looked* at your leg, Frankenstein's Bride?' Katie asked with a sassy kink to her eyebrow as she stood at the end of Sophie's bed.

She *had* seen her leg—there was a long row of perfectly formed stitches that had closed the gash on her leg—but she could still work. She could at least take calls.

'You need to stay off it for a few days.'

'Fine! Then just get me out of here at least.'

'I'll do what I can but you'll have to take it up with Ado when he comes around,' she shrugged.

'Did I hear my name?' Ado asked as he entered the room, looking as brisk and businesslike as usual.

'Thank goodness, she's all yours, doc. I'm outta here,' Katie sighed gratefully as she waved and left the room quickly.

'It's usually not a good sign when your staff are so eager to get away from you,' he said with a small smile.

'They're too bossy for their own good,' she muttered.

'They were very worried about you, as were a lot of people,' he said and pulled a chair closer to her bedside.

John had been beside himself when he came in earlier, and that was saying a lot considering she'd never seen the man unsettled by anything in the entire time she'd known him. Thankfully, Ian, the camper, only had a stable fracture of his T1 vertebrae, which accounted for the severe pain in his neck, but there was no paralysis. Poor John had been left with a patient and a missing partner, and she felt bad that he'd been placed in such a horrible predicament.

'You were extremely lucky, Sophie,' Ado said.

'I know,' Sophie said, tipping her head back against the pillow behind her, 'and I'm grateful to everyone who helped find me.' Everything that had happened between Zac finding her and the rest of that night was a blur of images she faded in and out of. She vaguely recalled opening her eyes to see Zac's face beside her, but the next morning when she'd awoken he wasn't there, and she hadn't seen him since. 'I didn't get a chance to thank everyone.'

'Zac was here until I sent him home,' he said, and Sophie's surprise must have shown on her face. 'He refused to leave your side, despite the fact he'd been out searching for hours before he found you. I had to send him home before he ended up in hospital too.'

'Is he okay? He hasn't been back.'

'I think Zac was a little shaken by the whole experience. Maybe he needs some time to come to terms with things.'

'What things? I don't understand.'

'Sometimes certain situations bring back painful memories. I think hospital rooms remind Zac of some very dark times.'

'His wife?' Sophie asked quietly.

Ado gave a sad smile and pushed up out of the chair slowly. 'I will arrange for you to be discharged, but I want to see you again in a few days' time,' he said before leaving the room.

Zac had been sitting right there beside her bed through that first night when she'd been brought in. Had he been reliving memories of watching his wife in a hospital bed like this as she died? She felt terrible putting him in that position, especially since he'd been the one who had basically saved her life.

⁂

'Okay, you're all set. Do you need anything else before I leave?' Margaret asked, adjusting the pillows she'd just placed behind Sophie's head like a doting mother hen. It was good to be home.

'Thank you, Margaret. I'm fine, really,' Sophie insisted, although she had to admit it felt kind of nice to have someone fussing over her a little bit. She really missed her mum.

Margaret and Garry had come in to take her home from the hospital after Ado gave her the all clear, despite her protesting that she could get herself home.

'Are you sure you don't want me to give your family a call?'

Sophie knew her parents wouldn't be happy if they found out she'd been in hospital without telling them, but she really couldn't bear to put them through that again. She was fine now and there was no need to make everyone panic over something that was over and done with. 'No, thanks, Margaret. By the time they got here I'd be ready to get back to work again. I'm fine.'

'Well, you call me if you need anything, alright?' she said firmly, making Sophie look at her.

'I will. Thank you for all your help.'

'We're family around here,' she shrugged lightly. 'That's what family do—they look out for each other.'

Sophie swallowed a lump in her throat at the kind words and managed a smile as Margaret and Garry left.

Later that afternoon Sophie heard a car pull up and Julie Spicer knocked on the door calling a cheerful 'Cooee' as Sophie called out to come in.

'I just thought I'd drop by with some things to help you pass the time while you rested up.'

'Would you like a cuppa?' Sophie asked, making to rise.

'I'll get it. You stay put,' Julie ordered, already on her feet and heading to the kitchen before Sophie could protest.

'I just love what you've done with this place,' she said as she carried the two cups out and handed Sophie hers. 'It feels like a home again.'

Sophie smiled at that—it did feel like home.

'Oh, I almost forgot,' Julie said, reaching for a plastic bag near her chair. 'I thought you might be interested in these.' She pulled out a large photo album. 'I was looking for something the other day and came across these old photos of the Spicers and thought you might like to see the one of Danny and Edith.'

Sophie reached out and took the album that Julie had opened to a page in the beginning of faded black and white portrait images. They were very old, the clothing was a giveaway of the time frame, somewhere in the late 1800s, Sophie guessed. The Spicers had very distinctive looks, and Len and Horrie could have never been mistaken for anyone other than a Spicer.

'This was the one,' she pointed over the top of the album at a photo. 'That's Danny, Edith and little Lottie.'

Sophie studied the photo. Danny Spicer looked very much like the Spicers of today with his long nose and dark hair. Her eyes moved to the little girl dressed in a white pinafore dress with black stockings, her long fair curls hanging around the chubby, cherubic face of a maybe three- or four-year-old child. When she moved to the woman in the photo she felt her hands go clammy and she had to blink away a curtain of tiny black dots that dropped in front of her vision.

'Sophie? Are you alright? You've gone as white as a sheet.'

Sophie couldn't drag her eyes from the woman in the photo. A strange sense of déjà vu washed over her as she studied the long white dress, and light-coloured hair pinned loosely and elegantly on top of her head. But it was her eyes that Sophie couldn't stop staring at. They were lighter than her husband's and daughter's, and seemed to fix upon Sophie's as though looking deep into her soul. It was the woman she saw in the water.

'Sophie!'

Sophie's gaze snapped up at Julie's sharp tone and she blinked to clear away the strange feeling that hung around her. 'I'm sorry, Julie. No, I'm fine . . . Maybe just a bit more tired than I first thought,' she said with a weak smile.

'Of course you are. You need to make sure you rest. I'll leave these here for you to look at later when you're feeling more up to it,' she said, taking the album from Sophie and placing it on the coffee table nearby.

She needed to get a grip.

'If you want anything, you just call, alright?'

After Julie left, Sophie eyed the album warily, her mind racing. How had she ended up on the side of the river that night? When she came to it seemed that she hadn't simply washed up, it was as though she'd been dragged ashore. She'd been well away from the water and she had no idea how she'd got there. There had to be a reasonable explanation and yet, she struggled to dispel the idea that the woman she saw in the water had been Edith Spicer. She couldn't have conjured up her face when, before today, she'd never even seen a picture of her. This was freaking her out big time.

Sophie slowly reached for the album again and placed it on her lap. As she opened to the page, the air rushed from her lungs as the sound of water roaring in her ears filled her senses. It had been her, she was positive. Slowly the sound subsided as she studied the woman in the aging photo. 'What is it you want?' Sophie said softly as she ran her fingertips across the image. Her gaze shifted from Edith's face to that of the little girl in the photo, with her chubby little arms and big, wide eyes, and Sophie couldn't help the smile that tugged at her lips. She'd been such a beautiful little thing. She could only imagine the pain and heartbreak Edith and Danny must have endured, losing a child. Then as she looked back at Edith's face she knew. It was almost as though she'd heard a little voice in the back of her mind, the faintest of whispers, the barest of murmurs. She knew what Edith wanted.

Two days later, Sophie stood at the Spicers' front door and knocked, waiting as footsteps approached.

'Sophie! Should you be up and about?' Julie asked, eyeing her cautiously.

'Yes, I'm fine, thanks.' She dismissed the other woman's concern with a wave of her hand. 'I've brought this back,' she said, looking down at the album in her arms. 'Julie, I have something to tell you, and then I need to ask a really, really big favour.'

To Julie's credit, she didn't ask any questions, but the curiosity written across her face as she stepped aside and invited Sophie to come in spoke volumes. Sophie took a deep breath and hugged the album tighter. She knew what needed to be done.

Thirty-four

It had been a week since Sophie had seen Zac after he'd spent the night at her bedside in the hospital. She understood that it must have brought back memories of his wife's illness, and losing her, and clearly he'd needed some time to deal with it, but what she didn't understand was why she hadn't seen him since. She was worried about him, but every time she went to call she was overcome with self-doubt. His continued absence was making it pretty clear that he didn't want to be part of her life, and yet it didn't really make any sense.

She should have told him that she'd turned down the damn job as soon as she'd returned from Sydney. He probably still thought she was thinking about taking it. But he'd been so worried about her—she'd heard the desperation in his voice when he'd found her. She knew he felt something for her, and she couldn't deny that she felt something for him too. She just wasn't sure if he wanted the same thing as she did anymore.

Luckily, she had enough things on her plate to take her mind off Zac, not the least being that the time had finally come to test Cobber. She was grateful to have the distraction but not so much the worry. Today was the day that Cobber was going to be released from the holding yards and smaller paddock she'd opened up to him over the past few weeks, allowing him back out into the rest of the property.

She wasn't entirely sure he was ready. When Alison had suggested that it was time to let him out, that his training was pretty well complete, Sophie had tried to argue that maybe they needed a few more weeks, just to make sure. She was terrified that once she released him from the small paddock he was in he'd take off for the bushland and she'd never see him again.

Alison had of course seen right through her excuses and patiently, yet firmly, assured her that it would be fine. Sophie, though, wasn't as confident. But she knew he wanted to get out of his confinement, and she often saw him sniffing the wind and looking longingly towards the wildlands he'd come from.

'Okay, boy,' she said as she took her time brushing him. 'You have to stay away from fences, and particularly Horrie Spicer's fences. We don't want any more injuries.' For Horrie's part, he'd stayed well clear of her. She hadn't so much as passed him down the street since their run in after Cobber's shooting. She still didn't trust him as far as she could throw him though.

'And if you need me for anything at all, you just come back up here, okay?'

Sophie sighed as she finished brushing the big animal and took off the halter, burying her face into his neck one more time and breathing deeply. *Please don't leave me.*

She pulled back and wiped her eyes, planting a quick kiss on the long nose she'd grown to love so much, then crossed to the gate and opened it. 'Off you go, boy.'

Cobber cautiously made his way to the opening and gave a few low nickers, tossing his head as though uncertain as to what he should do before setting off at a trot and straight into a full-stride gallop as he headed out into the open ground beyond.

Sophie felt a warm trail of tears follow the curve of her cheek and down along her jawline to her neck as she stood and watched the shape of a horse fade into nothing more than a speck in the distance. Eventually she turned away, her heart both heavy and full. The absolute joy in which he'd raced showed how much he'd yearned for his freedom. He was once more back where he belonged, but she'd miss him being here where she could see him.

She looked up when a shape detached itself from the fence and her step faltered slightly.

'Hi. I didn't want to interrupt,' Zac said as she approached him.

'It was time to let him go,' Sophie said, dropping his gaze that was full of sympathy. He knew what it cost her to release him, how attached she'd become. She couldn't handle kindness right now.

'You saved his life. He won't forget. You okay?'

His gentle concern threatened a new rush of tears, but she forced them away and quickly nodded. 'I'm fine. I wasn't expecting to see you.'

'I wanted to see how you were doing.'

Sophie glanced across at him briefly. 'I've been out of hospital for a week.'

He didn't miss the light insinuation she'd lent to her comment. 'Yeah, I'm sorry, I've been away at a conference. I just got back in town.'

'I see,' she said, trying to keep her expression as politely interested as possible.

'In case you thought I was avoiding you or something.'

Sophie shook her head quickly. 'No, I figured you were just really busy. I know I have been. I've hardly had a moment to myself all week.'

'Yeah, well, I didn't get a chance to speak to you after the accident . . .'

'I understand,' she cut in quickly. This whole conversation was becoming awkward, which seemed par for the course in their relationship. 'You don't have to explain.'

'I think I do, Sophie,' he said firmly. 'I shouldn't have disappeared on you like that,' he said, rubbing a hand across his chin before dropping it to his side. 'It caught me off guard. After the initial adrenaline wore off and we were in the hospital—I don't know, it all kinda bombarded me, the noises, the smells, how quiet it was . . . You lying

325

there with tubes in you . . . It was like seeing Christa all over again. I was sitting there, helpless to take away the pain. All I could do was watch as she faded away. It got a bit too much,' he said, wincing as he shoved his hands back into his pockets and hunched his shoulders. 'I went outside to get some air, but the next thing I knew I was walking, and I ended up at the cemetery.'

Sophie could see the torment written in his expression and felt his hurt.

'I've hardly been out there, Soph,' he said bleakly. 'Other than the day of the funeral and then the first anniversary. I couldn't bring myself to go out there anymore. It always felt so . . . final, I guess. I've been shying away from it for the past three years. If I didn't acknowledge it, it wouldn't hurt so much.' He looked at her for some kind of sign of understanding and she nodded. 'Ever since that day you turned up in the surgery with a poisoned cat, I've been fighting a losing battle. You made it hard to keep ignoring the pain. Or maybe you dulled the pain—I don't know. All I do know is suddenly in that hospital room it all came back and there was nowhere to hide from it.'

Sophie put her hand on his arm and searched his sorrowful eyes. 'I'm sorry that I put you in that position.'

Zac shook his head and stared down at her hand. 'When I heard what happened . . . When they couldn't find you . . . All I knew was I couldn't lose you too.'

Sophie's throat closed and she found it hard to swallow past the tightness his words evoked.

'I vowed if we found you, I'd stop wasting all this time the way I have been and I'd do something about it. But then I was in that damn hospital room and all those memories began swarming me . . . I'd forgotten all about the conference I was supposed to go on, and then it seemed like a good way to get some distance and do some thinking. So I left early without coming back to see you.'

Sophie was still trying to keep up, having spent too long dwelling on what he'd meant by *doing something about it* that she'd almost missed the rest of it. Her heart dropped. It seemed that he'd pretty much told her everything she'd already guessed. He'd had second thoughts about their relationship and now he was back here to tell her. 'It's okay, Zac. Really. I get it.'

'You do?' he asked slowly, eyeing her strangely.

'You needed to get away and sort everything out. I understand.'

'Do you want to know *what* I figured out?'

Sophie wasn't sure. *Did* she? Just when she'd thought she had things worked out, he'd disappeared. So far their relationship seemed to always be taking one step forward and two steps back.

'I figured out that being with you is the only thing that makes sense,' he said, taking a step closer to her. 'I had to make peace with my past. Before you came along, I was happy not to deal with it. It was the thought of losing you that made me wake up and realise that I wasn't really living. I hadn't been living since I lost Christa, I was just going through the motions. It took almost losing you to wake me up. I want to start living again, Soph, and I want to do it with you by my side.'

God knows she hadn't been thinking of a new relationship when she took this move—all she'd been thinking of was leaving her past behind and getting control back over her life. But he was right about one thing: if the past few years had taught her anything it was that life could be taken at any moment, and you had to make the most of every second you had.

Sophie closed the gap between them and lifted a hand to the side of his face, smiling when he turned his head and planted a soft kiss on her palm. 'For the briefest of moments when I was in the water, I thought about just letting go. I was so cold and so tired, but then I thought about you and I knew I couldn't. I don't want to waste any more time second-guessing all the decisions I've made in my life lately.'

'Me neither. Can we start everything all over, from now?'

'Yes, but only if you promise me one thing.'

'Anything.'

'The cat poisoning story is forgotten.'

'No way. It's the best "how did you two meet" story ever. You can't ask me to give that up.'

'Fine,' she sighed. 'Well, just make sure you remember to stress the *accidental* bit . . . I really hate being known as the cat poisoner.'

'Alright, deal.' He lowered his head and kissed her. It was a gentle, probing kind of kiss, the sort that said everything that couldn't be spoken and promised a lifetime of memories.

A loud whinny nearby broke the kiss. Sophie turned with a start and felt her heart swell when she saw Cobber prancing in the paddock nearby.

'See? He's come back to show you that he's not too far away.'

Sophie couldn't speak. She could barely swallow past the thickening of her throat as tears filled her eyes once more. She hadn't lost him after all. She hadn't lost either of them.

Epilogue

The sun shone down bright and warm on Sophie's shoulders as she stood at the end of the new grave and read again the wording on the restored headstone:

Edith Spicer
July 21st, 1865 – August 23rd, 1890
Loving wife and mother.
Lottie Spicer
December 4th, 1886 – May 23rd, 1890
Safe in her mother's arms again. Forever together.

'It's a good thing that you've done,' Bill said from beside her as he bent down awkwardly to lay a small bouquet of flowers on the freshly dug grave.

'It felt right,' Sophie said, looking across at Julie and Len who stood nearby. 'Thank you both so much for agreeing.'

Without their approval to exhume Lottie's casket from the original Spicer family plot, she would never have been able to make it happen.

'It's never sat well with me, what the old Spicers did to this poor woman. No mother should ever be separated from her child,' Julie said, delicately touching a tissue to the corner of her eye.

Surprisingly, it hadn't been as much of a red-tape nightmare as she'd been expecting, once Sophie had pleaded her case to Len and Julie. After getting the appropriate council approval, it had then been a matter of working with the local funeral director who had handled the rest.

The service to rebury little Lottie was brief but moving and done more as a token of respect than any real necessity, but it gave a sense of closure to the whole process.

The men began to move off but Julie remained and eyed Sophie curiously. 'Have you had any more . . . encounters?' she asked quietly, and Sophie gave a lopsided grin. She'd told Julie about the woman in the river that night who had reached out and saved her, even though she realised how insane it sounded. Surprisingly, Julie hadn't laughed at her.

'No,' Sophie said, 'but I feel . . . lighter somehow.'

'She's at peace now,' Julie nodded sagely as she looked down at the headstone. 'She knew you would help her.'

Sophie still wasn't sure what she saw in the water that night—she'd never been a believer in ghosts or the afterlife, but she couldn't ignore the pull she'd experienced in so many ways since coming to this place. Maybe Edith had been behind all the out-of-character decisions she'd been making, or maybe she'd finally found the place she'd always been meant to find.

Sophie glanced across at the other major undertaking that had happened in the past few months. Just prior to the hundred-year anniversary of the charge of Beersheba on 31 October, Bill had organised the local RSL sub-branch to add a plaque to Clarrie's grave and held a service to commemorate his part in the battle. She felt a protectiveness when it came to Clarrie. Through his diaries, she'd felt as though she'd come to know him and she understood that the things he'd seen and done during the war had scarred him badly. After returning home he didn't want to celebrate anything to do with war, but she hoped that he'd be alright with this. The sacrifices Clarrie and all servicemen had made for their country deserved to be remembered and never forgotten.

She'd donated the trunk and Clarrie's diary to the RSL where they were on display in the war memorial so that generations of Australians could learn what war was really like for the men who went away to fight in it—ordinary people doing extraordinary things in the name of mateship, country and freedom.

'Look who's decided to come to see what's going on,' Zac chuckled, coming up behind her and looking over her head.

Sophie turned as Cobber gave a loud neigh, shaking his head and trotting over. Behind him, three brood mares nervously watched and waited.

'Hey, boy,' she said, walking across to greet the other man in her life. 'How's things with the new ladies?'

'I'd say pretty good. He's living every guy's dream—a harem of willing women and freedom to run,' Zac said, stroking the other side of the horse's neck as he grinned down at her.

Sophie had become involved in the Heritage Horse Association and offered up her property as a place to keep some of the horses they brought out from the national park before they went on to be trained and rehomed so Cobber now had a new mob of his own.

'Oh? And is that your dream too?'

'Well, no. I'm having enough trouble satisfying one woman,' he admitted ruefully.

'Oh, I don't know. I'd say you're doing okay.'

'Speaking of which,' he said, moving closer, 'I say we ditch the stragglers and head back home. What do you reckon?' he asked, wiggling his eyebrows.

Sophie laughed. 'I say that's the best idea you've had in at least the last twenty-four hours.'

'Then what are we waiting for?'

Sophie rubbed her face against Cobber's neck and breathed deeply. God, he smelled good. Yep, she had everything a girl could ever ask for to feel complete: the love of a good man, beautiful memories and a horse. Life was good. With one last pat, she said goodbye to Cobber and glanced at the quiet little cemetery with a happy sigh. Everything was finally as it should be, the past settled and the future beckoning impatiently for her to hurry up. A movement in the corner of her eye drew Sophie's gaze to the big old tree nearby. A man stood there dressed in a khaki uniform, complete with boots, leggings and spurs, holding the reins of a black horse with a *white splodge on its forehead.*

She held her breath, not daring to even blink in case he vanished. *Clarrie.* She desperately wanted to look around and see if anyone else could see what she was seeing, but she couldn't drag her eyes away from him. Then, without a word, he gave her a lopsided grin and tipped a finger to the brim of his hat before turning and leading his horse away.

'Soph? You alright?' Zac's deep voice broke the spell and she looked up at him, blinking away the veil of tears that had come with Clarrie's unexpected visit.

'I'm fine,' she said, plastering a bright smile on her face. And she was. She was better than fine; she'd found this amazing man who had fallen into her life when she'd least expected it and given her a brand new chapter to look forward to. She had a home set in some of the most spectacular scenery this country had to offer. And she'd rediscovered the love for her career again and found a community who welcomed her with open arms. What more could a person ask for?

It was a very good day to be alive.

Acknowledgements

The inspiration behind this community came from an article I read about a small central New South Wales town called Tottenham, who banded together to save their ambulance station. The dedication and community spirit demonstrated by this town should be an inspiration to us all. Just imagine the things we could do if every community in Australia, rural or city, worked together like Tottenham did.

While I started out with the intension of setting Hilsons Ridge in Tottenham, a chance conversation when researching aspects of the book, suddenly made me realise that I needed to tie in the light horse story with its origin and so the town was packed up and moved to the New England highlands.

The Heritage Horse Association in the book is in fact a real group and one that I am a proud member of. The Guy

Fawkes Heritage Horse Association was formed to preserve the unique characteristics and bloodlines of the horses from the Guy Fawkes National Park. The brumbies that run wild in the Guy Fawkes National park today are direct descendants of the horses known as Walers, captured and sent to the Boer War and the First World War as part of the Australian Light Horse Brigade and are the only group of Australian wild horses to have this proven heritage value.

Hilsons Ridge is a fictional town, based on a now abandoned gold mining town. Its location is remote and roads are tricky, so while I have tried to stay true to the location, had this town still existed, I have also taken a few liberties with distances and travel times from major towns nearby. For more details on the stories behind the book, head over to my blog at karlylane.com

As always, there were so many people I turned to for information while writing this book. For the paramedic scenes I had some pretty amazing people help me out, and I'd like to thank them for giving up so much of their time to answer my questions: in particular, David Horseman and Paul Cue; also Karen Schutze, Caryn Hargrave, Nicki Edwards, Renae Haley and Leanne Jarvis. I really tried to get my facts correct when writing such important scenes, but I take full responsibility for anything that may be incorrect.

Big thanks to the Frank Partridge Military Museum in Bowraville. Thanks also to Sharon Selwood, Jacqui Turpin, Lisa Hall, Bec Belt and Cindy Eichmann, as well as my local vet, Rod Lamont. And to Kate Young from the Heritage Horse Association and Georgia Bates for their help with information on our amazing heritage horses and for their fantastic work with these very special animals. Thank you to Carmel Logan and the community of Tottenham, New South Wales for inspiring the fictional town of Hilsons Ridge.

And, as always, I'd like to thank the team at Allen & Unwin, my family and my amazing readers for all their wonderful support.

ALSO FROM ALLEN & UNWIN

Third Time Lucky

KARLY LANE

After a disastrous marriage, December Doyle has returned to her home town to try to pick up the pieces of her life and start again. She's also intent on helping breathe new life into the Christmas Creek township, so the last thing she needs is trouble.

Bad boy Seth Hunter has also returned to Christmas Creek, and trouble is his middle name. Wrongly convicted of a serious crime in his youth, Seth is now a successful businessman, but he's intent on settling some old scores.

As teenagers, December and Seth were madly in love, and seeing each other again reawakens past feelings. But will Seth be able to overcome his destructive anger about the past, and can December conquer her fear of heartbreak to make their relationship third time lucky?

By the bestselling author of *Second Chance Town*, this compelling novel is about betrayal, ambition and the power of forgiveness—and love.

ISBN 978 1 76029 182 2

Second Chance Town

KARLY LANE

Single mother Lucy Parker loves the quiet historical charm of her hometown of Bundah. Raising her teenage daughter Belle can be challenging and, in a small town where everyone knows everyone else's business, it's even more daunting than usual.

Newcomer Hugh Thompson is determined to put his chequered history behind him. Excited by the potential he sees in Bundah, he buys a rundown pub with big plans for a fresh start. But not long after Hugh's arrival, a spate of teenage drug overdoses starts to divide the locals and there are whispers they might be connected to the reclusive new publican who has a somewhat dark and mysterious past.

When Belle suddenly starts hanging out with the wrong kids and experimenting with alcohol, Lucy becomes fearful that drugs will be next. The very last thing she needs is for a man like Hugh to come along and disrupt her life. But it seems fate has other ideas . . .

Suspenseful and romantic, *Second Chance Town* is about fulfilling your dreams in life and love.

ISBN 978 1 76029 627 8

Tallowood Bound

KARLY LANE

When Erin Macalister leaves the city to take care of her beloved grandmother, she's relieved to be escaping the remnants of her broken marriage.

Arriving in the small rural community she grew up in, Erin finds nothing much has changed—including Jamie McBride, who is still as ridiculously good looking as he was when they were seventeen and madly in love.

Leafing through old photo albums evokes vivid memories for her grandmother of a soldier she once loved. Erin's curiosity about this mysterious soldier deepens when she finds an engagement ring he once gave her grandmother.

Meanwhile, Jamie McBride seems intent on rekindling his relationship with Erin, even though she's not at all sure she wants to risk heartache again.

From the bestselling author of *Poppy's Dilemma*, this poignant, heartfelt story of old loves and new possibilities is both inspirational and entertaining.

ISBN 978 1 74331 727 3